ULTIMATUM

Simon Kernick is one of Britain's most exciting thriller writers. He arrived on the crime writing scene with his highly acclaimed debut novel *The Business of Dying*, the story of a corrupt cop moonlighting as a hitman. However, Simon's big breakthrough came with his novel *Relentless*, which was selected by Richard and Judy for their Recommended Summer Reads promotion and then rapidly went on to become the bestselling thriller of 2007. His most recent thrillers include *The Payback* and *Siege*.

Simon's research is what makes his thrillers so authentic. He talks both on and off the record to members of the Met's Special Branch and the Anti-Terrorist Branch and the Serious and Organised Crime Agency, so he gets to hear first hand what actually happens in the dark and murky underbelly of UK crime.

Find out more about Simon Kernick and his thrillers at

www.simonkernick.com

www.facebook.com/SimonKernick

twitter.com/simonkernick

Also by SIMON KERNICK

THE MURDER EXCHANGE

Ex-soldier Max Iversson is hired to provide security for a meeting that goes disastrously wrong.

'From hardboiled cops to ruthless women on the make, Kernick generates a potent cocktail of thrills'
Guardian

THE CRIME TRADE

DI John Callan and DS Tina Boyd uncover a murderous conspiracy that will take them to the heart of London's most notorious criminal gang.

'A taut gritty novel in which Kernick uses every trick in the book to keep the narrative breakneck'
Time Out

RELENTLESS

Tom Meron finds himself on the run, pursued by enemies he never knew he had . . .

'This is the sort of book that forces you to read so fast you stumble over the words. Phenomenal!'
Evening Standard

SEVERED

You wake up in a strange room on a bed covered in blood. And you have no idea how you got there.

'If you like lots of non-stop action, this is for you'
Guardian

DEADLINE

You get home from work and your daughter is missing.
You know you will do anything to get her
back alive – but time is running out . . .

'So authentic that it completely takes your breath away'
Mirror

TARGET

Rob Fallon is the target of brutal killers. But what do they
want? Either he finds out or he's dead.

'A gritty mix of Jeffery Deaver and Harlan Coben,
with a distinctly British accent'
Books Quarterly

THE LAST 10 SECONDS

A man, a woman, a sadistic killer. As they race
towards a terrifying confrontation only one thing is
certain: they're all going to have to fight very hard
just to stay alive.

'Nail-biting . . . More twists and turns than a
boa-constrictor on speed'
The Times

SIEGE

A group of ruthless gunmen storm a London hotel,
shooting guests and taking others hostage.
Only one thing matters: who will survive?

'Fast and furious'
Daily Mail

Featuring Dennis Milne

THE BUSINESS OF DYING

Featuring DS Dennis Milne, full-time cop, part-time assassin.

'Taut, gripping, disturbing – a most assured and original debut'
Daily Mail

A GOOD DAY TO DIE

Exiled cop Dennis Milne returns to London to hunt down the murderers of a close friend.

'Great plots, great characters, great action'
Lee Child

THE PAYBACK

Two cops with pasts that haunt them, and a present that could see them both dead. They are about to meet. And when they do, it's payback time.

'It delights, excites and stimulates, and the only reason you consume it so quickly is because it's so damn good'
GQ

SIMON KERNICK

ULTIMATUM

arrow books

Published by Arrow Books 2013

2 4 6 8 10 9 7 5 3

This novel is a work of fiction. Names and characters are the product of the author's imagination and any resemblance to actual persons, living or dead, is entirely coincidental

First published in Great Britain in 2013 by Century

Arrow Books
The Random House Group Limited
20 Vauxhall Bridge Road, London, SW1 2SA

www.randomhouse.co.uk

Addresses for companies within The Random House Group Limited can be found at: www.randomhouse.co.uk/offices.htm

The Random House Group Limited Reg. No. 954009

A CIP catalogue record for this book is available from the British Library

Penguin Random House is committed to a sustainable future for our business, our readers and our planet. This book is made from Forest Stewardship Council® certified paper.

Typeset in Palatino (11/15pt) by
SX Composing DTP, Rayleigh, Essex

Printed and bound by [illegible] plc

For my daughters, Amy and Rachel.

One

07.25

His whole world collapsed exactly three seconds after the door opened.

In the first second, her pale, beautiful face peered through the gap, then disappeared as she moved aside to let him in. The next second saw him walking into the cramped front room and, with a rather foolish flourish, lifting up the small bunch of petrol station flowers he'd brought her. And the third was when the man in the hood appeared out of the shadows to his left and pointed a gun at his head while Mika closed the door, plunging the room into semi-darkness.

'What's going on?' asked Akhtar Mohammed in a voice several octaves higher than usual. 'Take my money, but—'

'Sit down and shut your mouth.'

Akhtar stole a glance at Mika – his beloved Mika. She was standing in the middle of the room in just a nightdress, her pale skin almost translucent in the dim light, her face set fast in an expression of pure fear. Tears ran down her cheeks and Akhtar wanted to reach out and hold her, tell her that everything was all right, but the gunman grabbed him roughly by the back of his shirt and shoved him towards the nearest chair.

'I said, sit down.'

Akhtar stumbled into the seat and turned to his assailant, putting his hands in the air so that the other man knew he wasn't going to do anything stupid. He was neither a brave man nor a foolhardy one, and he was fully aware that the only way he was going to get out of here was by cooperating.

The gunman stepped towards him and pushed the barrel of the gun against the side of his head. It felt cold and hard, and Akhtar swallowed. Was this some kind of divine punishment for his adultery? If it was, then he prayed God would be merciful. He'd never intended to hurt his wife or his children, nor to bring shame down on his family's head.

'I don't want any trouble,' he said, conscious of the fear in his voice.

'I'm going to give you a task, Mr Mohammed,' answered the gunman in a tone that was worryingly calm.

His accent was English, so Akhtar knew he wasn't Mika's pimp. So who on earth was he? And how did he know who he was? Even Mika didn't know his last name.

'If you carry it out as instructed, you'll be free to go and you'll never hear from me again. If you fail to do what you're told, however, I will kill your girlfriend here. Slowly, and very painfully.'

Mika gasped. She was still standing in the middle of the room, unmoving, and Akhtar wondered why she didn't try to escape. Then he saw the restraints round each of her ankles, separated by barely a foot of thick chain, and he realized she was as helpless as he was. He gave her a small, hopeful smile and she stared back at him with those big oval eyes of hers that had so bewitched him in the first place, and he wished by all that was holy that he'd never met her.

'And just in case Mika dying slowly isn't enough to motivate you,' continued the gunman, still keeping the gun pushed down on Akhtar's head, 'there's this.'

He held out a remote control and switched on the TV. For a couple of seconds the screen was blank and then an image of two people having sex on an unmade bed appeared – the woman on all fours facing the camera, the man kneeling behind her, his eyes closed. The gunman pressed another button and the couple began moving frantically on the screen, their joyful moans filling the room.

Akhtar cringed as he recognized himself. Had Mika set this all up? Had she hidden a camera when they'd been making love? He looked up at her and she shook her head silently. This was nothing to do with her.

The gunman switched off the TV and the room fell

quiet once again. 'I have more than an hour of footage taken on three separate occasions, showing you in various acts with Miss Donovic here, all of them as explicit as this. Some of them even more so.' The gunman chuckled. 'But then you knew that, didn't you? If you don't carry out the task, I'll have copies of the footage delivered to your wife, your mother, and the imam at your mosque.' He calmly reeled off the names of all three, and the addresses to which the copies would be sent. All of them were correct.

Akhtar felt his breathing increase and he began to tremble. If this happened, his life would be finished. No one would forgive him for such a rank betrayal of everything his community held dear. He'd be shunned. Exiled. Worst of all, his children would grow up knowing the terrible, sordid sins he'd committed.

'What do you want me to do?' he whispered.

'It's a very simple job that will take you less than an hour. You're to deliver that' – he pointed to a plain black backpack sitting on the floor next to the fleabitten sofa – 'to the address on the contacts section of this phone.' He dropped a BlackBerry into Akhtar's lap. 'It's a twenty-minute drive from here, half an hour if the traffic's bad. You need to be there for eight a.m., and I know you've got a TomTom in your car, so if you leave now you'll make it on time. Park right outside, then as soon as you're ready to go in, call me immediately. Do you understand?'

Akhtar nodded. He had no idea how this man knew so much about him, but the fact that he did made it imperative that he did what he was told. Then perhaps he could emerge from this nightmare unscathed and go back to living his life again. He would miss Mika – God, he would miss her – but in the end it would be a very small price to pay.

The gunman lowered his weapon and took a step backwards, motioning for Akhtar to get to his feet.

Pocketing the BlackBerry without even checking the address, he grabbed the backpack and hauled it over one shoulder, surprised at its weight. He wondered what was inside. Initially he'd thought it would be drugs, but it was far too heavy for that.

The gunman seemed to read his thoughts. 'Under no circumstances look inside that bag, Mr Mohammed. However tempted you are. Because if I find out you have – and I will find out – then our agreement's void, and I'll carry out my threat.'

The gunman stepped aside and Akhtar walked past him. He glanced briefly at Mika, and she gave him a hopeful look back.

'Please do what he says,' she whispered. 'He means it.'

'I will,' said Akhtar, opening the door and stepping out into the gloom. 'I promise.'

But not for you, he thought. For me.

Two

08.00

Martha Crossman opened the door to her local coffee shop and stepped inside.

The place was busy with the pre-work crowd – mainly businesspeople – and a powerful blast of coffee, conversation and central heating hit her straight away. The normality of the scene filled her with an intense jealousy. When Martha had last been here a few days ago, her life had seemed so normal and straightforward. Not happy – she hadn't been happy for a long time – but at least back then she hadn't been burdened by the secret she was now carrying.

She took a deep breath. She wanted to throw up. To run out of the café, find a cold, quiet spot where no one could see her and vomit up the few scrappy contents of her stomach. If it wasn't for her daughter, she'd end it all. There was no question. What had happened – what she'd found out – was so devastating that, in one single stroke, it had destroyed her will to live. But Lucy – dear, beautiful Lucy – was what kept her going.

That, and the need for justice to be done.

The man she was meeting, Philip Wright, was already there, sitting in a booth in the far corner next to the gleaming silver coffee machines on the counter, facing the door, with a large cup of coffee in front of him. She recognized him from the photos straight away, and it was clear he recognized her too. He gave a small nod, and she tried a smile in return as she walked over.

'Mrs Crossman, it's good to meet you,' he said, getting up from his seat and shaking her hand. He was a big man in his early sixties, and his grip was firm.

'Thanks for seeing me,' she said, taking off her coat and sitting down opposite him.

'Can I get you a drink of anything?' he asked. He had a gentle demeanour, and for the first time in days she felt her burden beginning to lighten.

'I'm OK for the moment, thanks.'

'You said on the phone that it was extremely urgent.'

She looked round the room, making sure no one was watching her. 'It is.'

'I have to admit, I'm surprised. As you know, my expertise isn't in an area where urgency tends to be an issue. And as we don't know each other, I'm assuming this isn't something to do with my personal life.'

'It's not. It's your professional opinion I need.'

He wrinkled his brow, still not quite understanding. 'Well, ask away.'

She put down her handbag but kept it close to her. It made her feel sick knowing what it contained, but at some point she was going to have to give it to him, otherwise there was no evidence. She looked him straight in the eye, saw a warm intelligence there, coupled with many years' experience in what he did, and felt reassured.

Leaning forward in her seat, she started talking, keeping her voice low.

Three

08.03

Akhtar Mohammed pulled up on double yellow lines several yards past his destination. The traffic had been bad and he was three minutes late. He still couldn't believe what was happening to him. It was like being stuck right in the middle of a nightmare.

He stared at the backpack on the passenger seat next to him, desperate to know what was inside, but not daring to look. He was scared out of his wits. He just wanted to get this thing delivered so he could get on with his life again, but he also knew it might contain something bad – something that could get him into even more trouble.

He cursed himself for ever getting involved with Mika. He cursed himself for—

The BlackBerry he'd been given started ringing, the ringtone a blaring horn. Akhtar spent a few seconds trying to find it with shaking hands before pulling it out of his back pocket. He pressed the green answer button.

'Where the hell are you?' demanded the gunman. 'I told you that you needed to be there by eight o'clock.'

'I'm here now,' said Akhtar. 'I've just parked.'

'Tell me the street, and the name of the shop next door to the right.'

Akhtar looked round hurriedly. 'I'm on Wilton Road. Just behind Victoria Station. There's a hairdresser's to the right of the coffee shop.'

'Good. Now I want you to stay on the phone while you go inside the coffee shop with the backpack. And I want you to act completely normally.'

Keeping the phone to his ear, Akhtar picked up the backpack with his free hand and pulled it over one shoulder. 'OK,' he said, getting out of his car and walking unsteadily over to the coffee shop door. His legs felt weak and he could hear his heart beating in his chest as he stood to one side to let two smartly dressed young women in the middle of a lively conversation come out with their takeaway coffees.

'I'm going in now,' he continued, squeezing through the door with his rucksack, the heat and noise of the place hitting him right in the face. The place was busy with commuters ordering their caffeine fixes, but he hardly saw them. They were just a blur.

'Can you see a woman in her early forties with

shoulder-length hair sitting anywhere? She'll either be on her own or sitting with a man with a grey beard.'

Akhtar scanned the room, forcing himself to concentrate on faces as he slowly approached the queue of people at the counter. He saw two people in the far corner. The woman had her back to him and appeared to be talking intently to the man, who had a deeply troubled expression on his face. 'Yes, I can see them.'

'I want you to take a seat as close to the woman as possible.'

'You don't want me to say anything to her?'

'Just do as you're told. Take a seat . . . nice and close.'

It was those three words that set off alarm bells. *Nice and close*.

It hit him then. He was carrying a bomb. He had to be. As soon as he found a seat close to the woman, the gunman would detonate it somehow – Akhtar had seen it done on all those TV shows – killing him, the woman, and everyone around them. And he, Akhtar, would end up getting the blame, because he would have been the one carrying the bomb, heaping even more shame on his family.

He looked over at the woman. She looked totally normal. White, attractive, well bred, with expensive clothes – and he wondered if he was wrong. Whether he was just being paranoid.

And then the woman turned his way and their eyes met, and even from twenty feet away he could see the fear and tension in them. He turned away quickly.

'Are you sitting down yet?' demanded the gunman.

'I'm trying to find a seat. It's crowded in here.'

'How close are you?'

It *was* a bomb. It had to be.

'Not too far, but she's sitting near the counter and there are a lot of people in the way.'

'Get as close as you can.'

The fear was so intense now that Akhtar could hardly walk. If he stayed here, he died. No question. If he put the bomb down and tried to evacuate the place, the man on the end of the phone would detonate it, and he still died, along with everyone else. And if he hung up, he also died. He was completely trapped, and only seconds from death. He had to make a decision.

Joining the end of the queue at the counter, he put the backpack down on the floor then, looking round briefly to check that no one was watching him, he walked towards the coffee shop door, making way for a young student couple coming the other way, trying not to look at their faces, knowing that he could be sentencing them to death.

He reached the door. 'OK. I'm just about to sit down.'

'How far away?'

'Five feet,' he replied, holding the phone against his

jacket to block out the sounds of the street as he stepped outside and immediately broke into a run.

When Martha Crossman caught the Asian man with the backpack staring at her, she thought the worst, but as he turned away and joined the queue she told herself to stop being so foolish. No one knew she was here. And even if they did, they wouldn't kill her in a public place.

She turned back to Philip Wright. His demeanour had changed since she'd told him about her secret. Beforehand he'd seemed reassuring yet cool, as if he was half-expecting to be wasting his time coming here. Now, the tension cutting across his features matched hers.

'You're talking about murder here, Mrs Crossman,' he told her. 'You're going to have to talk to the police immediately. I can't help you with this.'

'I don't want to involve the police yet. Not until I'm absolutely sure that what I've discovered is actually what I think it is.'

'OK,' he said, nodding slowly. 'I can understand that. And it's something I can authenticate very quickly. But I'm going to need to see it.'

She motioned towards the handbag on the seat next to her. 'It's in there.'

He frowned. 'You've brought it *here* with you?'

'I wanted you to see it as soon as possible. Listen,' she added, looking round, unable to see the Asian man any longer, 'I'm feeling a bit claustrophobic. Can we go somewhere quieter and more private? Please?'

He nodded. 'Of course.'

Martha felt faint, the need to vomit even stronger than it had been when she'd first come in here, and she stood up unsteadily.

He stood up too. 'Are you OK?' He put a hand on her shoulder. 'Let's go to my car. I'm parked up the road.'

She needed no encouragement. The room was spinning, and she could feel the beginnings of a panic attack – the first she'd had in years. With Wright holding on to her she hurried towards the fresh air and salvation.

'Excuse me, sir,' said a voice behind them. 'You haven't paid for your coffee.'

Martha turned back towards the waitress at just the moment the bomb exploded, the force of the blast caving in the windows and the Plexiglas counter and sending jagged projectiles hurtling through the enclosed space at more than two hundred miles per hour.

The bomb – five kilos of PETN plastic explosive surrounded by the same weight in assorted shrapnel – was designed to rip to shreds everything in its immediate proximity.

Neither Martha nor Philip Wright had time to react, or even understand what was happening. Wright was struck in the left eye by an industrial railway bolt that immediately pierced his brain, killing him near enough instantaneously, while Martha saw a single, all-consuming white flash, heard a roar like a great wave crashing over her, and then a sixteen-inch-by-ten-inch shard of Plexiglas that until a second earlier had been covering the muffin cabinet sliced effortlessly through her neck as if it was butter, taking her head, and her secret, with it.

Four

08.06

DC Tina Boyd was sitting in an unmarked CID car just down the road from the home of a wanted burglar, who'd beaten his most recent victim with a hammer and then promptly skipped the bail he'd been given by some half-witted magistrate, when she heard the explosion – a huge, decisive boom that sounded like it was some distance away but was still loud enough to make the car vibrate on its chassis.

Her colleague, DC Clive Owen, who was trying not to stare at a couple of teenage schoolgirls, who might have been sixth formers if he was lucky, turned to Tina. 'What the hell was that?'

From their position on the edge of an estate of modern mid-rise flats just west of Vauxhall Bridge Road, it was difficult to see too much, but as they looked in the direction of the blast Tina saw a thick plume of black smoke racing up into the sky between two buildings about half a mile away. 'Shit. It looks like Victoria Station. We need to take a look.'

'Hold on, we're on surveillance here, and we've got a good plot. We can't just up sticks and leave.'

Tina gave him a withering look. She'd only been paired with Owen for three days but already she could see he was a jobsworth who didn't like putting himself out, or taking risks. The force was full of people like him these days. They knew all the rules and regulations but seemed to have forgotten how to actually catch criminals. Tina might have found him more tolerable if he'd actually looked a bit more like his movie-star namesake. At least then she'd have something to look at. But he didn't. Nowhere even close.

'Look, we've been sat here the last two days waiting for our fugitive to turn up at the first place he knows we'll be looking for him, and he hasn't made it so far. I don't know what that tells you, but it tells me he probably isn't going to arrive in the next five minutes.'

'He might,' said Owen firmly.

'Well, if he does, then we'll just come back and get him.'

Switching on the engine, Tina reversed out of the dead-end road they were parked in and turned north in the direction of the smoke. She could do with some action. Since being reinstated to the Met nearly a month earlier (for the second time in her career), and placed as a DC in Westminster CID, the highlights had been scarce. They were currently on what the borough's chief super was calling a blitz on burglary, but there wasn't much of a blitz about it. So far, all three burglars they'd nicked were currently back on the street, and their one big raid on the home of a major suspect, with the local press in tow, had turned out to be the wrong address. By the time they'd got to the right one – the flat next door – the guy had gone out the back window and disappeared into the early morning gloom.

'It's definitely coming from somewhere near the station,' said Owen, peering through the windscreen, the radio in his hand. 'What the hell do you reckon could have happened?'

The smoke was showing no signs of abating as it poured skywards, forming a spreading black cloud. Whatever it was, it was bad.

At that moment the radio crackled into life. 'Attention all units,' said the female operator breathlessly. 'We have reports of an explosion at a coffee shop in Wilton Road, next to Victoria Station.'

Almost immediately another voice came over the airwaves. 'This is PCSO 2049. We've just seen an IC4 male running away from the scene of the explosion. He's heading east on Bridge Place in the direction of Belgrave Road. We're currently giving chase on foot.' The PCSO sounded knackered and Tina wondered if it was the overweight guy she'd seen occasionally down at the station. If it was, it was unlikely he'd be keeping pace for long.

The operator came back on the line. 'Keep a visual, 2049, but do not apprehend. Repeat, do not apprehend. We are calling in armed back-up to make an arrest.'

'Tango Four to base, we're also giving mobile pursuit,' said Owen into the radio. 'We're currently heading north on Tachbrook Street. ETA at Bridge Place, two minutes.'

'Approach with extreme caution, Tango Four. Keep a visual but only intercept if you can confirm he appears unarmed.'

This, thought Tina, was the kind of bullshit that policework had been reduced to. Everything was about health and safety and risk assessments these days. You couldn't just catch the criminals. You had to make sure you jumped through a dozen hoops and filled in all the necessary forms before you could actually finally get round to feeling a collar. It wasn't really any wonder they were losing the war on crime.

'All right, turn right up here,' Owen told her. 'Bridge Place is only a couple of hundred yards away. And for Christ's sake, let's be careful. I know what you're like, and if he's got a gun, I know it'll be me, not you, who ends up with a bullet.'

Tina made a hard right, and found herself driving up a narrow residential road with an unbroken line of cars parked up on either side. She was feeling a real burst of excitement for the first time in months. To her this was what being a copper was all about. The chase; the adrenalin; the collar. If, like Owen, you weren't willing to take a risk, then as far as she was concerned you should be working behind a desk.

'There he is!' Owen shouted, as an Asian man ran across the road in front of them fifty yards further on. He immediately grabbed the radio and reeled out an update on the suspect's location to Control, while Tina accelerated towards the junction, not listening to the operator's continued warnings to assess the situation before attempting an arrest.

And then, when she was barely twenty yards from the junction, a four-by-four pulled out from the side of the road, forcing her to slam down hard on the brakes, and flinging both her and Owen forward in their seats.

'Jesus, get back, get back!' yelled Owen as the woman driver sat staring at them with a face like thunder, her oversized car blocking the road. He pulled out his warrant card and waved it out of the window. 'Police!' he screamed. 'Get out of the fucking way!'

The woman yelled back, clearly furious about something, and she wasn't moving.

Bollocks to this, thought Tina, and jumped out of the car, leaving the engine running. She took off up the road at a sprint, knowing she was breaking all the rules, but not caring. A man had run away from a building just after an explosion. She'd like to think the fact that he was Asian, and possibly Muslim, had no bearing on her reaction, but she couldn't help thinking that this could well be terrorist-related, in which case there was no way she could let him escape.

As she turned the corner, Tina saw him up ahead. He was a good forty yards away and running towards the Vauxhall Bridge Road, which struck Tina as odd, since it was roughly the direction he'd come from, suggesting he hadn't spent much time planning his escape. He was already clearly slowing as he tired, so she was confident she could make up the distance between them.

But then he turned and spotted her and accelerated, disappearing up a side street. Tina went to the gym five times a week. Religiously. It was one of her few pleasures these days, and consequently she was very fit, and still young enough to be fast. She picked up her pace, going flat out now, and as she rounded the corner she saw that there was now less than twenty yards between them.

He looked back over his shoulder a second time, which was when Tina got a good look at him. He was youngish, probably early thirties, and smartly dressed in pressed trousers, black work shoes and a shirt and tie beneath his jacket. Which again struck her as odd. As did the look of pure panic on his face. Criminals sometimes looked scared when they were being chased by the forces of law and order, but not like this. This man seemed utterly terrified, as if he was a victim rather than a perpetrator.

'Police!' she yelled. 'Stop now!'

He ignored her, kept running, his arms flailing in front of him. Two Lego-like blocks of flats loomed to her right and standing out in front of them was a large group of schoolboys watching the chase, several of them pulling out mobile phones and filming Tina as she ran past, gaining now. Fifteen yards and counting.

Akhtar's lungs felt like they were about to burst. He'd been running ever since he'd left the coffee shop. In the sheer chaos of the situation he'd run right past his car, just as the explosion had hit, temporarily throwing him to his knees. Knowing he had to get away from the shop, he'd jumped to his feet and carried on running, his ears ringing from the sound of the explosion, before he'd realized his mistake. By that time it was too late. Two police officers had appeared on the other side of the road and had started chasing him. He'd thought he'd outrun them and then, suddenly, this woman in jeans and trainers was right behind him, shouting for him to stop.

He didn't know how much longer he could keep going for. A part of him even wanted to give up, to throw himself at the mercy of the authorities. But there was no way he could do that now. As far as the world was concerned, he'd planted a bomb in a busy café. A bomb that had almost certainly killed many innocent people. He had to escape. There was no choice. There never had been.

There was a main road with flowing traffic directly ahead of him. If he could get across that, put a bit of distance between him and the woman, he might just make it. Gritting his teeth against the pain, he forced his legs to keep going, not even hesitating as he charged into the road. A horn blared as a car was forced to brake suddenly, and another much louder horn blasted to his left.

He turned and saw a lorry bearing down on him, its pistons hissing as its driver tried to stop.

But it was too late. Akhtar just managed to let out the first second of a terrified scream, throwing up his arms in a desperate protective gesture, before he was struck by a screaming wall of metal, and the whole world seemed to explode.

Tina saw it all. The car skidding as it swerved to avoid him; the man continuing to run across the road oblivious to the lorry coming the opposite way; the impact as the lorry struck him with a loud bang, sending him flying across the tarmac like a rag doll; and then the man being crushed under its wheels amid a futile wail of brakes.

It all happened in the space of a few seconds while Tina stood frozen with horror, wondering if there was anything she could have done to stop him, and knowing that once again she'd given her many enemies a stick to beat her with.

Five

08.18

The gunman was watching Sky News when the pretty young anchor interrupted the sports round-up to announce in serious tones that reports were coming in of an explosion near London's Victoria Station. This was immediately followed by live footage from a helicopter of the view above the street in question showing a blazing shop front with people milling about outside, some of them clearly hurt, and several others lying on the ground. There were emergency services personnel on the scene but they appeared to be in short supply.

He switched off the TV. The job was done, but he took no great pleasure in it, even though the whole thing had been a huge risk and had required precision planning. The bomb had been powerful, and plenty of people were dead – cut down for no other reason than that they were in the wrong place at the wrong time.

The outrage would be immense. Just as they wanted it.

Mika sat at one end of the sagging sofa, her head resting on one shoulder, a dark bloody hole in the centre of her forehead. She too was collateral damage, which was unfortunate. She'd done her job well, if under duress, but she knew too much to be allowed to live.

He took out the mobile he'd used to detonate Akhtar Mohammed's bomb, and phoned the main switchboard at BBC Radio London. Clearly it was a bit early in the morning for them because it took a good minute before the call was answered by a male operator.

Speaking into the high-spec voice disguiser that made it impossible to detect either his age or ethnicity, he began his short prepared speech. 'A soldier from Islamic Command just struck a blow against Crusader forces by detonating a bomb right in the heart of your corrupt capital city. The British Crusader government has until eight p.m. tonight to make a public statement promising to withdraw all its troops from Afghanistan and cease support for its American puppet government with immediate effect, or a far greater attack will take place somewhere in this country that will bring fire down on all your heads. Remember, the deadline is eight p.m. You have been warned.'

The operator started to speak but the gunman ended the call. He didn't turn off the phone, though.

Instead he wiped it down with a cloth and threw it on the sofa next to Mika's corpse. He was pretty sure he hadn't left any of his DNA inside the flat. On the two occasions he'd visited he'd always worn gloves and had tried to minimize his contact with any of the surfaces. To make doubly sure that the police had nothing to go on when they came to this place, though, he picked up a second backpack from behind the sofa and placed it in Mika's lap. It too contained a bomb of similar destructive capacity to the one he'd given to Akhtar, but this one was on a timer, primed to explode at 10.35 a.m., which he'd estimated would be around the time the police arrived, having traced the location of the phone. A second bomb in the boot of a car nearby was primed to explode at the same time. Hopefully, between them the bombs would take out a few of the security forces; but even if they didn't, it wouldn't matter. The point of all terrorist campaigns is to sow fear and especially panic among the civilian population, and there was nothing more effective than apparently random attacks to do just that.

He took a last look round, one final check that he hadn't left behind any telltale evidence, then put on a pair of glasses and a baseball cap, pulling it low over his face, and left the flat, keeping his head down against the cold February air, confident that even if he was picked up on the inevitable CCTV cameras round here, no one would recognize him.

Six

08.24

There was no denying it. Prison decor really was shit.

Prisoner number 407886, William James Garrett, better known to the international media by his codename Fox, sat on his bunk staring at the four grimy, pockmarked walls that marked the borders of his home, and wondered who on earth had decided to paint them lime green. The bright colours didn't make him feel any more positive about his situation, as he was sure they were meant to do. They just gave him a headache.

Fox couldn't stand prison. In his mind, keeping a man in a tiny cage without hope for the rest of his days but giving him glimpses of the outside world through TV and the net was far less humane than killing him outright. What surprised him was the number of men in the cells around him – men who were here for many years, and a few who were in for the rest of their lives – who'd become so institutionalized that they no longer had any desire to experience life on the outside. One old lag had even told him that if the gates to the prison were suddenly to be opened one day, 99 per cent of the prisoners would opt to stay behind bars.

Not Fox. He wasn't going to end up like some sort of zombie, subservient to the establishment as he counted down the days until he finally pegged out, unloved and unmourned, a pantomime hate figure for the masses.

Yet the charges he faced were enough to keep him inside for ten lifetimes. He was the sole surviving terrorist of a bloody siege at a London hotel that had left more than seventy people dead, and there were a whole host of witnesses who'd seen him kill at least five of them in separate incidents in what was widely acknowledged to be Britain's worst terrorist atrocity. There was absolutely no doubt that he would be found guilty at his trial. Even his defence team had conceded as much, but, since the taxpayer was paying them by the hour, they were still prepared to give it a go. And there was no doubt either that the sentence he'd be handed would be a whole-life tariff. In other words, there was no hope of him ever getting out.

And yet . . .

Fox's head hurt. Three days earlier he'd had his first taste of prison violence when he'd been attacked by another prisoner armed with a homemade shank.

He rubbed a finger along the wound where the blade had torn across his scalp, touching each of the nineteen stitches. It felt tender to the touch but he ignored the pain. It would heal soon enough, as would the deep cuts on his right hand and his left and right forearms, which he'd lifted to ward off his attacker's blows. He'd been bloodied, as he had been on more than one occasion in his life, but, as always, he remained unbowed.

The TV in the corner of his cell was switched to BBC *Breakfast News*, as it was every morning. He liked to find out what was happening in the outside world while he ate his breakfast, even though it was rarely anything exciting. But today something was actually happening. The well-scrubbed male presenter had interrupted the fawning interview he was doing with some fourth-rate actor to say that the BBC were getting reports of a bomb attack on a café in central London.

He got up from the bunk and pressed the call button on the wall. Prison was, he thought, much like staying in a very cheap and tatty hotel, which was probably why so many of the prisoners quite liked it.

Outside he could hear the early morning noises of the prison: the clanking of doors; the shouts; the rattle of keys; the occasional burst of laughter – the sounds of a closed, insular community, but a community nonetheless, and he almost wished he could be out there as well. But for the moment he was being held in protective custody on the governor's orders in case there was a further attempt on his life, and it didn't look like that was a situation that was going to be changing any time soon.

A few minutes later, the flap on the cell door opened and the face of Officer Fenwick, a bearded screw at the wrong end of his fifties who'd have trouble stopping a clock let alone a riot, appeared in the gap. It almost amused Fox that Fenwick, unarmed and way too old, was one of the few men standing between him and freedom.

'Good morning, Mr Garrett,' said Fenwick with a cheery smile as if he was addressing his next-door neighbour rather than a man who was about to stand trial for his part in arguably the worst mass murder in modern British history. 'What can I do for you?'

'Good morning, sir,' said Fox, pressing his face up to the gap, pleased to see the other man flinch slightly at his closeness. 'You know it's less than a month to my trial?'

'I do.'

'And you know what I've been charged with?'

'I do.'

'And you know I haven't said a word to the investigating officers about any of the people involved alongside me?'

'Are you going somewhere with this, Mr Garrett, because I'm actually very busy?'

Fox nodded. 'Absolutely.' He stared coolly at the

other man. 'I want to cooperate, Mr Fenwick. I want to tell the police everything I know about the people behind the Stanhope siege. And I want to do it right now.'

'You know the procedure, Mr Garrett. You'll need to make a formal request.'

'It's urgent.'

'So are a lot of things.'

'I've just seen on the TV that there's been another bomb attack in London. And I know it's the same people behind it.'

That stopped Fenwick. He frowned. 'How could you possibly know?'

Fox stared him out. 'I just do,' he said firmly. 'And I need to speak to the governor. Now.'

Fenwick nodded slowly, clearly deciding that Fox's announcement was too big to be ignored. 'I'll inform him of your request.'

'And something else.' Fox paused to make sure even Fenwick couldn't get this next part wrong. 'There's only one person I want to talk to.'

Seven

08.50

Tina stood on the pavement, next to a graffiti-strewn wall, smoking a cigarette, her hands still shaking with the shock of what she'd seen.

The road had been sealed off for fifty yards either side of the lorry, and the place was crawling with emergency services vehicles. The man Tina had been chasing had now been removed in an ambulance, after increasingly desperate efforts by the paramedics to save him had come to nothing. Now there was only a large, irregular bloodstain on the tarmac where he'd been.

The driver of the lorry looked shell-shocked. Two traffic officers had put him inside one of the squad cars furthest away from the scene to breathalyse him and take a statement, where he wouldn't have to look at the evidence of what he'd done. It would be Tina's turn to give a statement soon, but so far all available manpower had been sent to the scene of the explosion near Victoria Station. Thick, bilious smoke still rose above the nearby buildings and helicopters circled lazily overhead like vultures waiting for the kill. The sound of sirens was everywhere.

She sighed. Barely a month back in the force and already it had all gone horribly wrong. It wasn't that she hadn't done her job – she had. The suspect had been running away from the scene of an explosion that had almost certainly been caused by a bomb. She'd identified herself clearly and yelled at him to stop. If he'd been innocent, he would have done. But he'd run for his life, hadn't looked where he was going, and it had ended badly. If it had been anyone else doing the chasing, Tina would have been hailed a hero. But because it was her, she wouldn't be. In the opinion of far too many of her police colleagues, Tina was a magnet for tragedy.

DC Clive Owen wandered over. He had a sympathetic look on his face. 'Are you all right?'

She took a long drag on the cigarette. 'I've been better.'

'Look, you did the right thing. The word is this guy planted a bomb in a café in the middle of rush hour, and there are big casualties. What happened, serves him right. Saves the taxpayer the cost of keeping him behind bars for the next forty years.'

Tina thought about the look on the terrified suspect's face when he'd seen she was chasing him. He hadn't looked like a hardened terrorist.

'I'll stand up for you if there's any shit,' continued Owen. He looked over her shoulder. 'And I think it might be coming now.'

A gleaming Audi A6 had pulled up on the other side of the police tape. A second later the door opened and Tina's boss, DCI Frank Thomas, stepped out. He spotted them immediately, and marched over. He was a big man with a florid expression and a strong desire to make DCS, and he looked extremely pissed off. He hadn't wanted Tina on his squad in the first place, and doubtless his view had just been reinforced.

'This is a major bollocks-up,' he said in his strong Welsh accent, sounding just like a cut-price version of Tom Jones, as he stopped in front of her and Owen. 'We've got a bomb attack with multiple casualties, and the only suspect' – he made the word 'only' stretch twice as long as it should have – 'is run over and squashed by a lorry before we get a chance to question him. And to top it all, the copper doing the chasing, who left her colleague behind in the car—'

'It wasn't quite like that, sir,' said Owen.

'Shut up, Clive. The copper doing the chasing is none other than the Black Widow herself, probably the most controversial figure in the Met, Miss Tina Boyd.' He glared at her. 'Not only have we now got a mountain of paperwork, and a high-profile IPCC investigation to contend with, but the one man who could point us in the direction of the rest of his terrorist cell is dead.'

'What would you have preferred, sir?' said Tina, holding her ground. 'That I let him get away?'

'She's right, sir—'

'Clive, I told you to shut up.' DCI Thomas turned back to Tina. 'What I would have preferred is that you had maintained a visual on him but kept well back, as I believe you were told to do, and as is standard procedure in this kind of scenario, because that way . . .' He paused. 'That way we would have got him alive.'

'I did what I thought was right,' Tina insisted.

'You did what you thought would cover you in glory. There's a big difference.'

'Sir, I was trying to catch a criminal. That's what I thought we were meant to do. It was just bad luck that he got hit.'

'Bad luck seems to follow you around.'

Tina sighed. She couldn't argue with that. She'd also worked out that it was better to be conciliatory than confrontational. 'But I was twenty yards behind him, sir, well back, when he ran straight into that lorry's path.'

'Do we know he's part of a terrorist cell, sir?' asked Owen.

Thomas gave a single decisive nod. 'Yes. There's been a call claiming responsibility from some Islamic outfit that no one's ever heard of. They say there's going to be another attack today. A bigger one. It might be bluster, but the whole Met's on full alert.

Which is why we needed him in one piece so badly.'

'I'd like to make amends, sir,' said Tina.

'Well, unfortunately you're not going to get a chance to.'

'You're not suspending me, are you?' Tina felt the disappointment like a blow. Despite her frustrations with the way the Met was run she loved her job, and knew she was good at it.

'I'll be honest, DC Boyd, a part of me's sorely tempted, but apparently you're needed elsewhere. I've been told I have to temporarily release you from CID with immediate effect. I've also been given a number for you to call.' He fished a business card from his pocket and handed it to her. 'You'll still need to make a full statement on what happened here later today, and you'll have to make yourself available to the IPCC when they come calling. But as of now, you're free to go.'

Tina stared at the handwritten mobile number on the card. At first she thought it was some sort of joke, but it really wasn't a day for jokes. She exchanged puzzled glances with Owen – clearly he didn't have a clue what was happening either – then turned back to Thomas. 'Thank you, sir,' she said, having to shout above the noise of a rapidly approaching helicopter.

She waited for it to pass before dialling the number. It was picked up on the first ring, and straight away she recognized the voice on the other end.

Mike Bolt. A man she'd shared far too much history

with, but whom she hadn't seen or heard from in well over a year.

'I hear from your boss that you've been involved with the suspect from the coffee shop bomb,' said Bolt, with none of the usual preliminaries as to how she was.

'That's right. Is that what you're dealing with too?'

'Indirectly,' he said cryptically. 'I need you for something.'

Tina took a last drag on the cigarette and crushed it underfoot. 'What?'

'You remember Fox, the captured terrorist from the Stanhope siege? Well, he wants to cooperate, and for whatever reason – and I cannot think for the life of me what it could be – he wants to talk to you. I need you over here right away.'

'But I haven't got transport, and the roads around Victoria Station are gridlocked. I also haven't got a clue where you are, or even who you work for these days. It's been a long time, remember?' She resisted asking why he hadn't bothered to call before now. She already knew the answer to that one.

'We're a ten-minute walk from where you are now. I'll text you the address.'

He ended the call, and Tina took a deep breath. It was barely nine a.m. and already this was turning into one of the most dramatic days of her career.

Eight

09.12

Crack cocaine can be an excellent moneymaker. It's one of the most addictive substances known to man. That first hit on the pipe is meant to be like having a five-minute orgasm multiplied by a hundred while simultaneously finding out you've won ten million on the lottery. Addicts will do near enough anything for their fix – forever chasing, but never quite managing to replicate, that very first high – and there are plenty of them out there living on the periphery of everyone else's world, unseen and unloved.

So if you're running a crackhouse selling rocks at ten pounds a hit, you can easily end up taking two, three grand a day. Of course you've got overheads. You've got to buy the coke to make the end product, and you've got to hire security, because there are plenty of people out there who'd rob you blind if they could, but even so, you're still left with the kind of profit margins most legitimate businesses struggling in the recession would kill for. And you don't even have to pay tax on them.

Most crackhouses are run by individual dealers who let their places go to shit, attract the attention of the local housing authority and even, God forbid, the cops, and end up getting shut down. But if you're an entrepreneur with a bit of intelligence, and you keep your dealing discreet, then you can operate under the radar for months, years even, building up a network of establishments. And if you actually import the coke you use to make the crack yourself, then you can end up a very rich man.

Nicholas Tyndall was one such entrepreneur. A well-established gangster with good contacts among his fellow criminals, and even within the police service itself, he ran eleven crackhouses across north-east London that were reputed to net him more than two hundred grand a week. And they were never shut down because one of Tyndall's front companies bought the properties being used to sell the dope as well as the properties next door (usually at knock-down prices) so that complaints from neighbours were kept to a minimum, which meant the cops weren't too interested either. If no one reports a crime, there's an argument that a lot of target-obsessed senior coppers subscribe to that says it's not actually being committed. Ergo, everyone – dealers, addicts, civilians, the law – stays happy.

One of the headaches you've got as a crack entrepreneur, though, is getting the cash out of your establishments and into your own grubby mitts. You need men you can trust for this. Men who are reliable, and who scare the shit out of people. One such individual was LeShawn Lambden. Now this guy was a man mountain. Six feet five inches tall and two hundred and fifty pounds of pure, rippling, three-hours-a-day weight training's worth of muscle, with a face like a bull and the kind of coal-eyed glare that puts the fear of God into citizens and criminals alike.

Every few days LeShawn and his crew would travel round to all of Tyndall's establishments and collect 80 per cent of the takings, the other twenty being paid to the dealer who ran the premises. In order to minimize the risk of being stopped by the cops or, worse, being ambushed by people keen to get their hands on all that cash, LeShawn always varied the days he carried out his collections, and the order he visited the crackhouses in, and he liked to use different vehicles. Street legend had it that in all the time he'd been doing the job, no one had ever held back cash from him, or tried to take it.

And now all that was about to change.

The job had been planned down to a tee. LeShawn might have worked hard to keep his movements unpredictable but it was his leather jacket that let him down. It was a knee-length black thing that he always wore when he was out on business, supposedly because it made him look cool and menacing, like Arnie in the first *Terminator* movie. It hadn't been very hard to get a GPS sewn into the lining. A quick and silent break-in at one of his girlfriend's places when he was staying over a couple of nights earlier, and five minutes later there were four of them planted, so if one ran out of batteries we could just switch on another. The GPS units were attached to a laptop in which the coordinates of all eleven crackhouses had been entered. As soon as LeShawn visited two of the addresses within fifteen minutes of each other, an alarm sounded, letting us know that he was almost certainly on one of his collection runs.

So there I was, sitting in a Volvo C60 on a grimy, litter-strewn council estate in south Tottenham, with Cecil in the driver's seat next to me, watching the GPS's progress on his mobile phone. Three minutes earlier LeShawn had stopped at crackhouse number eleven, the last on his list, two hundred yards from where we were parked.

Cecil was short, wiry and very, very hard. He had a very small bald head that reminded me of a fly's, and the kind of terrifying glare that sets all but the most physically confident men on edge. He was looking at his watch, counting down the seconds. LeShawn and his crew didn't like to hang around any longer than they had to at the places they visited. They went in, got the dealer to hand over the contents of the safe, gave him his cut, and left. It wasn't their job to see if the money tallied with the amount of coke entering the premises. This was done separately by Tyndall's finance people. The average length of time from the moment LeShawn's car stopped outside a crackhouse to the moment it started moving again was four minutes and fifteen seconds. The one he was visiting now took slightly longer at four minutes and fifty, because there was a bit more of a walk to and from the front door.

Which meant it was time to move.

Cecil gave me a curt nod. 'You ready?'

'Sure,' I said, sounding calmer than I felt. The adrenalin was pumping through me, heightening my senses. This job may have been planned to the last detail, but both of us knew better than most that in fast-moving, violent situations, the first casualty is usually the plan itself. The key when things go wrong is to ride with the punches and not panic.

Cecil switched on the engine and pulled out, taking a left at the end of the road.

The area was vaguely rundown but money had been spent keeping the streets clean and the walls free from graffiti. Low-rise sixties council blocks painted a tasteless mud-brown stretched out on either side of us. The road was quiet. Not many people commuted to work round here, and those kids who weren't bunking off were already in school.

Halfway down, a gunmetal-grey BMW X5 was parked illegally on the pavement outside one of the blocks. It was one of the cars LeShawn sometimes used, and a young black guy sat in the driver's seat.

Cecil drove towards him. The road was narrow with cars lining one side, and he had to go quite slow. LeShawn always carried the bag containing the takings with him, never letting it out of his sight as he went into each of the crackhouses, and he was always accompanied by one of his crew. So the plan was to relieve them of the cash when they were en route back to the car. That way we had the whole three-man crew together where we could control them. But the thing was, it required perfect timing. If we were too early making our approach then we'd have to come back round the block again, and as soon as the X5 driver saw our car a second time, he'd be as suspicious as hell. These guys were armed, and if they got nervous, anything could happen. Plus, there were only two of us, when really you needed four or five for a job like this.

It struck me as we crawled towards our targets, and my heart thudded hard and fast in my ears, that this really wasn't such a clever idea.

But then, lo and behold, there was LeShawn and his wingman sauntering across the stretch of grass at the front of the building towards the X5 with the kind of confidence that only men with guns have. LeShawn had the holdall with the loot slung over one shoulder, and both men had their right hands in the pockets of their jackets, doubtless clutching weapons.

LeShawn's head turned slowly in our direction.

'OK,' said Cecil, still staring straight ahead, speaking as casually as possible. 'I'm going to count to three, then you do it.'

Without looking down, I removed the jacket that had been sitting on my lap, revealing a brand-new Heckler and Koch MP5 machine pistol and the type of black police cap worn by armed CO19 cops.

One . . . two . . .

LeShawn and his mate were only five yards away from the X5. He was still staring straight at me as he walked, but making no move for his weapon.

Three.

Our car was still moving as I threw open the door, lifting the MP5 and flinging on the cap, and leapt out. 'Armed police! Get on the ground now!' I ran towards them, MP5 pointed straight at LeShawn, who I knew was the one most likely to go for his gun. 'Now! Now! Now!'

This is the pivotal moment. You've made your move, now you've just got to wait that single second to see how they react. Most people are so caught out they instinctively do as they're told, but a few are wired differently. They either bolt for it or, very occasionally, they stand and fight. And if anyone was going to stand and fight it was going to be LeShawn Lambden.

LeShawn didn't move. Neither did the other guy. They just stared at me, calling my bluff.

I kept coming, yelling at them to get down, pulling

the cap down, trying to obscure my face, knowing that if I fired I'd ruin everything, and if I didn't fire I'd ruin everything as well. Out of the corner of my eye I saw the X5 driver try to reverse the car, then heard Cecil's barked commands followed by an explosion of gunfire from his MP5 as he blew out the car's front tyres and one of its headlights.

The sound of automatic gunfire's a hell of a lot louder than most people expect, and if you're on a narrow street without ear protectors on, you jump when you hear it.

I took another step forward, my finger tensing on the trigger. 'On your knees now, both of you, or I'll blow your fucking heads off!' I didn't bother shouting 'armed police' again since it was abundantly clear now that we weren't. If anything, though, this did a better job of securing their cooperation, because they both finally did what they were told.

LeShawn stared me down, a look of simmering anger in his coal-black eyes. 'You don't know who the fuck you're dealing with here,' he spat.

'Yeah, I do. An idiot who gets caught with his pants down because he's too cocky. Now remove your hand from your pocket nice and slowly and throw away the gun you've got in there.'

'I haven't got a gun.'

'Just fucking do it.'

'I'll kill you for this. You're a dead man, you understand?'

'You've got three seconds to comply or you'll be the dead man.' I lifted the barrel of the MP5 slightly so it was pointed right between his eyes, my aim absolutely steady.

The key is to establish control, but LeShawn was still delaying. Behind him, faces were appearing in the windows of the council block, attracted by the noise of gunfire. Any second now the cops would be called, and there could be an ARV right round the corner. We had to move.

I started counting. 'One! Two!' My finger tightened on the trigger, and I pushed the stock back into my shoulder, preparing to fire.

Which was when LeShawn caved. Reluctantly he brought his hand out of his pocket and threw a Glock pistol on to the grass in front of him.

'Throw the holdall over to me. Now.'

He hesitated, and at the same time Cecil came over, pushing the X5 driver in front of him using the barrel of his MP5, before kicking his legs from under him. 'What the fuck's going on?' he demanded, pointing his weapon at LeShawn. 'Do as he tells you or you're dead.'

Slowly, LeShawn heaved it off his shoulder and threw it over.

I grabbed it, slung it over my own shoulder, impressed by its weight, and took a step back.

'You,' I said to LeShawn's wingman, the third member of the crew. 'Bring out your gun.'

'I ain't got one,' said the guy, taking his hands out of his pockets. They were empty, and now he looked scared.

I told him to put his hands on his head and, while Cecil picked up LeShawn's gun from the grass, I gave the guy a quick search, keeping the barrel of my MP5 pressed against the base of his skull. He was holding a knife but that was all, which is the great thing about Britain's gun laws. The baddies can't get hold of decent weaponry very easily any more, which gives men like us an advantage.

I pocketed the knife and told the guy to keep his hands on his head, which he did without arguing. It wasn't his money and he wasn't prepared to die in order to protect it, which seemed to me to be the sensible option. I'd have done the same thing. Most sane people would. But then with these guys it's all about respect, and having a rep on the street, and being made to go down on your knees in a public place and give up your stash and your weapons is an insult of the most heinous kind.

Which was why, in the end, I suppose the whole thing was always going to go tits up.

It happened when I was crouched down behind LeShawn, gun pressed against the back of his head. I was about to give him a brief once-over just to check he didn't have another gun somewhere, while Cecil covered me from the front. By this point the whole thing, from the moment I'd jumped out of the moving car, had lasted no more than forty-five, fifty seconds tops, and was running pretty smoothly. We were ten seconds away from making our getaway when Cecil cursed and looked towards the council block behind me. I heard shouts too, and turned round.

A lanky white guy with wild hair, wearing a pair of tracksuit bottoms and nothing else, had appeared out of the building's main entrance and was running towards us, waving a carving knife and clearly off his nut on crack.

Cecil opened fire over the guy's head, the noise deafening, and the guy had the good sense to hit the deck, dropping the knife in the process. But I'd let my guard down, and suddenly LeShawn swung round, grabbed the barrel of the gun, and tried to yank it out of my hands. I fell forward, resisting pulling the trigger, and fell over him, landing in the grass, twisting round so I could still keep a grip on the gun.

LeShawn fell on top of me, shoving the barrel to one side, one beefy hand going round my throat and squeezing with such power that it cut off my air supply instantly. I tried to kick out, but I didn't have the room to do any damage. LeShawn roared, spittle forming at the corners of his mouth as he used his free hand to slam the MP5 down into the ground, twisting my arms in the process. He lunged at me, trying to take a bite out of my face, but I managed to free up a hand and smack him hard on the underside of his chin, making him bite his tongue.

He roared with frustration and lunged at me again, which was the moment the left side of his face suddenly disappeared in a welter of red, and I was splattered in warm blood. His grip on my throat weakened as his whole body slumped. He let out a loud grunt, and I had to put up a hand to stop him falling on me.

I kicked him off me and jumped to my feet, wiping the blood from my eyes as I made sure the holdall was still on my back.

'Come on, move it!' yelled Cecil, retreating rapidly.

The other two members of the crew were lying on their fronts, still alive but clearly not wanting to get involved, while the wild-haired guy was back on his feet and dancing round with the knife, but still sensible enough not to get too close.

Cecil glared at me as we ran for the car. 'What the fuck were you doing?'

I didn't answer as I chucked the holdall in the back of the car while he ran round the front and jumped in the driver's side.

And then, just when things couldn't get any worse, they did.

A marked patrol car pulled into the road behind us. There were no lights or sirens, so it wasn't responding to an emergency call. It had arrived on the scene purely by accident and was driving in our direction. I looked at them, and they looked at me, slowing up at the same time as they took in the sight of a man in a police cap with a submachine gun and a face covered in blood.

The terrible thing was, I recognized them. PCs John Nolan and Gloria Owana. I'd met them both when we'd worked out of the same station. Even so, I didn't know them well, and I was pretty damn sure they wouldn't recognize me in the state I was in.

But they still presented a threat, and it was time I showed Cecil what I could do. As their car stopped, I opened fire, swinging the gun in a steady arc as I blew out the tyres, feeling that intense satisfaction that only pulling a trigger can bring, watching as both ducked out of sight. Out of the corner of my eye I saw the wild-haired guy charging me and I swung the gun round, ready to pop him if I had to, but he took a flying dive and landed face down on the pavement with an angry thud, the knife clattering on to the tarmac.

Then, as Cecil gunned the engine, I turned and jumped in the car, and he pulled away in a screech of tyres.

The whole thing had been a disaster. A man was dead; cops had been shot at; half the Met would probably be on our tail in the next five minutes. But in the end we still had the money.

Although if I'd known what it was going to be used for, I'd have flung it out the window there and then.

Nine

09.19

'Have you got any idea why William Garrett might want to talk to you?' asked Mike Bolt, leaning forward in his seat and fixing Tina with a cool, formal stare that belied the friendship they'd once had. They were in his office in a large Georgian townhouse just off Green Park, facing each other for the first time in almost two years.

Tina shrugged. 'I've got no idea. It's not as if I've ever had any contact with him. All I am these days is lowly CID.'

'Although you still manage to get yourself right in the thick of things. It's a pity we lost that suspect.'

'You're the second person today who's told me that, Mike. It wasn't my fault.'

'I know, but we've now had confirmation that the explosion earlier was a powerful rucksack bomb, delivered by the suspect you were chasing. We've already had a very plausible claim of responsibility from an unknown outfit calling themselves Islamic Command, and they've given us an ultimatum. Either the government acquiesces to their demands – which are the usual stuff, promising to pull out of all Muslim lands – by eight o'clock tonight or there'll be a much bigger attack.'

'It all sounds very similar to the Stanhope siege.'

Bolt nodded. 'It does.'

The Stanhope siege had been a short but brutal terrorist incident just over a year earlier. It had involved a team of white mercenaries, allied with Arab gunmen, who'd set off two bombs in London before taking over the Stanhope Hotel and holding hundreds of guests hostage. When the whole thing had ended six hours later, more than seventy people were dead, and the psyche of the nation had been left badly scarred. Almost all the terrorists had died – one of them at the hands of Tina herself, who'd killed him in self-defence while rescuing the kidnapped children of one of the senior officers involved (an act for which she'd narrowly escaped charges) – but, since that night, there'd been no further arrests, nor any clear sign of who was responsible. Theories had abounded. Some claimed the terrorists were working for al-Qaeda; others for an unnamed Arab government, or the Iranians; and some claimed the real organizers were even closer to home and members of a domestic neo-Nazi organization seeking to foment discontent.

But the problem was that only two of those involved had survived. One, a member of the Met's Counter Terrorism Command called John Cheney, who'd been the terrorists' inside man, had been found hanged in his cell a few weeks afterwards. And the other, a former soldier called William Garrett, who'd gone by the codename Fox, and who was now in prison awaiting trial, had kept his mouth resolutely shut.

Until now, it seemed.

Tina frowned. 'So Fox has suddenly decided that he wants to cooperate?'

'Apparently he saw footage of the explosion this morning and told the governor he knew who was behind it, but wouldn't give any further details.'

'The suspect I chased this morning was south Asian. Probably Pakistani. Definitely not a white mercenary, and not the kind of guy likely to be working as an Arab government agent.'

'So it might be nothing to do with Fox or any of his friends. But initial reports are saying the explosives used were PETN, the same as those used at the Stanhope, and that the bomb looked sophisticated. The thing is, there just aren't that many terrorists with access to that kind of weaponry, particularly homegrown Islamic extremists.' Bolt paused. 'There's something else as well. There was an attempt on Fox's life three days ago.'

'I didn't hear anything about that.'

'It's being kept under wraps. Cheney died before he

could stand trial. If they lose Fox as well, it's going to make the government, and this country, look like a bunch of incompetents. He was attacked by another prisoner armed with a homemade blade. He got a slash across the head and defensive cuts on his hands and arms, and ended up with a lot of stitches. But he managed to fight his attacker off and put him in hospital as well.'

'Do we know why he was attacked?'

'The other prisoner's not talking. He's Category A and violent, so it could be any number of reasons, but the timing, just days before a new bombing campaign, is the kind of coincidence that sets alarm bells ringing.'

Bolt absent-mindedly stroked the biggest and deepest of the three small scars that dotted his right cheek – the result of a car crash many years earlier. Because of his big build and closely cropped hair, they helped to lend him a thuggish appearance that was only partly offset by his incredibly blue eyes, and looking at him now, Tina remembered how attractive she'd once found him.

'Anyway,' he continued, 'Fox is a tough bastard, but the word is the attack's shaken him up, so what he has to say could be useful. It might also be nothing, of course, and if he's after immunity from prosecution, then he's pissing in the wind. But I want to give it a shot.'

It struck Tina how little she knew about Mike Bolt

these days. The building they were in now was a four-storey Georgian townhouse on a quiet residential Mayfair street, with a brand-new plaque outside the front door identifying the occupants as Lowe Robertson Real Estate. She'd walked through an open-plan office with a handful of men and women working on high-end PCs to get to the room she was in now, but the place was hardly buzzing with activity.

'So, what is this place and how are you involved?' she asked. 'The last I heard you were working for SOCA.'

'I'm in CTC now, working counter terrorism. I'm running a unit called Special Operations, but you won't find anything about us in the brochures or on the Met website. We've been set up specifically to identify, locate and gather evidence against the people behind the Stanhope siege – the ones who bankrolled it, and provided logistical support to the terrorists.'

'That sounds a lot more fun than what I've been doing these past few months. Fancy seconding me?'

Bolt smiled properly for the first time since Tina had walked into his office. He was, she thought, still a good-looking guy, perhaps even more so since he'd hit his forties. His hair had begun to turn from blond to silver, and the lines on his narrow, aquiline features had become more pronounced, but the changes actually enhanced his appearance, and she wondered suddenly if he was still single.

'It sounds a lot more exciting than it actually is,' he

said. 'We do all the usual no-frills policework: sifting through available intelligence in-house, talking to informants, running taps and surveillance ops. But it's a long job, and I've got to be honest with you, it hasn't generated many good leads. The people we're looking for aren't known to us, and they've proved very adept at covering their tracks.'

'I heard from various sources that the Stanhope siege was bankrolled by an unfriendly Middle Eastern government.'

'According to sources within MI6, there was financial backing from Arab sources within the Middle East, and at a high, possibly governmental, level, but there was help for the attackers from within the UK as well, and given the fact that half the terrorists were white former soldiers it's very likely that it came from extreme right-wing elements, and ones with money. That's why Fox could be so important to us. I need you to find out what he has to say.'

'Sounds good to me,' said Tina. 'But I want to be a part of your team. I'm not cut out for recycling low-level scumbags through the courts system, which is what I'm doing at the moment. Is there any way you can get me on board in a more permanent capacity?'

Bolt sighed. 'The work we do here's low-key and secretive, and I don't want someone who's going to go on a one-woman crusade for justice, put herself and everyone around her in danger, get her face plastered all over the media, and end up compromising all our work. I'll be straight with you, Tina. You're a hothead, and it's got you in a hell of a lot of trouble in the past. That's why you're a DC in a small CID office.'

Tina had heard this all plenty of times before as she'd fought to get herself reinstated, but it still hurt coming from a man she'd once considered a good friend. 'I'm still a good copper. You know that. And I get results.' She leaned forward and looked him right in the eye. 'Give me a chance, and you have my word that I won't do a thing to compromise any part of your work. I mean it.'

Bolt stood up, looking uncomfortable. 'I'll see what I can do. In the meantime, you need to get going. Interviewing Fox is top priority, and that comes all the way from the top. There's a helicopter waiting at New Scotland Yard to take you up to the prison where they're holding him. I'll get one of our people to give you a lift over there.'

Tina got to her feet, feeling relieved and disappointed at the same time. She was glad to be in the thick of things again, but sad that her relationship with Bolt had become so distant. Theirs had always been a complicated one, yet he'd always stood by her when things had been tough. She owed him a lot more than he owed her, and it was a debt she knew she'd never be able to repay.

'One thing before I go,' she said. 'A lot of people died in the Stanhope incident, and the inquiry to find out who's behind it has got to be pretty major. So, why does this place feel so empty?'

'We're a small team. Manpower's a problem these days. With all the cuts going on, and the resources they've pumped into the phone-hacking scandal, the Met's running extremely low on detectives.' He shrugged, seeing her expression. 'I know, I don't like it either, but that's just the way it is. Also, up until about an hour ago, we've effectively been working on a hunch. We've always believed there was UK involvement, but there's never been any proof. And there's another reason too. The smaller the team, the less chance there is of a leak to the bad guys. The fact that a senior CTC man like John Cheney was working for the terrorists scared a lot of people. That's why I've agreed to work with you, Tina. You're a hell of a lot of things, and not all of them good, but one thing's for certain: you're definitely not corrupt.'

Tina smiled. 'I'm flattered.'

They looked at each other, and something – a flash of their old friendship – passed between them.

'It's good to see you again,' he said. 'Considering what you've already been through this morning, you look great.'

'It's good to be back,' she said. And she meant it.

Ten

09.50

There are no noble causes.

They tell you there are, but they're lying. When they sent me to Iraq they said we'd be liberating a downtrodden people from the shackles of a brutal dictatorship, but all we did was destabilize the whole region and start a civil war that's still rumbling on today, losing a lot of good people in the process. And in Afghanistan they said we'd be in the forefront of the fight against global terrorism, and helping to keep the streets of Britain safe for present and future generations.

Bullshit.

The streets are no safer because we went there. In fact, they're probably a lot less safe. The world's Muslim extremists – the kind we were supposed to be defeating – can come and go inside Britain as they please, safe in the knowledge that, thanks to the

Human Rights Act and the parasitic lawyers who uphold it, they can't be deported. And they hate us even more because of what we're doing in Muslim countries. We're international aggressors and domestic appeasers, which seems to me to be the worst kind of combination there is.

And the politicians who sent us to those God-forsaken countries are sitting pretty at home, eating their vol-au-vents, fucking their secretaries, and fiddling their expenses, while harping on about freedom and sacrifice and all that shit, even though it's not them who've lost limbs in IED attacks, or seen their best mate's brains splattered all over some dusty rock thanks to a sniper's bullet.

I did two tours of Afghanistan and we didn't change a damn thing. Not a jot. The moment western forces leave, the Taliban will be all over the country like a rash. And you know why? Because they don't want our democracy. Most of them don't even have a clue what it is, and the few who do think it contradicts God's law anyway, so won't have anything to do with it. Democracy to them just means corruption – and one look at the western-backed government in Kabul and you can see they've got a point. So the whole thing will have been a complete waste of time, money and, most of all, the blood of far too many good men.

We changed cars less than a mile from the scene of the robbery, switching to a Renault Mégane saloon Cecil had parked under some trees next to a stretch of deserted waste ground near the Lockwood reservoir. No one saw us as we torched the car we'd used for the robbery, along with the police caps. We kept the guns, though. In a country like Britain where even semi-automatic weapons are almost impossible to come by, they were way too valuable, and after putting them and the money in the boot, we changed into suit jackets and ties, got in our car, and drove off in the direction of Enfield. All without being seen. Even in the centre of a city like London you can still find some lonely places where people don't go at ten o'clock on a cold, grey February morning.

I was still pumped up with a mix of adrenalin and anger. The plan had been to hold up LeShawn and his men and make them give up the cash with threats, a few shots into their car, but no actual violence. That way, even if there'd been witnesses, and the police had found empty shell casings at the scene, the crime would never have been reported. LeShawn was hardly going to say anything, and people who live near crackhouses tend to learn to look the other way. In other words, it should have been perfect.

But now LeShawn was dead. He might have been an arsehole and I might not have pulled the trigger, but that wasn't much consolation. First off, the robbery had been a joint enterprise, which meant I was just as responsible for his murder as Cecil was in the eyes of the law. And second, I'd shot up a cop car, ripped the front of it to shreds, and scared the living shit out of the people inside, thereby making myself a very active participant. Worse, pulling the trigger had felt way too good.

My name's Jones by the way. Richard Burnham-Jones to be exact, but I always hated the names Richard, Rick, Richie, and especially Dick, and I'm not a big fan of double barrels, so it's always been Jones, which suits me fine. And I'm not a bad man either, whatever first impressions might suggest. You could say I've got in with the wrong crowd, and you'd be absolutely right, but not quite for the reasons you might think.

It was a cold day but I could feel the sweat on my brow, and I used my forearm to wipe it away.

'What the fuck happened back there, Jones?' demanded Cecil, fixing me with one of his trademark glares. 'You almost let me down.'

The two of us have known each other a long time. We've served together in a war zone, and that creates a bond that other men just don't have. That didn't mean Cecil didn't scare me. He did. He scared everyone. He might only have been a short bald guy, but he was also lean and wiry, with an intense energy that seemed to emanate from him in waves, and eyes like pieces of flint. Even his voice, with its hard Belfast growl, spelled aggression. Luckily, I knew how to handle him.

'If I'd fired when we were fighting, I could have hit

anyone, including you,' I said. 'That's the problem when there are only two of us on the job. It was always going to be risky.'

'You're not going soft on me are you, big man?' Cecil didn't care that he'd just killed someone. As far as he was concerned, they'd disobeyed instructions, got what was coming to them, and now he'd moved on. That was what he was like.

'I just shot up a cop car, Cecil, so no, I'm not going soft. We needed a bigger team, that's all. I told you that before we got involved. I thought you had friends we could use.'

'This was a test, Jones. To check your loyalty.'

'I'm not interested in tests. You know you can trust me. We've got history.' And we did. We had secrets too, forged on the battlefields of Helmand Province.

There was a pause, and then he nodded slowly. 'I think it may be time to go up to the next level,' he said, finding a gap in the parked cars at the side of the road and pulling up. 'But first I've got to make a quick phone call.'

We were outside a parade of shabby-looking shops, and I watched as Cecil passed a group of even more shabby-looking drunks on a bench shouting incoherently to each other in what sounded like Polish. As I looked on, one tried to stand up and simply toppled over on his side, landing against a large overflowing litter bin, much to the mirth of the others, before rolling over on the pavement while somehow keeping his drink intact. A young woman in a business suit hurried past, head down and giving them a wide berth.

No, there are no noble causes. If you fight for something you believe in, innocent people will always get hurt, and even if you achieve whatever goal it is you've set yourself, it'll always end up being a hollow victory, because everything comes at a price.

Cecil walked back to the car, giving the drunks a sideways look that temporarily silenced all of them, and got back inside.

'There's someone who wants to meet you.'

And that was when I knew I was in.

Eleven

10.26

The man was parked in a deserted stretch of woodland bordering a golf course just inside the M25 when he got off the phone to Cecil. He had an iPad on his lap and was watching Sky News as they continued their frenetic coverage of the coffee shop bomb attack. So far, actual hard news was scarce; they were relying on eyewitness reports and continued footage of the scene from the Sky News Copter. The fire in the café was now out, but the street was still full of emergency vehicles. According to the rolling newsreel on the bottom of the screen six people had so far been confirmed dead, with more than thirty wounded, but the death toll was expected to rise. There were also unconfirmed reports that a previously unknown terror group had claimed responsibility, that the bomber himself had fled the café before the explosion, and that he'd been arrested.

This last rumour concerned him. They'd used Akhtar Mohammed so that the attack could be blamed on Islamic fundamentalists. If it was revealed that he'd been blackmailed into delivering the bomb, then their plan fell to pieces. Worse still, Mohammed would be able to identify Martha Crossman as the intended target.

There was nothing he could do about this now, though, so he sat patiently, staring at the iPad's screen, waiting for the signal to go to the next stage.

Sure enough, a little over five minutes later it finally came as the anchorwoman interrupted her interview with the Sky security correspondent to announce further breaking news. Viewers had been calling the newsroom to report that large numbers of armed police had surrounded a block of flats in Bayswater, barely a couple of miles from where the coffee shop bomb had exploded, and were in the process of evacuating the surrounding area. A minute after that the security correspondent announced live on air that he'd received confirmation from a source at New Scotland Yard that an ongoing armed operation was underway.

This was the amazing thing about modern life, thought the man. The speed with which news travelled was almost instantaneous. There were plenty of positives in this. It meant citizens were generally kept well informed. It made it difficult for dictatorships to hide their guilty secrets. Unfortunately, it also allowed the bad guys to monitor the progress of the security forces highly effectively.

The screen had switched back to the Sky News Copter which was now circling above the block of flats where he'd shot dead Mika and booby-trapped her body over two hours earlier. Dozens of black-clad police were moving like ants round the front of the building as they formed a cordon around it and evacuated residents from the surrounding flats. Clearly they'd traced the mobile phone he'd used to make the call claiming responsibility for the café bomb, as he'd anticipated. Of course, they wouldn't be reckless and go storming in, even though he could see that a number of them were CO19, with their trademark Heckler and Kochs. First they'd need to secure the area, finish the evacuation of any civilian within a hundred yards, then make a risk assessment, before even thinking of trying to get into the flat where the dead woman lay with the bomb and the phone on top of her. The whole thing would take hours. The man smiled. He knew this would happen, which was why there was a second bomb in the boot of one of the cars in the parking area directly in front of the building. The device contained twenty kilos of PETN explosives in two large bags, surrounded by a further twenty kilos of assorted shrapnel – and, like the bomb on Mika, it was timed to go off in two minutes exactly.

So far no one seemed to be taking any notice of the

parked cars, although the senior officers on the scene would get round to checking them fairly soon. They'd probably already blocked the mobile phone signal in the immediate area to prevent any booby-trap bombs being set off remotely. Secondary devices were a known hallmark of Islamic terrorists. At the moment, though, the situation on the ground was still in its early semi-chaotic stages.

The man looked at his watch. One minute to detonation.

He took a cheap mobile phone from the outer pocket of his jacket and speed-dialled the single number stored on it. 'This is the Islamic Command,' he announced into the voice disguiser as the man on the *Evening Standard* news desk picked up. 'Two more bombs are about to explode. There will be no further attacks if our demands are met.' He ended the call and switched off the phone, throwing it out of the window into some bushes.

The Sky News Copter was still filming the scene when there was a huge flash of light, accompanied by a very loud bang, from among the parked cars, followed moments later by a second blast from inside one of the flats. The camera shook and the helicopter banked, temporarily losing its view of the scene as the programme suddenly went to split screen, showing a visibly shaken anchorwoman with her hand on her mouth as it became clear to her that she'd just witnessed a second bomb attack.

The man shut the iPad case, and pulled away from the kerb.

It was time to meet their new recruit.

Twelve

10.40

HMP Westmoor was a very big, very bland-looking modern prison set slap bang in the middle of glorious rolling Hertfordshire countryside. It was, Tina thought, like some kind of immense fortified municipal library, and it had been an act of architectural barbarism to put it in such a beautiful place.

As she walked towards the reception area, it struck her that she could very easily have ended up in a place like this. It was only a little over a year since she'd killed a man with a single blow to the head. The fact that the man in question, twenty-one-year-old Liam Roy Shetland, had been one of the terrorists involved in the Stanhope siege and was about to murder two kidnapped children was still not perceived as sufficient justification for what she'd done.

Although she and Shetland had been fighting, and Tina had sustained a number of injuries herself, he'd had his back to her when she'd hit him with a piece of piping, and for weeks afterwards charges had been hanging over her head. She'd been lucky. Public and political pressure had helped her, as had the fact that Shetland was going for a gun at the time. Tina was a hero in some people's eyes, the kind of tough, no-nonsense cop that the UK was sorely lacking these days. 'Dirty Harriet' the *Daily Mail* had called her, which was far more preferable than 'The Black Widow' moniker that had haunted her ever since one of her colleagues had been killed on a job they were both working on. Politicians, sniffing an opportunity as always, had also got involved, singing her praises (but with plenty of caveats, of course), several of them pushing for her reinstatement in the force, which was how she'd finally ended up in Westminster CID.

Westmoor was a maximum-security prison, housing only Category A offenders, and those awaiting trial for the most serious crimes. It was built in a wheel shape, with the six spokes representing separate wings, each of which could be sealed off from the others, and a separate prison-within-a-prison section in the centre where only those guilty of, or charged with, the most serious crimes were held, and it was here that Fox was currently residing.

Having filled out all the forms and passed through security, Tina's first port of call, however, was the governor's office.

The governor, a tall white-haired man in his sixties

with a slight stoop, a bow tie, and the air of a weary academic, got up from behind a cluttered desk next to the room's only window. 'I'm Jeremy Goodman,' he said, giving her a surprisingly firm handshake and a quick once-over, before motioning her to take a seat opposite him. 'So you're the famous Tina Boyd. I've read a lot about you over the years.'

'All bad I'm sure.'

Goodman didn't smile. 'All very interesting,' he said after a short pause, his silence confirming that yes, it had all been bad. 'And you're here to see William Garrett?'

'That's right. I understand he was attacked three days ago. Can you tell me what happened?'

Goodman nodded, an expression of distaste sitting all too easily on his face. 'It was a most regrettable incident. We pride ourselves here at Westmoor on the peaceful, tolerant environment we've fostered, and as such, relations between individual prisoners, and between prisoners and staff, are generally very good. This fight was a rarity. There was a confrontation between Mr Garrett and another Category A prisoner, Eric Hughes, inside the main recreational area toilets of the prison's Central Maximum Security Section, where they're both housed. Both prisoners were injured, and were hospitalized in separate sections of the hospital here. They've since been released from the hospital, but we don't know what caused their altercation, since both prisoners refused to cooperate with the police when they were interviewed yesterday.'

'Was it captured on film?'

'No. The camera covering the main area of the toilet was out of order. By the time the control room realized it wasn't working, and had organized someone from maintenance to examine it, the fight was over.'

'So it suggests a degree of planning.'

'I honestly don't know,' said Goodman defensively. 'Two of our officers heard the commotion from the toilets. They ran inside and intervened.'

'You describe it as a fight, but Mr Garrett sustained some major slash wounds. It sounds like he was attacked by the other man.'

'We can't be certain. The camera in the corridor outside recorded each man going into the toilets approximately thirty seconds apart, but it was impossible to see which one was carrying the knife. And when the officers went in, the two men were struggling violently on the floor, with Mr Garrett on top of Mr Hughes, punching him, even though he was losing a lot of blood. The homemade knife that was used was a few feet away. It's been taken away by the police for examination, and we're awaiting the results.'

'Can you tell me about the other prisoner – Mr Hughes? What's he in here for?'

'Murder. I'm afraid Eric Hughes is a man with a very violent background. He killed a man during an aggravated burglary eight years ago – one of a series of similar crimes that left a further two people seriously injured.'

'When's he due for his parole hearing?' asked Tina, unable to quite hide the cynicism in her voice.

'The minimum tariff for Mr Hughes set by the judge was eighteen years, so it'll be another decade at least before he can be considered for release. He may have a violent past but his behaviour since he's been at Westmoor has generally been very good prior to the incident on Monday.'

'I'm going to need to speak with him while I'm here.'

'As I said, he's already been interviewed by the local CID, and he refused to cooperate.'

'Maybe I can sweet-talk him into admitting something,' said Tina with a slight smile.

'Maybe you can. I'll see what I can arrange,' Goodman answered tightly, as if it was an inconvenience.

Tina was used to certain people taking an instant dislike to her – it was the kind of thing that happened when you'd attracted the sort of headlines she had – but she was a little surprised by the cold reception she was getting here. She'd expected more from a man running one of the country's toughest prisons. 'Thank you, I'd appreciate that. As for Mr Garrett, I understand he wants to cooperate with the inquiry into the Stanhope attacks.'

'Yes. He made contact with one of the prison officers this morning, after he saw footage of the bomb in London on the news. He said that he knew who'd done it, but refused to talk to anyone other than you.' He raised his eyebrows. 'Do you have any idea why that might be?'

Tina shook her head. 'No. I've had no contact with him whatsoever. I'm not even working on the inquiry. At least I wasn't until an hour ago.'

'I'm just hoping that he's not going to attempt to' – Goodman paused, clearly looking for the right word – 'manipulate you.'

'I'm not easily manipulated, Mr Goodman. Tell me, does Mr Garrett sound genuinely interested in cooperating?'

Goodman thought about this for a moment. 'I think the altercation he was involved in scared him. It shocked all of us. Both men were very lucky not to have been more seriously injured.' He paused. 'But Mr Garrett worries me. He's quiet, he's controlled, and he's well behaved and polite to the staff. In that sense, he's been a model prisoner – at least up until this latest incident. But there's also no sense that he's remotely concerned with the gravity of the crimes he's committed. I'm a great believer in the power of rehabilitation, Miss Boyd, something which I know isn't a particularly fashionable view among a lot of people in this country. But I believe we could gain a great deal from the Scandinavian model of treating prisoners as individuals who've made poor life choices, rather than as amoral monsters who need to be locked up for as long as possible. However, I believe Mr Garrett might be an exception to that rule. I very much doubt that he *can* be rehabilitated. I've spent enough time with him, and the psychiatrists who've interviewed him, to know he feels no real remorse for what he's done. Given that it's likely he personally killed at least five people, and was responsible for the deaths of many times that number, that makes him extremely dangerous. Coupled with that, he's highly intelligent. Whether you're easily manipulated or not, I'd bear this in mind when you're dealing with him.'

'Thank you, sir, I will.'

'We've prepared an interview room in the Central Section for your meeting. He should be there by now, so if you've got no further questions, I'll have you escorted down there.'

'I think you've answered everything for me,' said Tina, getting to her feet.

'I must admit,' said the governor as they shook hands a second time, 'I'm surprised that he asked to see *you* here, and alone too. It seems odd to me, given your own involvement in the Stanhope siege.'

Tina swallowed her continuing irritation at the way she was being talked to. 'It was my *involvement* that helped bring the siege to a successful conclusion, Mr Goodman.'

'Surely over seventy dead civilians can't be judged to be a successful conclusion.'

'It can when you have five hundred hostages and a building wired up to be blown to smithereens. And whatever you or Mr Garrett may think, I'm good at my job.'

Goodman raised a sceptical eyebrow. 'In my opinion, your methods leave a great deal to be desired, Miss Boyd, so I'd request that when in my prison you work according to my rules.'

Tina held his gaze for a long second, sorely tempted to kick him in the nuts, or at the very least come up with a rude rejoinder, but in the end she thought better of it. 'Of course, sir.'

The guard who escorted Tina to the prison's Central Section was the same one who'd taken her to the governor's office. His name was Thomson, and he looked like he'd been doing the job for years.

'Did the governor give you his talk on rehabilitation?' he asked as they walked.

Tina gave a derisive grunt. 'He said a few words on the subject.'

'He's big on rehabilitation,' Thomson said. 'He says it's the whole purpose of the job – that there's good in everyone, even if in some cases it's very well hidden. But he spends most of the time in his office, and he doesn't see what we see.'

'And what do you see?'

'I see hundreds of bad men. Every day of my life. Men who wouldn't think twice about cutting your throat, or raping your daughter. Or even your son. And do you know what the worst part of it is, Miss Boyd?'

Tina looked at him. 'What?'

'The public think we run this place. They think the governor and the guards run every prison.' He frowned. 'But we don't. We don't run any of them. The prisoners do. Right now, the only way we keep order is by treating this lot with kid gloves, and cutting them slack. The minute they decide they don't want to take orders from us any more, they won't. It's as simple as that.'

'I can believe it.'

'Maybe if you were running the shop rather than the governor, things would be a bit different.' He let slip a small smile to let her know he was joking.

Tina laughed. 'I'm not patient enough, and I can't stand being nice to people who don't deserve it.'

'You wouldn't last long here then. This place is a tinderbox, Miss Boyd. And when it goes up, there'll be nothing any of us can do about it. I think about that every day I'm here.'

Beyond the corridor walls, Tina could hear the faint sound of cell doors clanking and the staccato shouts of prisoners. The air felt hot and artificial, with an unpleasant undercurrent of cleaning products, reminding her of a hospital. The guard's words unnerved her, even though she'd heard the same thing from different sources plenty of times. It was always disconcerting to know that however hard you fought, the war against the bad guys was ultimately unwinnable.

'The whole country's a tinderbox, Officer Thomson,' she said. 'The riots in 2011 showed that. We've just got to make sure we do our bit and keep blowing out the matches.' She decided to change the subject. 'This attack on Garrett by Eric Hughes. Do you think it was spontaneous, or planned?'

'It's difficult to tell. Hughes is a nasty piece of work – they both are – but there was no history of conflict between the two of them. The men in here are some of the most dangerous in the country, and they're living in unnatural conditions, so their behaviour can get unpredictable.'

'What about the camera? I heard it was tampered with.'

'It was broken, but we're not sure it was deliberate.'

'Do you know how long it was broken for?'

Thomson shrugged. 'Things like that are meant to be fixed straight away for health and safety reasons, but we're like everyone else. Short of money and short of staff. So it could have been a while.'

'Would the prisoners have known the camera was out of order? I mean, it would explain why Hughes attacked Garrett where he did.'

'I honestly don't know,' he answered, but Tina's

antennae picked up something in his voice that made her think he might be lying. She filed it away for future reference.

They stopped at a set of heavy double doors and Thomson used a card to swipe them through. He nodded at a guard on the other side, who unlocked another set of doors, and then they were into the maximum-security section of the prison. It was far quieter in here, and the smell of cleaning fluids stronger, making Tina feel slightly nauseous.

Thomson turned to her as they walked down a windowless tunnel illuminated with garish strip lighting. 'Be careful of our Mr Garrett. He might be polite and quiet, but I wouldn't trust him an inch.'

'Don't worry, Officer Thomson. I can look after myself.'

'So I've heard, Miss Boyd. So I've heard.'

They stopped outside a door where two more prison officers stood guard.

'He'll be handcuffed for the duration of your interview, and there's a panic button in case he tries anything. Press it and we'll intervene immediately.'

Tina smiled. 'Thanks, but I'm sure he won't do anything stupid. He knows there's no way out of here.'

Officer Thomson nodded. 'Exactly,' he said, opening the reinforced door. 'Right now, he's got nothing to lose.'

Thirteen

10.58

William Garrett, the man the media knew as Fox, was possibly the most dangerous prisoner in the UK out of a population of close to a hundred thousand. Although it was another three months before his trial was due to start, and the reporting of his alleged crimes had been kept to a minimum so as not to prejudice any future proceedings, the prosecution case against him was as close to watertight as you were ever going to get. Positively identified by witnesses, and caught at the scene of the crime with traces of blood and gunshot residue on his person, as well as a phone which he'd just used to send a message to a fellow conspirator, it was well known that he'd been one of the lead terrorists involved in the Stanhope siege. There were numerous reports of him killing hostages without compunction or conscience, and he'd been fully prepared to blow up the building along with hundreds of people inside it.

And yet the man sitting on the other side of the desk holding a mug of lukewarm tea between cuffed hands didn't look much like a ruthless terrorist to Tina. He looked more like a washed-out PE teacher who'd been in an accident. He was of medium height and medium build, with neatly cut, short sandy hair, and pale, almost translucent skin, which was probably the result of spending too many months behind bars. The signs of the attack on him were obvious. The top of his head was bandaged, and he had dressing running up his right forearm from wrist to elbow. There were also several minor defensive wounds on both hands, one containing a few stitches. His face was on the thin, almost gaunt, side, as if he exercised too much or had stopped enjoying his food, but the wide, clearly genuine smile he gave Tina as she entered the room suggested he remained in good spirits. Only the calculating expression in his narrow grey eyes suggested something darker.

'Thanks for coming,' he said in a confident voice that carried the faintest of West Country burrs. 'I'd shake your hand but it's not very easy with these on.'

'I'm sure I'll get over it,' replied Tina, taking a seat opposite him and making a point of not looking at the red panic alarm button just beneath the lip of the desk. She didn't want him thinking he intimidated her.

'I heard you got reinstated in the Met. How did you manage that?'

Tina leaned forward in her seat, meeting his gaze. 'We're not here to discuss my career, Mr Garrett. You told the governor you had information regarding the people involved in the Stanhope siege.'

He looked down at the pockmarked table, then back at her. 'Do you know why I asked to see you specifically?'

'No. I've got to say I'm surprised. I'm not even working on the Stanhope case.'

'The reason is I trust you. And I also think you can get things done. Most people do what they're told, fill in the forms they're meant to fill in, and let their bosses make the big decisions. That's why this country's in such a parlous state. Nobody likes taking responsibility any more. If it had been any other copper sitting where you are today, things would move slowly. With you, I think we might be able to get somewhere.'

Tina resisted telling him that as a DC in a mid-sized CID department, she really wasn't in that powerful a position. 'I'll do what I can,' she said.

He nodded slowly. 'I know you will. I hear there's a team still investigating the events at the Stanhope. I'm assuming they briefed you before you came here.'

'I've had some background,' said Tina non-committally.

'How are they getting on? I haven't seen news of any arrests.'

'I can't discuss ongoing enquiries with you, Mr Garrett.'

'And I bet the bombs this morning gave them something of a shock.'

'Bombs?'

'Don't tell me I'm better informed than you are.' He smiled, showing teeth. 'There were two more bombs about half an hour ago. I saw it on TV in my cell while I was waiting for you. The police were about to raid a flat of someone involved in the first bomb when there were two separate explosions. It looks like it was a trap.'

Tina resisted asking him for more details. She'd been blindsided by this information. She was annoyed that Mike Bolt hadn't phoned her straight away, and surprised that the governor hadn't known either. Or maybe he had, and the bastard had just chosen not to tell her. 'The bomb, or bombs, this morning are a CTC matter,' she told him.

'It all looked very sophisticated. That's what they kept saying on the news. And I'm willing to place a very big bet that the people behind it are the same ones who planned the Stanhope siege.' He looked round the empty, windowless room. 'Is this being recorded?'

'Right now, anything you say is off the record. You have my word on it.'

He put his elbows on the table and rested his chin on the backs of his cuffed hands. He was watching her very carefully. 'If, hypothetically speaking of course, I was to provide you with information that helped you, how would I benefit?'

'It depends what the information is.'

'The names of the people behind the Stanhope siege and today's attack.'

Tina kept her expression neutral. She was surprised by his confidence that the people he was talking about were responsible for both attacks. He'd been behind bars for fifteen months, after all. 'I'll be straight with you,' she said. 'You're never going to walk free. Not after what you've done. You know the evidence against you is massive, and that your chances of acquittal are almost nil, no matter what kind of representation you have. Which means you're going to be convicted of premeditated mass murder with zero extenuating circumstances.' She paused. 'But there are different ways of doing the time.'

'I need to know there's a release date.'

Tina shook her head. 'I can't promise you that. There'd be a public outcry if you were let out after what you've done.'

Fox seemed to think about this before nodding slowly, as if accepting the inevitable. He dropped his hands and leaned across the desk again, his face coming too close to Tina's for comfort. 'I expect you're wondering how I know that the people behind the Stanhope siege are responsible for today.'

'It crossed my mind, yes.'

'Check the bombmaker's signature. It'll be the same man who built the bombs used at the Stanhope. But the people involved will be covering their tracks. So whatever you or your bosses may think, I'm your best chance of finding them and building a case against them.'

'And you do know who they are?'

'Absolutely. These are the organizers, the ones providing the funds and the resources. But they stay a long way from the action. And they're not finished yet.'

'Are we talking about unfriendly Arab governments?' asked Tina.

'There was Arab involvement in the Stanhope operation,' said Fox. 'They wanted to pay the UK government back for interfering with Muslim affairs, and occupying Muslim lands. Iraq, Afghanistan, Libya. You name it, they were pissed off about it. But there was involvement within this country too. From people who, let's say, were sympathetic with what the attacks on that day were trying to achieve. They've even got a name. They call themselves The Brotherhood.'

Tina wrote the name down. 'And what are The Brotherhood trying to achieve?'

'In their opinion, the UK's lost its culture; it's overcrowded; it's being taken over by immigrants. A lot of citizens resent this, but the problem is they don't resent it enough. They need something to push them over the edge. To get them so angry that they reach a point where they'll vote for someone pushing a radical right-wing agenda. And the best way to achieve that is through terror attacks that can be blamed on immigrants and the children of immigrants. That's what the Stanhope was about. I reckon that's what the bombs today are about too. And there'll be more to come because the more people die, the greater the effect.'

'And were . . . are you a member of The Brotherhood?'

Fox smiled. 'No comment.'

Tina eyed him closely, still surprised by how ordinary he looked, even though she knew that most killers look just like everyone else. 'And do you have evidence against these people?'

'More than you can imagine. And not just for Stanhope. For other crimes as well. And there's one man at the top of the chain you're going to be particularly interested in.'

'How do you know about all this?'

Fox stared at her. 'Because I used to work for him. If you can give me a guarantee that I'll be sent to a secure, safe environment, and that I won't serve more than ten years, then I'll help you bring him and everyone involved to justice.'

'You know as well as I do, Mr Garrett, that judges decide sentences in this country. Not politicians. And definitely not the police.'

'But I also know there's flexibility.'

'There is. But it's going to take time.'

'We haven't got time. That's why I asked for you.

There was an attempt on my life three days ago, just before the attacks today. That tells me, and it ought to tell you, that it wasn't random. It was done for one reason and one reason only. To silence me. Like they silenced John Cheney. And they're going to try again. Especially if they know I've been talking to you. You need to get me out of here, and fast.'

'Give me a name. Something for me to go on.'

'I need some guarantees.'

'If your information's good enough, I'll get you out of here, I promise.' Tina was lying, but she had to get something from this meeting in a claustrophobic little room with a brutal murderer. And she could tell from the renewed tension in his body language that he was thinking about it.

The room was silent.

Tina waited. Counting the seconds in her head.

'Jetmir Brozi.'

'He doesn't sound much like a British neo-Nazi.'

'He isn't. But he's involved.'

Tina wrote the name down. 'In what way?'

But Fox was already getting up. She could tell that, as far as he was concerned, this meeting was over.

'Look, a name's no good to us on its own. I need something that shows you're not bullshitting me.'

Fox ran his handcuffed hands through his hair, trying to avoid the bandage on his head, then winced and rubbed his injured arm. If the attempt on his life had been staged, it had been a damn authentic job.

His eyes were cold as he looked at her, and for a moment Tina could imagine what it must have been like for the hostages on that frigid November night when they'd been staring down the barrel of his gun.

'The weapons and explosives for the Stanhope siege came from Kosovo,' he said at last. 'The man who set up the deal from this end was Jetmir Brozi. He's based in this country – a failed asylum seeker, if memory serves me correctly. He's an Albanian with strong links to former members of the KLA – the Kosovo Liberation Army – who are still sitting on a lot of weaponry left over from the conflict. If the explosives used today are the same as at the Stanhope, Brozi will have been the broker.'

'Where can we find him?'

'He runs a brothel in an old warehouse near King's Cross, or at least he did when I was dealing with him eighteen months ago. It's on a place called Canal Street, about halfway down on the left if you're heading north, and I think the name of the building is Mill House, although I couldn't say for sure. I don't know where he actually lives, but he's known to the authorities under the name I've given you. He ran over a cyclist once, while driving without insurance or an MOT, and put the guy in hospital for six weeks with a fractured spine. It turned out that Brozi shouldn't even have been in the country because he'd had his asylum application and two appeals turned down already. Even then they couldn't get rid of him because, before the case got to court, he married a girl with a British passport and got her up the duff. Then he got his legal-aid-funded lawyers to say that separating him from his wife and child breached his right to a family life under the Human Rights Act. Hence, he's still here.' Fox couldn't resist a cold smile. 'It's a great country we live in, isn't it?'

Tina didn't react as she wrote down the details, even though hearing stories about the weakness of the justice system and the vagaries of the Human Rights Act annoyed her as much as anyone.

'I always made it my business to find out as much as I could about the people I did business with,' continued Fox, 'just in case it ever came in useful. Like now. Don't waste what I know, Miss Boyd. Because if I die, my secrets go with me. And I have secrets that'll make your hair stand on end.'

Tina replaced the notebook and got to her feet too. 'I'll be in touch,' she told him, making no effort to shake hands.

'You know, I admire you,' said Fox, looking her up and down. 'You might have caused us a lot of problems at the Stanhope, but I can't help thinking that in other circumstances, we might have got on.'

'Don't flatter yourself,' said Tina, turning away and signalling for the guard to let her out.

Fourteen

11.08

There are no noble causes.

When I left the army, after twelve years' service, I decided to become a cop. I'm still not entirely sure why. It just seemed like a good idea at the time. After my last tour of Helmand Province, I was sick of the military, and the way we were being hung out to dry out there. I wanted to try something different, something that didn't involve sitting in an office all day or losing my legs to an IED, and being a cop seemed like it might be an interesting alternative.

It wasn't.

I did three years in the Met, and I did a good job, no question. I put up with a lot of shit from the scum out there on the streets – and I tell you, there are one hell of a lot of them, people who know every last one of their rights, and think the world owes them a living. They didn't have an ounce of respect, or fear, for the law or the uniform. The Human Rights Act put paid to all that. To them, we were just a joke. But I learned to turn the other cheek and get on with the job. I filled out all the pointless forms, followed the thousands of pedantic little rules, took the diversity courses, watched the senior officers fiddling the crime figures so they met their targets – never actually doing much in the way of fighting crime, but knowing that at the end of the day I was earning OK money and supporting my wife and daughter.

To alleviate the boredom, I applied to join CO19, the Met's specialized firearms unit, and got in on the first attempt. And although I knew the chances of getting any real action were slim, I remember thinking that life was looking up for me.

Which was, of course, the moment it all went wrong.

It was just over a year ago, and I was part of a team who raided a shitheap of a property in Hackney where a couple of small-time crack dealers lived. We'd heard they kept a gun on the premises that was supposedly for protection – one they'd used in a mugging the previous year where some kid had got shot – as well as a pitbull. So we went in armed and mob-handed. We broke down the door, shot the dog – which was a pity because he had nothing to do with anything – then stormed through the place making a lot of noise, like you do when you're an armed cop.

It was a real mess in there. There were overflowing rubbish bags and old takeaway cartons wherever you looked, dog shit on the floor, and an army of cockroaches lording it in the kitchen among all the grime-encrusted dishes. The whole house stank like the lions' enclosure at a zoo. But that's often par for the course in those types of places. As a cop, you learn fast that it's not just the law that the criminal classes have no respect for. Most of the time they don't respect themselves either.

I was one of the first upstairs, and that's where I found her. She was fifteen years old, a runaway from a local care home, and she was tied to a stinking mattress in the back bedroom, semi-conscious and out of her head on God knows what. She was stark naked, with friction burns round her ankles and wrists where she'd struggled to break free. I had no idea how long she'd been there for, but she'd peed and crapped herself, and when the doctor examined her afterwards he said she was massively dehydrated, so it must have been a fair while. They'd been using her for sex. Just fucking her and, from what we could work out, charging other men to fuck her. Apparently she owed them money for dope, hadn't paid up, and this was her punishment. They got her wrecked, then held her prisoner. Threatened to burn her alive if she ever told anyone.

Most right-thinking members of the public have no idea this kind of thing goes on, often only within walking distance from their front doors. But it does. It's happening all the time.

We never knew how many men had raped her. These days, thanks to *CSI* and all those other programmes, the bastards are all forensically aware, so they used condoms and made sure they didn't leave any of them behind for us to find. The girl herself wasn't sure. She'd been too wrecked to know what was going on most of the time, but she'd suffered some pretty major injuries, so we knew it was a good few of them, and they hadn't been gentle.

The problem was, when we raided the place only one of the two dealers was there. He was a cocky little sod, name of Alfonse Webber. Only eighteen and already a career criminal. He said he didn't know anything about the girl, and blamed his friend, the other dealer. But when we tracked down the other dealer, he denied everything as well. We tried to get the girl to talk but she was scared stiff; all she wanted was to be left alone. And you couldn't blame her. She had to live round there.

So that was that. What could we do? To top it all, we only found a few rocks of crack in there, and no gun. Webber went to court and got a suspended sentence. He claimed the gear was for his own use, and that he didn't have a clue how the girl had got herself tied up in the bedroom. The judge didn't believe him – at least I hope he didn't; sometimes it's hard to tell. But the prisons are full, and there wasn't enough evidence to convict him of anything major. So he got a suspended sentence, and walked.

To be honest, what happened with Webber was no worse than a dozen other incidents I'd had to deal with, but the thing was, it acted like the culmination of all those other incidents. I'd had enough. When he came strutting out of the court with his lawyer, the little bastard saw me and laughed – this braying, mocking noise like a donkey. Even now, I remember perfectly the rage that went through me. It was so intense it actually made me start shaking. Then he started bragging in this ridiculous street patois about how the Feds would always be too stupid to get one over him – that sort of thing. His lawyer, this nerdy little bald guy with glasses, tried to get him to stop, and the cop I was with, well, he could see the effect it was having on me, so he put a hand on my shoulder and told me just to ignore it.

I almost managed to as well. I started to turn away, to think about something else.

And then he said it. The one thing that was always going to tip me over the edge. He said that he was looking forward to fucking my daughter some day soon.

My beautiful little daughter, who was three years old.

I snapped. The strange thing was that, as he said it, the vision that came into my head wasn't of my daughter. It was of a young squaddie called Max, who got hit by an IED in Helmand on my first tour there. He was ripped to shreds, left with half an arm and no legs, and he ended up stuck in a council flat ignored by the army and the government and the council and everyone, while this piece of shit – this dirty fucking piece of shit who'd never done a day's work in his life, who'd never done anything to help anyone else ever – got to deal crack, torture young women, and threaten police officers, all with total impunity.

So I went for him. Hard. His lawyer tried to stop me but I broke the slimy bastard's nose with one punch. Webber was off like a shot, but his jeans were hanging halfway down his arse and he was wearing these huge trainers that looked like they weighed more than him, so he was never going to get away. I jumped on his back and drove him face first into the pavement. I had his head in my hands and I kept slamming it down on the concrete. The blood was splattering everywhere. Jesus, it was a sweet feeling. I would have killed him, no question. It never even occurred to me to stop. I would have smashed his head into pieces and stamped on the remains, but thankfully I never got the chance. There were a lot of people in the vicinity, including cops and security guards, and eventually they managed to pull me off him. But I was still lashing out. One of the court security guards got an elbow in the face that knocked out two of his teeth, and the cop I was with ended up with a busted cheekbone.

I was arrested on the spot. There was no way of avoiding it really. Alfonse Webber was hurt pretty bad. He was in hospital for a week and had to have extensive plastic surgery to repair the damage to his face. I was suspended immediately and charged with grievous bodily harm. When I appeared in court two days later, I was remanded in custody. Even though it was my first offence, even though I was a decorated war hero, even though a psychiatrist who interviewed me subsequently concluded I was suffering from post-traumatic stress disorder, even though Alfonse Webber was a violent lowlife who'd gone out of his way to provoke me . . . Even after all those things I was looking at a three- or four-year stretch minimum.

And then someone offered me a deal.

We drove through the back streets of north London, passing through Edmonton and then Enfield, and all the time Cecil kept checking his rearview mirror to make sure we weren't being followed – although I had no idea who might be following us. If it was the cops, they would have arrested us on the spot, seeing that Cecil had just killed a man. But I kept quiet and let him get on with it.

The continuous swathes of clogged-up London suburbs eventually gave way to identikit executive housing communities, golf courses, and the first hints of the green belt, and then when we were only just the other side of the M25, Cecil pulled into a quiet country lane and stopped twenty yards short of an abandoned-looking barn nestling on the edge of a small beech wood.

'This is a bit of an out-of-the-way place to meet someone, isn't it?' I said, looking round.

'You can never be too careful,' said Cecil, reaching over and pulling a mobile phone-shaped electronic device with an antenna on the end from the glove compartment. When he switched it on, a red light appeared on the side.

'What the hell's that?' I asked, knowing full well what it was.

'It's a bug finder. If you're wearing a wire, it'll pick it up.'

'It might have escaped your notice, Cecil, but we've just committed an armed robbery together, so I'm hardly likely to be setting you up.'

'The man we're meeting's paranoid. And orders are orders.'

I let him do the honours, knowing there was no point arguing. The machine didn't beep.

'You want to search me as well?'

Credit to Cecil, at least he had the dignity to look embarrassed as he got out of the car after grabbing the holdall with the money from the back seat. 'Come on.'

I followed him up the track towards the barn. The air was cold and fresh, and the sun was just managing to fight its way through the cloud cover. The constant stream of traffic from the M25 was no longer audible, and the only sound among the trees, and the fields beyond them, was the occasional shriek of a crow. There were no other cars around, which meant that the man we'd come to see hadn't arrived yet, or he was keeping a very low profile.

It struck me then that this would be an ideal place to kill someone.

We stopped outside the barn. One side of it was open to the elements and it was empty inside bar a cluster of rusty oil drums and some ancient farm machinery.

'Where's the guy we're here to meet?' I asked, rubbing my hands together against the cold.

'Here,' came a voice behind us.

I turned round and saw a figure in a long coat emerge from the outbuilding behind us, from where he'd clearly been watching our approach, and walk over to us. Even though he was dressed casually, he was wearing an expensive-looking pair of leather driving gloves.

'Sir, this is Jones, the man I was telling you about.' Although he tried to hide it, Cecil's tone was deferential.

The man who stopped in front of me was a mass of physical contradictions. On the one hand he was tall, lean and fit-looking, with the classic bearing of an ex-army officer, but on the other, his complexion was pale to the point of illness, and he had a prominent vein running down one side of his face like a worm beneath the skin, which I had difficulty taking my eyes off.

'Mr Jones, pleased to meet you.'

'Jones is fine on its own,' I said. 'And you are?'

'My name's Cain,' he said, his voice surprisingly deep and sonorous. 'Cecil's been telling me about what happened to you. That you were sent down because you doled out some real justice to someone who deserved it. That's this country all over.'

'It hasn't done me any favours.'

'It hasn't done any of us any favours.' He looked at me sharply, and I thought I saw the vein move beneath his skin. 'You were lucky you only got sent down for a year.'

That was my weak point. The length of sentence. 'It was long enough,' I told him. 'Especially for an ex-cop. I wasn't the most popular man on the block.'

'I can believe it.' He gestured towards the holdall Cecil was holding. 'How much did we make?'

'We haven't counted it yet,' said Cecil, 'but it feels like a lot.' He handed it to Cain who motioned for us to follow him into the barn.

Inside, Cain put the holdall down on one of the oil drums and opened it up, revealing a whole heap of cash. He immediately started to count it out, placing each individual wad on one of the other drums. I'm not a greedy man but I felt a slither of excitement as I stared at it. Apparently, LeShawn always insisted that the money was counted before he arrived to pick it up, and it had been divided into single-denomination five-grand wads.

'What happened out there?' asked Cain as he

carried on counting. I was counting too and I'd already got to ninety grand.

'LeShawn didn't want to play ball,' said Cecil. 'He went for Jones's gun. We had to shoot him.'

'Who pulled the trigger?'

'I did.'

'How come *you* didn't shoot him, Jones?'

'I didn't get a chance.'

Cain gave me another look. His eyes were a watery grey but there was a fierce intelligence in them.

'I shot up a cop car,' I told him.

Cain smiled thinly. He was still counting the money. We were at a hundred and forty now. 'I apologize for all the secrecy, but you were a cop once, and we have to be very careful who we trust.'

'Well, thanks to what happened an hour ago I'm now an armed robber,' I told him. 'I think that means you can trust me.'

As I said this, I realized almost with a shock that I was now just like the criminals I'd been trying to put away. The only reason I'd agreed to do the armed robbery in the first place was because I'd thought we could get away with it, but now I'd compromised myself badly.

'You're not an armed robber, Jones. You're a soldier raising funds from some bad people for a good cause. There's a big difference.'

Cain finished counting. Two hundred and twenty-five grand plus change.

'Cecil told you how the split worked, didn't he? Fifteen grand each for you two?'

I nodded. 'Seems like you get a very big cut.'

'Firstly, I planned it. And second, the money isn't going to me.'

I stared him down. 'We could have done with some help out there today. The reason it went wrong was because there were only two of us. If there'd been three of us, the whole thing might have run a lot smoother.'

'Come on, Jones,' said Cecil, intervening. 'You knew the score when you took the job.'

'But that's the problem,' I said, turning back to Cain. 'I still don't know what the score is. Because no one's actually told me. Cecil said there might be an opportunity for me to make some money and get involved in fighting the government, but so far all that's happened is I've risked my neck and taken part in a very public murder, all for the price of a mid-range saloon car.' I gestured at the wads of money. 'So, where's all this going?'

Cain and Cecil exchanged glances. Then Cain turned back to me. 'Let's take a walk.'

I followed him outside. Beyond the barn, a fallow field stretched away to some trees in the middle distance, and we started towards it.

'We're fighting a war, Jones, and in a war you need weapons. The other side have got weapons. Did you hear about the bombs this morning?'

I shook my head. We hadn't had the car radio on at all on our way up here. 'What happened?'

'A bomb went off near Victoria Station three hours ago. Nine dead already, but the toll keeps rising. And then another two less than an hour back at a block of flats in Bayswater, which looks to have been aimed at the police. Four dead in that one so far. The Islamics have already claimed responsibility.'

'And is it them? I remember in the Stanhope attacks there were white guys, ex-soldiers, involved.'

'The coffee shop bomb was delivered by a suicide bomber who, according to the news, got spooked at the last minute and ran off. Ended up under the wheels of a lorry, but word is he's a local Asian.' Cain stopped and looked at me. 'This country's under attack, Jones. The Islamics are going to keep launching attacks like this because the government hasn't got the backbone to fight back. They'd rather innocent British civilians died than stop people who don't belong here pouring into the country and trying to destroy us. Cecil tells me you've got a family.'

'I've got a daughter,' I said carefully, reluctant to have Maddie dragged into this.

'Do you want her to grow up as a minority in her own birthplace? Because that's what's going to happen if the government keep going with their multicultural experiment. The whites are going to end up outnumbered. There'll be mosques on every street, and the government won't do a damn thing to stop it because, like always, they're too interested in showing how PC they are, and lining their own pockets. Look at Tony Blair. He's a multimillionaire now on the backs of all those soldiers he sent to war.' Cain's vein was throbbing angrily in his cheek. 'Cecil tells me you're interested in fighting back.'

So, this was it. If I answered him correctly, I could be joining what was possibly the most dangerous terror cell in the country. I thought of my family. Thanked God they weren't anywhere near central London. 'Yeah,' I said, looking him firmly in the eye, 'I am.'

'Cecil says you killed in Afghanistan.'

I shrugged. 'I fired my gun at the enemy plenty of times.'

'That's not what I meant,' he said quietly. 'He said you *killed*.' He emphasized the last word, stretched it out.

So, Cecil had told him the secret that we'd carried since Afghanistan, something we'd all sworn we'd never repeat.

Cain gave me a predatory smile, his upper lip curling to reveal a perfect row of white teeth. 'Your secret's safe with me, Jones. But I want to know how far you're willing to go in this war.'

'I'll do whatever it takes, Mr Cain,' I said steadily. 'You know my background. You know the shit I've been through. I only want two things. Revenge on the system that ruined my life and career, and humiliated my family. And money. I need money, so I can pay for my ex-wife and my kid. I don't much care what I have to do to get either.'

So that was it. I'd laid my bait.

Cain was silent for a long few seconds before he spoke again. 'I can get you both, Jones. I'll put you on a retainer. Three grand a month cash. For that you need to be available at short notice for jobs which may involve guns, like today. Every time you do a job, there'll be a serious bonus paid up front. How does that sound?'

I nodded slowly, not wanting to appear too enthusiastic. 'It sounds OK.'

'Good. Then do we have a deal?'

I said we did, and we shook on it.

He pulled a phone from his jacket and handed it to me. 'Keep this on, and keep it with you. The only person who'll phone it is me. Have you got any plans for today?'

'Nothing that I can't put on hold.'

'Good. I'm trying to set up a meeting with some business associates on neutral ground. It may well happen later today, and I want you and Cecil there to back me up. I've done business with them before, and they're generally pretty reliable, but there's money involved, and money can sometimes make people do stupid things, so you'll both be armed. The bonus is another grand.'

'Who are the people we're dealing with?'

'The prisons are full of people who talk too much,

Jones. With us, everything's on a need-to-know basis. It's a lot easier for everyone that way.'

I turned away from him, looking across the field to the woodland. 'Still don't trust me, eh?'

'Let me tell you something,' said Cain, lighting a cigarette with a gloved hand. 'When I was in Lashkar Gah a few years back, we had an interpreter called Abdul. He came from a good family. Not exactly pro government, but not exactly anti it either. One of his brothers had been murdered by the Taliban, so he was considered safe. He was a nice guy too. Well educated, even quite enlightened by Afghan standards. He often used to eat with the men, and would ask us all these questions about England. What was the Queen like? Did the police really not carry guns? He liked talking about football too.' Cain chuckled. It was an odd, artificial sound, as if he'd been practising it but still had some way to go. 'I remember, Abdul supported Liverpool. He could name their 1978 and 1981 European Cup-winning teams. We used to test him, and he was never wrong.

'One day, he was chatting with a couple of the privates over tea in one of the sangars. The next thing we heard a burst of gunfire, followed by screams. We rushed over there, weapons at the ready, just in time to see Abdul come walking out. At first we thought he'd been hit, and then he lifted up one of the privates' SA80s and pointed it at us. His expression was totally calm, almost dreamy, as he started firing. I always remember that. He wasn't a bad shot either. He hit one of my corporals who made the mistake of hesitating a couple of seconds because he couldn't believe what he was seeing, before the rest of us opened up and finally shot Abdul dead.

'When we got inside the sangar we found the two privates Abdul had been talking to lying on the floor. One of them, a Geordie called Peterson, was already dead. The other was this big Fijian with an unpronounceable name who we used to call Hula and, although he was in a bad way, he was still conscious. He told us that one minute they'd all been chatting away like good friends, and the next, Abdul had grabbed Peterson's gun and opened up on them. No rhyme. No reason. Hula never made it. Neither did Abdul, so we never did find out what motivated him. Whether he was a sleeper agent all along, or whether the Taliban had got to him somehow.' Cain shrugged. 'Personally, I believe it was the former. Not that that matters to either Peterson or Hula. Either way they're still dead. But the point of the story, that's easier.' He gave me a hard stare. 'You can never be too careful.'

And that was what was worrying me.

Fifteen

11.22

Tina called Mike Bolt from an empty interview room. She'd asked the warder if she could smoke since the prisoners seemed to do so with impunity, but was told she couldn't, which pissed her off no end.

'Jetmir Brozi,' she said when he picked up. 'Apparently he was involved in procuring the weaponry for the Stanhope siege, and Fox reckons he may well be involved in the attacks today too.'

She gave Bolt a brief rundown of the details of the interview.

'He's sure the attacks this morning are linked, and by the way, Mike, it would have really helped me if I'd known there'd been a second bomb before I spoke to him. I felt a right fool when he told me about the Bayswater attack.'

'I called you as soon as I had the chance, but your phone was on silent.' He sounded stressed and tired, which wasn't like him at all.

'How many casualties have there been so far?'

'Nine dead from the first bomb. Five from the two in Bayswater. The Bayswater attack was designed to take out police officers attending a flat where they'd traced the phone used to claim responsibility for the first explosion.'

'So it was a sophisticated attack, and similar to the bombs set off prior to the Stanhope siege.'

'Very much so. But that doesn't mean they're connected. Our one suspect is a British national of Pakistani origin. The ID he was carrying says he's Akhtar Mohammed, aged thirty-one and married with three children. He's not on any watchlists, but then neither were the 7/7 bombers. But the point is, nothing links this man to any previous attacks. I'll get our people to find out what they can about Jetmir Brozi, but I reckon it's going to be a long job to gather any evidence against him.'

'We've got to do it though, surely?'

'We'll do what we can, but right now everyone in the Met is focused on what's going on in central London. The terrorists are threatening a much bigger attack, and if their track record so far's anything to go by, God knows what they could be planning. I need more from Fox. If he's serious about cooperating, we need the names of everyone involved in these attacks. And we need them now.'

'He wants to be moved to a safehouse first.'

'We can't do that, Tina. He's an extremely dangerous and high-profile remand prisoner.'

'He says his life's in danger.'

'Do you believe him?'

Tina thought about this for a moment, remembering his injuries. 'Yes, I do. And after what happened to John Cheney, it's possible the people he worked for are trying to silence him. If it's OK, I'm going to stay round here to interview the man who attacked Fox. See if I can find anything out that way.'

'Good idea. Keep me posted. And thanks, Tina. You're doing a good job.'

They ended the call, and Tina put the phone back in her pocket, a familiar excitement in her gut.

Sixteen

11.28

Mike Bolt took a deep breath. It was a strange feeling being back working with Tina after all this time. He'd always had feelings for her. One time, four years earlier, when they'd last been working together at SOCA – the soon-to-be-disbanded Serious and Organized Crime Agency – he'd made a pass at her. They'd kissed, but things hadn't gone any further, and it had ended up souring their friendship. As a result, she'd transferred back to the Met. Since then he'd stuck his neck out for her on more than one occasion, even though at times it had seemed as if Tina was on a mission of self-destruction, and it had almost cost him his job.

Most people, and not just those in the upper echelons of the force, thought Tina Boyd was bad news. And in many ways she was. She wasn't a team player, and she did things her own way, often with very little respect for the law she was meant to be upholding, and that made her dangerous. Yet it felt good to have her on the team, even if it was only temporary. She'd squeezed a name out of Fox, which was something. Bolt had a vision of her grabbing him by the hair and battering his head on the interview room desk, demanding answers. It brought a smile to his face, even though he knew it wasn't entirely outside the realm of possibilities. That was the thing with Tina. She always brought an energy to everything she did. She also brought something to Bolt's own lonely life, a spark that had been missing a long time – although he preferred not to think about that right now.

He went down to the next floor and found one of his team, DC Nikki Donohoe, a fiery-looking woman in her late thirties with short, fashionably cut red hair and the first sign of a bump where her third child was, due six months down the line. Nikki was their IT expert, a woman with an uncanny ability to dig up any information, however obscure.

'Hello, boss,' she said with a tight smile. 'Any more on the attacks?'

Nikki was usually a livewire, but like everyone else in London that morning what had happened had shaken her. Her two kids went to school barely a mile from where the last two bombs had exploded.

'We've got a lead.' He told her about Jotmir Drozi. 'Drop everything and find out anything you can about him, particularly his current location.'

'You think he might have something to do with the attacks?' She looked hopeful.

'Tina Boyd got the name from Fox, so it's worth prioritizing.'

'I'm on it,' said Nikki, turning back to her PC.

'So the Black Widow actually got something, did she?'

Bolt looked up to see DC Omar Balachi come into the room. Balachi was a tall, lean black man of Somali origin, in his late twenties, with finely sculpted features, who looked like he should be modelling sharp suits on the catwalk rather than wandering round in jeans, trainers and a hoodie, as he was now. He'd been with the team for most of the past year, and he was a good worker, albeit one with an attitude. He'd already made it known to Bolt that morning that he was annoyed that he'd spent so much of his time on the team doing donkey work while Tina had simply breezed in and been asked to interview the one man they'd all been wanting to talk to.

'That's right,' said Bolt, turning to face him. 'And I told you already, the reason she went there is because Fox insisted on it. I don't like it either, but that's the way it is.'

'But you've still seconded her to the team.'

'Temporarily yes, but only while she's dealing with Fox.' Bolt didn't like having to justify his actions to members of his team – it set a bad precedent – but he knew what a sensitive issue this was.

Omar nodded slowly, clearly still not liking the situation. 'Is there anything I can do to help?' he asked. 'With all this stuff going on, it seems a bit of a waste of time trawling through bank statements and phone records for the thousandth time.' He was currently looking into the backgrounds of all the ex-soldiers who'd worked for the security company Fox had run for some years prior to the Stanhope siege. It had been a long and time-consuming task, and Bolt knew Omar was bored stiff by it.

Ordinarily he'd have told him to persevere with it. After all, it was what detective work was all about. But this wasn't an ordinary day. 'Help Nikki with Jetmir Brozi, can you? I need everything you can find on him, and I need it ASAP.'

He went back up to his office, grabbing his fourth coffee of the day en route. Like Omar, he felt frustrated. He wanted to be out there hunting down the terrorists, but their only suspect was dead, and no use to anyone. In the meantime, they just had to wait for the next attack. This was the weakness of living in a multicultural democracy like Britain, where people could come and go as they pleased. You were exposed and vulnerable. The Stanhope siege and the bomb blasts earlier this morning had shown that a handful of men could bring a city of ten million people to a standstill, and effectively hold it to ransom.

He took a sip from his coffee and looked out of the window. The sun was shining, and the clouds were beginning to thin and break up. It looked like it was going to turn into a fine winter's day. Sirens still blared in the distance, their sound only just audible through the glass. Outside, innocent people were being killed, and there was nothing that he or his colleagues could do about it.

The sound of one of the three mobile phones he carried stirred Bolt from his thoughts. At first he didn't recognize the ringtone – a loud pealing of church bells – then he remembered the contact he'd assigned it to, and he frowned as he picked up the phone.

'We need to meet,' said Jones. 'Urgently.'

Seventeen

11.50

Heathrow's Terminal 5 offered the kind of welcome to the UK that gave tourist chiefs sleepless nights. The queue started almost as soon as you were in the building – thousands of people shuffling along in a thick unruly line, as if the arrival here of the planes that had been carrying them had been completely and utterly unexpected. Young Asian staff with funky haircuts and big badges on their shirts claiming they were 'Here to Help' barked orders like prison guards as they shepherded the passengers down the escalators, before wedging them like cattle on to the shuttle trains, which then deposited them a few minutes later at the back of an even bigger and more chaotic queue in the cavernous Arrivals Hall.

Luckily for Voorhess, he wasn't in a hurry. The man next to him, a bald-headed Australian in a tailored suit, was. He kept repeating what a disgrace it was being treated like this, and that this was the last time he would travel through Heathrow. A couple of other passengers murmured in agreement, others talked in hushed tones about the bombs in London that morning, but Voorhess just looked ahead, an amiable expression on his face. He was being paid for his time here. There was no point getting distressed.

It took close to an hour from leaving the plane to finally reach Passport Control. It amused him to see that of the dozen or so officials manning the desks, all but one of them was Asian. It was, he thought, more like arriving in New Delhi than London.

The only white passport officer, a severe-looking lady with a turned-down mouth and beady eyes, inspected Voorhess's Irish passport. The document was a fake, but a near perfect one – one of a batch from within the Irish Passport Office itself – and there was no way either she or the computer would spot it. Voorhess gazed at her with the same amiable, slightly vacant expression he often wore in public as she inspected both it and him. He was a big man, both in height and broadness, and he had an imposing presence that was only partly diluted by the thick head of curly black hair, the boyish swirl of freckles, and the twinkling green eyes – Irish eyes – that he got from his mother. The powerful build came from his father, an Afrikaner farmer who'd somehow managed to tempt his mother to live on his bleak homestead at the arse-end of the Eastern Cape.

The woman gave him back his passport with a reluctant thank you, her tone making it clear she wasn't actually thanking him at all, and Voorhess headed straight for the Nothing to Declare channel at customs, joining the many others swarming through. There were only a handful of customs officers on duty, although he knew more of them would be watching through the tinted screens above the exit door.

The last line of defence against the bad guys. When you were through that door you were in the country and able to disappear at will, yet they seemed to be letting everyone in, including Voorhess himself, which would turn out to be a very serious mistake on their part. Today he was one of the bad guys, here to commit a crime that, for a short space of time at least, would capture the world's attention and spread fear like a contagion.

The thought didn't bother him. Voorhess was a professional. He did what he was paid to do, and those who hired his services knew that he could be relied on to carry out his orders, as long as the money was right and the risk manageable. He'd always been good at killing because he was able to disassociate himself from the fact that those he killed were human beings. He just killed them. It was as simple, and as complicated, as that.

He remembered the first time, all the way back in 1982, when he'd been a young conscript in the South African Defence Force, fighting the SWAPO Marxists in Angola. The captain of his platoon, a man named De Koch, had considered Voorhess soft. It was his boyish face, and those twinkling eyes. They always made people think he was soft.

They'd been on patrol one morning down a narrow back road through forest and had run straight into a patrol of SWAPO coming the other way. Both sides had been completely surprised at running into the other, and for a moment everyone just stopped and stared. Voorhess had felt no fear. Just a single burst of adrenalin. He hadn't seen people. He'd seen targets. And crucially he was the first to react. He'd cut down three of them before De Koch and the others had even raised their weapons. Two rounds to the chest in each one, killing them stone dead. It was something he'd been doing periodically ever since – first for the military, and finally for himself.

The previous night he'd received an email from the client telling him that a rental car was parked ready for him on the third floor of the long-stay car park, and when he got there he was pleased to find it was a Mitsubishi Shogun, similar to the one he drove back home. The keys were on top of the front passenger side tyre, as instructed, and when he got inside there was a blank envelope on the passenger seat containing an address and two front door keys.

This was how Voorhess liked to do business. Anonymously. With the exception of some of his victims, no one ever saw his face, and that included the people who hired his services. That way it protected both them and him.

He switched on the engine and shoved the heating on to full blast to banish the damp English cold, before reversing out of the space. His stay here was going to be brief. He was already booked on a flight out of Heathrow to Bangkok first thing the following morning.

And, if all went according to plan, he'd be leaving mayhem in his wake.

Eighteen

12.14

There are no noble causes. Even those with the purest motives taint themselves in their pursuit of justice.

I was thinking that as I watched Mike Bolt walk towards me through the park. He'd approached me a year earlier, after I'd been charged with GBH over the incident with Alfonse Webber, and had offered me a straightforward deal. Work for him and get a short sentence – no more than a year – or take my chances with the courts and risk going down for three or four. Maybe even more. Webber had sustained serious injuries. A campaign – Justice for Alfonse – had been set up in his name, fronted by a high-powered human-rights lawyer who clearly cared a lot more about Webber's rights than those of the girl who'd been tied naked to a bed in his flat. There was serious media interest amid claims of police brutality and racism. The point was, I was on my own.

At the time, I didn't think the police were able to make deals like that. I'd always been led to believe that it was up to judges to set prison sentences. Since then, I've learned a lot of things I didn't know about.

Bolt was heading up a team trying to find out who else had been involved in setting up the Stanhope attacks, and it seemed he had a lot of clout. He was also convinced that one of the terrorists involved – William Garrett, aka Fox – could provide the answers. The idea was that I'd be placed on remand alongside him, my brief being to build up a rapport and try to glean what information I could from him, and then pass it back to Bolt and his team. As an ex-soldier, just like Fox, who'd served in Iraq and Afghanistan, and who'd also committed a serious crime, I was the perfect candidate.

There was another reason too. I'd lost someone in the Stanhope siege. I wouldn't say I'd ever been that close to my cousin Martin, but we'd seen a lot of each other as kids, and we'd met up at family events now and again, and we'd always got on well. He'd died inside the hotel trying to disarm one of the terrorists, and I remember how angry that had made me. He was one of the good guys, and he'd died a hero, murdered trying to protect other people, just because he'd ended up in the wrong place at the wrong time. Just like those people in the café this morning.

You see, that's the thing with terrorists. They don't care who dies in the pursuit of their cause.

Well, I did. Which was why I'd agreed to help Bolt.

I spent six months in the cell next to Fox. I talked to him a lot in that time. I'd even say we got on quite well, given our shared background. But he was no fool, and he steadfastly refused to talk about his part in the siege, so I was never able to give Bolt anything of use. No names. No evidence. Nothing.

When I came out, having served eight months for my crime – much to the anger of Alfonse Webber and his extremely vocal supporters – Bolt wanted me to continue working for him, and the man he wanted me to go after was none other than Cecil Boorman, one of my old army colleagues. Cecil was suspected of being an associate of some of those involved in the Stanhope siege, and being part of a larger network of extreme right-wing terrorists. I found that part difficult to believe. Cecil was a hard man and a stone-cold killer, but the evidence against him seemed pretty scant.

I could have said no. Should have done really. I was under no obligation to continue helping Bolt. I'd been given my sentence and served it, so there was no way of putting me back inside. But in the end, what else was I going to do? I was an ex-con; I'd been fired from the Met; my criminal record prevented me from going back into the army; my wife had left me. I was facing the scrapheap. At least doing this gave me a chance for some excitement.

My brief had been simple: find out what Cecil is up to and who he's working for.

At the time he'd been running an outfit providing security for nightclub doors in north London and the occasional bodyguard work, and I'd asked him for work. We might not have seen each other for close to five years, but we'd hit it off again straight away. I was an angry man after my time inside, and it hadn't been hard to convince him of my right-wing credentials. Nor to let him believe that I would be up for more lucrative, illegal work if it was available.

I knew straight away he was involved in something bad, but like Fox, he was very careful not to give too much away. So I'd made the classic mistake and compromised myself to gain his trust.

The robbery should have sorted everything. We'd hold up a scumbag drug dealer, put the fear of God into him, and leave with plenty of cash, knowing that he'd never report what had happened to the police. But you know the rest. And now suddenly I was in a lot of trouble. If Cecil went down, he'd take me with him. I'd debated long and hard this morning whether I should say anything to Bolt, but in the end I'd decided I had no choice. I needed to see this through, and if I played my cards right, when Cecil went down he'd have no idea that I'd been the one to betray him.

All I had to do was make it happen.

Nineteen

12.15

As Bolt walked past a small café on his left, his informant, Richard Burnham-Jones, got up from where he'd been sitting at one of the outside tables and fell into step beside him. He was dressed in jogging gear and carrying a bottle of water. Jones was a tall guy, close to Bolt's height, with thick dark hair and handsome chiselled features that were enhanced rather than spoilt by a thin, twisting scar an inch and a half long above his left eye, which he'd received when he'd been hit by a piece of skull bone from a fellow soldier who'd just been shot in the head.

'So?' Bolt said without looking at him as they walked on through the park.

'I'm in. Cecil introduced me to a guy called Cain who's obviously the boss. Cain wants me to work for him and he's willing to pay good money. My first job's to accompany him and Cecil to a meeting today. He wants us to provide security.'

Jesus, thought Bolt, it was all happening today. He'd been running Jones as an informant for close to a year now with virtually nothing to show for it, and now he had a breakthrough on the day when London had once again come under terrorist attack. 'Did you get a photo of him?'

'No.'

'Why not? That's what I gave you the camera for.' A month earlier, Bolt had supplied Jones with a Nike baseball cap with a tiny camera sewn into the front lining. To take a photo, the person wearing the cap pressed a button in the side lining, an action Jones could easily have disguised by scratching the side of his head.

'It was just too risky. Cecil searched me before the meet, and I told you before: I've never worn a baseball cap in my life. He'd have noticed, and then if he'd searched it and found the camera . . .'

'He wouldn't have. It's too small.'

'It's the kind of thing he looks for. Cecil knows what he's doing, and he's paranoid as hell. If he'd found it, it would have got me killed.'

Which Bolt had to admit was true. Cecil Boorman was a difficult customer. A former soldier, he'd been ID'd as an occasional associate of several of the mercenaries involved in the Stanhope siege, and at one time had done work in Iraq for the security consultancy that Fox had run. The only problem was, there was nothing concrete linking him to the siege itself, and he was seriously adept at counter-surveillance, making an intelligence-gathering op against him near enough impossible. Bolt, though, had always thought he was worth pursuing, and if Cecil was being that careful about covering his tracks, it meant he had to have something big to hide.

'Describe Cain to me.'

'My height, early forties, short blond hair, lean and very pale – almost vampire pale – with a big vein running down his right cheek that really stands out. He doesn't look ordinary, put it like that. He's also ex-military, an officer by the looks of him, and speaks with a middle-class Home Counties accent. He served in Lashkar Gah a few years ago, and there was a green on blue incident in his battalion.'

'Green on blue?'

'Where an Afghan working with coalition forces attacks them. A translator called Abdul shot two of Cain's men while he was there. If you look hard enough, you should be able to get an ID on him from all that.'

Bolt nodded. He was recording the conversation so there was no need to write anything down. 'Did Cain mention anything about the bombs this morning?'

'Yeah. He said that it was Islamic terrorists, and gave me this spiel about how if I worked for him, I'd get a chance to fight against all the people doing the country harm. He was pretty extreme in his views.'

'But he didn't suggest that the bombs might be something to do with him?'

'You think they might be?'

Bolt sighed. 'I don't know.' He needed more than this if they were ever going to get a breakthrough. Even if they managed to ID Cain from Jones's description, it didn't push them any further forward. 'This meeting Cain wants you to go to. Do you know what it's about?'

'He didn't give many details, but I get the impression he's buying something, and that he doesn't trust the people he's buying it from.'

'Did you get a look at his car?'

Jones shook his head. 'He was on foot when I saw him.'

'The thing is, he may not be as good at counter-surveillance as Cecil, so it's possible we can get a tail on him. Have you asked Cecil about him?'

'Cecil's keeping very shtum about Cain, and if I ask too many questions he'll get suspicious.'

'You're entitled to act suspicious too, you know. You're being hired by someone you know nothing about, to do work you know nothing about, but which involves guns. How do you know that he isn't a cop trying to set you up? Ask Cecil that. The point is, if you put yourself in the position of a man who's looking for illegal work, you'll get the answers you're looking for.'

'That *you're* looking for, you mean. I'm doing this for you, remember?'

Bolt looked at him sharply. 'No, Jones, you're not. You're doing it for the ordinary man in the street, who just wants to go about his business without someone trying to blow him up in aid of some shitty little cause. You're doing it for your family. For your cousin who died at the Stanhope. For your daughter. Remember, she and your ex-wife could have been in that coffee shop when it blew this morning.'

Jones took a deep breath, staring off into space. 'Yeah, I know.'

Bolt knew he was laying it on thick but he was frustrated. He sympathized with what had happened to Jones. By all accounts he'd been a good cop who'd lost his head one day, and the result was that he'd also lost his job, his pension, his wife and, most humiliating of all, his liberty. He'd sacrificed a lot for his country, and the people in it, and all he'd received was a lot of shit in return. But it also meant that he was a perfect informant, because if anyone was justified in feeling the kind of rage needed to become involved with extremists, it was him. But there are strict rules in the UK on the police's use of informants, and Bolt was bending them seriously. He'd been told by his boss, the head of Counter Terrorism Command, that due to the seriousness of the terrorist threat he had some flexibility about who he used, and how he used them. But he also knew that if everything went tits up, he'd be the one taking all the flak.

'If you go to this meeting I want you to wear a listening device,' he told Jones.

'I told you: they search me.'

'This thing's tiny, and it's basically only a tape recorder, so no bug finder will be able to find it. It's just to gather evidence, so try to get these guys talking.' He reached into his pocket and pulled out an envelope. 'There are two GPS units in there as well. They're the size and thickness of postage stamps, and we can turn them on remotely. The bug finder won't find them either. They operate to a completely different frequency. If you can, plant one in Cain's car after the meet, and one in Cecil's car as well if it's at all possible. Then call me, and we'll switch them on.' He handed Jones the envelope, glancing round as casually as possible to check no one was paying them undue attention, but the park was quiet. 'We're not going to be tailing you. I don't want to compromise things, and right now we haven't got the manpower. You're on your own out there today.'

Jones grunted derisively. 'I've been on my own since the very beginning.'

'The most important thing is to ID Cain. No more. Once we've done that, you can pull out. And don't, whatever you do, compromise yourself by doing anything that's going to get you into serious trouble.'

Jones scratched the scar on his forehead. He still

looked unhappy. 'I've got one major request, Mike. I need you to make sure no one ever knows I've been involved. I don't want anything to do with a court case, or an inquiry. Nothing like that. And I don't want to do anything that puts my family in danger.'

'When you're done with this, you're out, I promise,' said Bolt, knowing this was a promise that might become very hard to keep. 'Listen, I've got to go. Things are chaos at the moment with these bombs. Keep me posted, OK?'

They turned and went their separate ways, Bolt already preoccupied with the terrorists' threat that if their demands weren't met, in less than eight hours there'd be another even bigger attack on the city he called home.

Only later did it occur to him that this was the first time they'd met up when Jones hadn't asked him for payment for his services.

Twenty

13.45

Voorhess's target was a young entrepreneur called Azim Butt who lived alone in a modern townhouse, three storeys tall, with an attached garage and a roof garden full of exotic plants that looked from the street like a miniature rainforest amid the urban concrete.

It had been easy enough to get inside. Mr Butt's Filipina cleaner came every Monday and Thursday between the hours of 10.30 and 1.30, and she'd been in residence when Voorhess had arrived earlier. She always turned off the hi-tech synchronized alarm and central locking system that supposedly made the house intruder-proof, so Voorhess only had a single non-alarmed lock to pick on the front door, which he'd done in the space of thirty seconds. The cleaner was working upstairs, so Voorhess had shut the door quietly behind him, made his way through a gaudily furnished front room, and planted himself in a downstairs toilet that she'd already cleaned, and which didn't have any motion sensors in it.

He was in there now, half an hour on, using the toilet as a seat, his holdall of tools at his feet, eating some sushi he'd bought at a small takeaway outlet on a nearby street. The cleaner had gone, having re-set the alarm, and Voorhess was pleased he hadn't had to kill her. He might have to be in the house for a while, and if she was missed during that time, it could be problematic.

According to the dossier the client had prepared for him, Mr Butt was the primary investor in a number of businesses in the central London area, which he visited regularly in between working from his office in Moorgate and also from an office in his house. In other words, he could turn up at any time.

Voorhess twisted open the lid of the tiny plastic bottle of soy sauce that came with the sushi – no easy feat with gloved hands – and poured half the contents on to a tuna roll, which he ate in one bite. The fish was bland and the rice stodgy. Not like back home where the tuna was caught in the nutrient-rich waters of the Western Cape coast, and prepared by people who, like him, actually cared about food. He felt a twinge of homesickness. He wanted to hear the crash of the waves breaking on the beach near his house, and feel the warm African sun on his back while he grilled a nice piece of fish on the barbecue, and enjoyed a crisp, cold glass of Pinot Grigio.

A picture of Mr Butt dressed in a loud Hawaiian shirt and a garland of flowers hung on the wall opposite the toilet. He was on a beach somewhere, with a vivid blue sea in the background, and he had his arms around the shoulders of an attractive leggy blonde who was having to bend down to get her face in the shot. Mr Butt was a short, slightly built but undeniably good-looking man, with a thick shock of black hair. He looked younger than his thirty-one years, and the big smile he was wearing suggested he enjoyed life, and didn't take it too seriously. Sadly for him, things were about to take an extremely serious and unpleasant turn, and what was most intriguing for Voorhess was that, unlike so many of his victims, Mr Butt would never understand why he'd been targeted. He had no enemies. He lived an unremarkable bachelor lifestyle. He was even apparently honest.

And yet someone somewhere had marked him for death.

Two loud bleeps coming from the front room broke the silence. It was the alarm being turned off from the outside. Voorhess popped the last sushi roll into his mouth and, still chewing, reached into the holdall.

The front door opened and closed, followed by footfalls coming past the toilet. Voorhess waited a few seconds until he heard the clatter of cupboards opening, and then he stepped outside and walked down the hall towards the kitchen.

Mr Butt was standing next to one of the worktops with his back to the door, wearing an expensive-looking suit, his hair sticking up on his head like it was some kind of unruly sculpture.

Voorhess wasn't a believer in the sixth sense. He'd crept up on far too many people without being noticed to know that it existed only in people's imagination. But even though he'd moved in near silence, Mr Butt turned round, an empty mug in his hand and a shocked expression on his boyish face.

'Who are you?' he asked, fear cutting right through his voice.

'Your new lodger,' said Voorhess, and shot him with the Taser.

Twenty-one

13.55

'According to the Border Agency, Jetmir Brozi's last known address is 60 Roman Road in Islington, although they haven't checked on him for the past three months. They're overstretched apparently.' A life-sized colour mugshot of a hard-faced man in his late thirties or early forties, with bad skin and collar-length black hair, appeared on the screen.

Tina was back in the Special Operations office in Mayfair, listening while one of Bolt's team, DC Nikki Donohoe, gave a rundown of the information they had on the man Fox claimed had played a pivotal part in supplying the weaponry for the Stanhope siege.

Aside from Tina, Nikki and Mike Bolt, there were two other people in the main open-plan office on the second floor of the building: DC Omar Balachi and DS Mo Khan, a short, stocky Asian who'd worked with Mike Bolt for as long as Tina had known him, and who'd never had too much time for her.

Bolt had introduced Tina to the others, and they were all still sizing each other up. Tina felt uncharacteristically nervous. Everyone had been polite to her as they'd shaken her hand in turn, but there was a coolness there, not least from Mo Khan, a feeling that she wasn't the sort of person they wanted to get close to. It was something Tina had encountered many times before, but which she'd never quite grown used to.

'It seems that Mr Brozi got a British passport holder pregnant,' continued Nikki, reading from a sheet of A4 paper, 'which is why the authorities can't kick him out of the country, even though he's a failed asylum seeker and a convicted criminal. Apparently he has a right to a family life in this country, even though he's not actually living with the woman or their child.'

There were groans around the room at this and a couple of people made comments, but Tina was keen to press on.

'Fox told me that Brozi spent time at a brothel in King's Cross as well,' she said, 'and was involved in running the place. It's where they met to discuss the arms deal last year.' She repeated the address Fox had given her.

Omar turned towards her, a sceptical expression on his face. 'Wow, this guy knows how to play the system. He's got the Border Agency wrapped round his finger, plus he's a brothel keeper and an arms dealer too. It all sounds pretty unlikely. Are you sure Fox isn't messing with you?'

Tina met his gaze. 'What would be the point?'

'Maybe he's bored. To be honest I wouldn't know, because none of us got a chance to talk to him.'

Tina noticed Omar was looking at Bolt when he said this.

'Listen, I know how it looks, but he was attacked three days ago, and it didn't look like a set-up to me. He ended up with more than twenty stitches, and he came across as scared. He wants protection, and he wants to do some kind of deal.'

'Did you get to interview the prisoner who attacked him?' asked Bolt.

Tina nodded. 'I did, but it was just the usual run of no comments to every question I asked. Eric Hughes is a lifer with another ten years minimum to serve, and he's straight out of "violent thug" central casting, so there wasn't anything I could scare him with. He knows the score, and he knows that if he stays quiet he'll just get another few months tagged on to his sentence. But the way the attack was carried out, with Hughes following Fox into the toilet armed with a homemade knife and attacking him in an area where the CCTV camera was broken, suggests that it was a pro job, not an argument. Which means Hughes must have got paid for his services. He wouldn't have got the money in prison, and since he's in for life, we have to assume that the payment was made to someone on the outside, and someone close to him.' Tina paused for a moment, pleased that the others were looking at her with interest now. 'I checked with the governor and, although Hughes has never been married, two of his three children are with the same woman, and she visits him regularly. I think maybe we should lean on her as well.'

'Good idea,' said Bolt. 'But our first priority is Brozi. I've just had confirmation that the explosive used in both bombs this morning is PETN – the same explosives that were used in the Stanhope attacks. So if Brozi is some kind of arms dealer, as Fox is claiming, it's possible he's got direct links to today's terrorists.' He looked round the room at everyone in turn. 'I don't need to remind anyone of the terrorists' ultimatum. And I'm reliably informed that the government have absolutely no intention of meeting any of their demands, so we're now in a race against time to locate the bombers. And Brozi might just be the person who leads us to them.'

Twenty-two

14.15

If there was one thing that DS Chris Hancock hated most about policework, it was delivering death messages.

According to those in the force who knew him, Hancock had the right temperament and look for it, his sad eyes and hangdog features putting people at ease as he gave them the bad news about the sudden, occasionally brutal, demise of a loved one. He'd done it no fewer than two dozen times during his time in the Met, and every time it had been excruciatingly painful. People tended to react in much the same way. First disbelief, then a profound sense of shock that seemed to sweep over them like a shadow. They were usually very quiet. 'How did it happen?' they would ask in hushed tones as the enormity of their loss slowly sunk in.

Only once had anyone ever reacted dramatically.

That had been a young mother – thirty-two years old if memory served him correctly. Hancock had had to tell her that her nine-year-old son, an only child, had been killed in a hit-and-run incident at a zebra crossing. She'd fallen apart, screaming, throwing crockery, howling with grief, her voice echoing round the room as she'd turned from an attractive young woman with a welcoming smile into an unhinged, wild-eyed banshee. It was as if she was trying to get rid of all her energy and strength in one tremendous burst so that she'd be too overcome with exhaustion to feel the pain. Hancock had had sleepless nights for weeks afterwards. He'd felt that woman's loss, tasted it in his mouth. He too was the parent of an only child, a daughter aged seventeen, and he couldn't begin to imagine what his life would be like if something happened to her.

Now that he was working for Counter Terrorism Command he'd hoped that his days of delivering dark news were behind him, but it seemed they weren't. It had been only six hours since the first of the three bombs that day but they'd already had their first positive ID of a victim, and he and his colleague DC Marie MacDonald had been tasked with delivering the death message.

The recipient was the owner of a major City-based IT company, a man called Garth Crossman. DS Hancock had done some brief research on Crossman on his way over (he always liked to find out a little about the people he was giving such bad news to, so he could at least try to get some idea of how they were likely to react). A self-starter and entrepreneur who'd left school at eighteen with poor exam results, Crossman had founded Logical Solutions two decades earlier, and was now a millionaire many times over. However, as DS Hancock knew from experience, all the money in the world can't protect you against tragedy.

At first when they turned up at the front desk of Logical Solutions' head office in Leadenhall, the receptionist hadn't wanted to disturb Mr Crossman. Apparently he was in an important meeting with investors. Only when Hancock showed her his CTC ID and told her it was an emergency did she finally relent, suddenly looking very worried.

Two minutes later, Crossman appeared in reception. He was a fit-looking, silver-haired guy in his late forties, a little on the short side, smart but casual in an open-necked shirt and dark, neatly pressed trousers. He fixed Hancock and MacDonald with a welcoming yet puzzled expression – he clearly had no idea what two officers from Counter Terrorism Command could want with him – and after shaking hands, ushered them into an adjoining boardroom.

DS Hancock never saw the point in delaying the inevitable. 'I'm afraid we have some very bad news,' he said, looking Crossman firmly in the eye. 'A woman we believe to be your wife was killed in the café bombing this morning.'

Crossman's face tightened, and Hancock could see he'd had a number of recent Botox injections. 'I, er . . .' He stayed silent for a moment as the shock of Hancock's message hit home. 'Oh God.'

'Would you like to sit down, Mr Crossman?' asked DC MacDonald, motioning towards one of the chairs round the boardroom table.

'No, no, it's OK. How sure are you that it's her?'

'There's no doubt, I'm afraid,' said Hancock. 'A DNA sample taken from her body matches the one we already have for her on the central database.' Two years earlier, Martha Crossman had been convicted of drink driving, making identifying her far quicker and easier than if her DNA hadn't been on file.

'I tried phoning her earlier,' said Crossman, his voice shaking. 'You know, after I heard about the bomb, and the message said the phone was switched off. I didn't think anything of it. I mean, you don't, do you?' He looked at them both in turn, his eyes wide and gleaming. 'It's a terrible shock. God, I'm going to have to tell the children.' He wiped a sheen of sweat from his forehead, and ran a hand down his face. 'Do you need me to . . . to identify her? My wife, I mean?'

Hancock shook his head. 'No, that's all taken care of. We'll release the body as soon as we're able, but it may not be for a while yet.'

'Did she suffer?'

'Your wife was very close to the bomber. She would

have died almost instantly. In fact, she probably never felt a thing.'

'And there's no doubt?'

'No. There's no doubt at all. I'm sorry.'

'Thank you, officers. It must be a very hard job you have to do.'

A long time afterwards, DS Chris Hancock remembered this being the point when he thought there was something wrong with Crossman's reaction. He was acting more like a politician doling out well-earned praise than a man who'd just lost his wife, but at the time all Hancock experienced was an uneasy feeling he couldn't quite put his finger on.

Crossman must have seen something in his expression. 'I have to admit, my wife and I were planning to split up,' he informed them. 'We've had a number of arguments and she was planning to move out in the next few weeks. Even so, it's still a terrible loss to our family.' He took a deep breath, and looked up towards the ceiling.

DC MacDonald put a hand gently on his arm. 'If there's anything we can do, Mr Crossman . . .'

'No, it's fine,' he said, wiping his eyes with the sleeve of his shirt. 'I'll do what has to be done.'

'It may be best for you not to be alone. We can organize a grief counsellor to come and talk to you and your children.'

'I really appreciate your offer, but we can manage.'

There was a finality in his tone that told them that

they were done here. They left the boardroom and walked back through reception, nodding at the receptionist as they left.

'God, I hope we don't have to do any more of those for a while,' said DC MacDonald when they were outside.

'I wouldn't bet on it,' said Hancock. So far, twelve people – not including the bomber – had been confirmed dead, a figure that was still rising. 'I always seem to get these jobs.'

'I thought he took it pretty well in there, considering.'

'So did I. Too well.'

'Really?'

He shrugged. 'There was something about him I didn't like.'

'I think you're beginning to get cynical in your old age, Chris.'

'I disagree,' he said, as they got into the car. 'I can see the good in people. But I can also tell when it's missing. And it was missing in there.'

Back in the boardroom, Garth Crossman sat in contemplative silence. He'd made numerous presentations in this room to investors, shareholders and clients, yet in many ways the one he'd just made to the two police officers had been the most important. It was essential they believed in his grief, and he was pretty certain they had.

He sat back in his seat and allowed himself a small smile. There'd been some unnerving moments, but so far his plan was working perfectly.

And the exciting thing was, it was only just beginning.

Twenty-three

14.30

Jetmir Brozi's name alone wasn't a huge help to Bolt's team. At the moment they only had the word of a suspected mass murderer that he was involved in the Stanhope siege and today's attacks, and Tina knew this meant a major and possibly lengthy evidence-gathering mission. The first priority was to locate him, which was why Mo Khan and Omar Balachi had been dispatched to keep watch on the brothel in King's Cross, while she and Bolt had just turned off the Pentonville Road and were driving to his house in Islington. A surveillance team from Tina's old station, Islington nick, was already there at Bolt's request, keeping an eye on the place until they arrived.

Bolt was driving and, as he approached some red lights, Nikki Donohoe's voice came over the radio to tell them that Brozi had been positively ID'd leaving his house, and was now being followed by the surveillance team.

'Christ, I hope they don't lose him,' said Bolt, bringing the car to a halt.

'How big's the team they're using?' asked Tina.

'Six.'

Tina frowned. 'Is that all?'

'Right now, everyone's on the hunt for the bombers, and this is just one of a hundred leads. We were lucky to get anyone at all.'

Most police surveillance teams were an absolute minimum of eight strong, with twelve being the average, while the terrorist chasers in MI5 liked to use up to twenty-five people to follow one suspect. As far as Tina was concerned, sending six was worse than sending no one at all, because they were more likely to get spotted, ruining everything.

It wasn't long before they were driving past the address they'd been given for Jetmir Brozi – a well-kept Georgian townhouse on a leafy residential street not far from Liverpool Road. 'Not bad for a thug who should have been deported years ago,' Bolt remarked.

They found a spot thirty yards further down the road, and took up position facing his front door. Now it was just a matter of waiting for authorization to carry out a covert entry on Brozi's house and plant cameras and audio equipment inside. Usually this could take days, but Bolt had asked his boss, Commander Thomas Ingrams, the head of CTC, to do everything he could to fast-track it and, given Brozi's record as a known criminal, they were both hopeful they'd get it sooner rather than later.

The car fell silent bar the radio chatter coming from the surveillance team as they followed Brozi through heavy traffic on the Pentonville Road. Tina recognized a couple of voices as cops she used to work with, and wondered if she'd end up running into any of them later.

'So, how's life, Mike? Are you still with that girl? The one you were engaged to?'

'Claire. It didn't work out.' He shrugged. 'It's not easy to hold down a relationship in our line of work.'

'That's true, but it's not impossible either. How come you broke up? I thought she was meant to be the one.'

'Blimey, Tina. What is this? *Twenty Questions*?'

Now it was her turn to shrug. 'I'm just interested, that's all.' But it was more than that. She was interested in *him*. She wanted to find out why a tall, good-looking, charismatic guy like Bolt couldn't hold down a relationship. She wanted to know if he still had commitment issues. And the reason was simple. Since seeing him that morning for the first time in two years, the attraction she'd once felt had suddenly, and totally unexpectedly, been rekindled.

'Anyway,' he said, turning things round, 'how's your love life?'

She laughed. 'Non-existent. I'm about as good as

you at holding down a relationship, so I guess I shouldn't be lecturing. I split with my last boyfriend because he wanted me to tie him up and spank him. Can you believe that?'

'I've been a copper for more than twenty-five years. I can believe anything.' He grinned. 'I'd have thought that was right up your street, Tina. Knocking men about without getting into trouble.'

'What got me was that it all started off totally normally. He was a really nice guy. Smart, good-looking. Good taste obviously.'

'Obviously.'

'We even went to meet his parents in Vancouver. Then one day he tells me out of the blue that he's always wanted to be dominated sexually, and he asks if he can call me Mistress when we're on our own.'

They were both laughing now.

'I reckon you'd make a good mistress.'

'I tried to play along – I like to think I'm a game girl – but it all just got a bit silly.'

They both fell silent, looking at each other, and she remembered how close she'd come to falling into bed with him last time, and she could feel the same thing happening now.

They were interrupted by the voice of Nikki Donohoe coming back over the radio. 'Control to Alpha One. Authorization for the creep at suspect property given. I'm emailing through the paperwork now. Over.'

'Alpha One to Control,' said Bolt into the radio. 'Received and understood. Over.'

According to the surveillance team chatter, Brozi was now heading north on the Caledonian Road, away from home, which meant it was safe to go inside and plant the bugs.

'Who wants to go in?' said Bolt. 'Me or you?'

Tina smiled. 'Can I go? You know me. I like a little bit of excitement, and my housebreaking skills are still bang up to date.'

Bolt nodded. 'I have no doubt of that. OK, I'll wait here. But be quick.'

'I'm on it,' Tina said, slipping on a pair of gloves and slinging the handbag containing the recording equipment over her shoulder. 'But make sure you watch my back. The last thing I need with my reputation is Mr Brozi coming home unexpectedly.'

'I've always got your back, Tina,' he told her, and their eyes locked for just a second too long.

She got out of the car and crossed the road, walking as casually as possible. The street was empty, bar a couple of builders working on some scaffolding a hundred yards further down, but you never knew who could be watching inside one of the houses. Covert entry was a highly delicate procedure, and there were always far too many things that could go wrong, especially when it was done in broad daylight.

She passed through the front gate, noting where they could plant a camera later under cover of darkness, which would kick into life whenever anyone passed in or out of the house, then rang the front doorbell. When there was no answer, she rang a second time, just to make sure, at the same time removing a set of picks from the handbag. She'd already seen that there was no sign of an alarm, so went straight to work on the door's standard Yale lock.

It took her longer to do than she'd expected, and she was conscious of the fact that Bolt was watching her. She pushed him out of her mind and concentrated on getting the movements of each pick just right, until finally the lock clicked and the door opened.

Tina stepped inside without looking over her shoulder, and shut the door behind her. She was in a narrow hallway with a staircase directly in front of her. The place smelled of mothballs and cheap spices, the walls were dirty and bare, and the cream carpet stained and thinning. In Tina's experience, criminals were rarely houseproud and did little to stamp their personality on their homes. A detective she'd once worked with back in CID had said it was because they knew they'd never be staying in the same place long, and Tina thought he had a point.

Feeling the illicit excitement that comes from creeping through someone else's house, she got to work. She'd been provided with the latest microscopic video cameras, long, thin devices with threading on one end, which could be used to replace the screws in wall sockets, making them almost undetectable. They were motion sensitive and apparently provided excellent sound quality. She moved through the house, putting one in each room, working her way upwards, making sure she had pretty much the whole place covered.

It was in the TV room that she found the gun. Aside from the TV itself – an immense thing that blocked out most of the bay window – and two leather chairs facing it, the only furniture in the room was a chest of drawers. The top drawer was slightly open and Tina figured that, while she was there, she might as well have a quick look through Brozi's possessions to see if there might be anything of interest. It seemed that he was pretty cavalier with his criminality because there'd been no attempt to hide the gun. It was sitting there in the drawer next to two three-inch-thick wads of used fifty-pound notes – a brand-new Glock 17 pistol. She picked it up and inspected it with gloved hands, releasing the magazine. It was fully loaded with live ammunition. Ordinarily Tina would have removed the bullets, but these weren't ordinary circumstances. If she did that, Brozi would know that somebody had been in his house, and the whole op would be compromised. But she was pleased with the find. It showed that Fox hadn't just been yanking her chain. It also meant that if they had to arrest Brozi quickly, they had something serious to charge him with. The minimum recommended sentence for possession of a gun was five years, which gave them some decent bargaining power.

Tina looked at the money. There was probably ten grand in there. She had to admit that, for a moment, she was tempted to take some. She wasn't paid a huge amount and she'd developed a taste for travel that was difficult to afford. A few hundred quid would pay for a flight to Asia or South America, and there was no way he'd miss it. The two piles weren't even, and she doubted Brozi had counted them. But in the end she knew it would only bring her another step closer to the people she chased, and that if she did it once, she'd do it again. She thought about Dennis Milne, the corrupt cop she'd met in the Philippines a couple of years ago, who'd gone from Met detective to killer for hire with God knows how many corpses to his name. She thought of Fox and his remark about them being similar, and with a sigh, she slid the drawer back to the position it had been in when she'd found it, and continued up through the house to the last floor.

As she reached the master bedroom, the radio crackled in her pocket. It was Bolt.

'What's happening?' she whispered.

'The surveillance team have lost Brozi,' he told her.

'Great. Where did they lose him?'

'On the Caledonian Road. He did a U-turn and shook them off.'

'So he saw them?'

'I don't know, but I want you out of the house right now. And no messing about, Tina, please.'

Tina looked round the bedroom. It was tidier than the rest of the house with a huge double bed with mirrors facing it on two walls, and a large cupboard at one end. It was the desk with the PC next to the window that caught her attention. 'OK, I'm coming.'

'Now,' Bolt said firmly, ending the call.

Tina figured she had another minute or two, and went over to the PC. The screen was dark, so she hit the return key and it immediately lit up, showing a freeze frame from an amateur porn movie. In the bottom corner of the screen there were two more internet icons. She tapped the first one and an email account appeared, showing an empty space where the new emails should have been. She wrote down the address, then saw that there was an email in the drafts section on the left-hand side of the screen. Using the drafts section to communicate was a much-used trick of terrorists, as well as the more organized criminals. If two or more people had access to the same email address they could write messages to each other in draft, which could then be read without the messages themselves ever actually being sent across the internet, meaning they couldn't be monitored by the authorities.

Tina pressed the drafts icon, and the message appeared. It was several sentences long and written in an indecipherable language that was presumably

Albanian. She made the text as big as she could on the screen and photographed it, before switching back to the original email account screen, and shrinking it so that the freeze frame from the porn film would be the first thing Brozi saw when he switched the PC back on again. She had no idea whether it was a useful lead or not, but it felt promising, and it gave her an excuse for not having left the house immediately.

Tina was conscious of the time but she also knew that she might not get another chance like this to bug Brozi, and if truth was told, it gave her an adrenalin rush just being in his house. She hadn't had much in the way of excitement these past few months, so she was making up for lost time. Working fast, she fitted a keystroke tracker to the PC, so that they'd be able to monitor every word he typed, and she was just looking round the room for a good spot to place another camera when the radio crackled into life again.

'What the hell are you doing, Tina?' demanded Bolt. 'They still haven't found Brozi. You need to get out right now.'

'OK, OK, I'm coming—'

'Oh shit.'

'What?'

'A car has just pulled into the street.' He paused. 'It's parking ten yards away. Yes, it's definitely Brozi. Tina, switch off your radio and stay put. I'll let you know when he comes out again.'

Tina shook her head. She'd messed up. The rules on

covert entry were always the same. You could only bug an individual's house while someone was watching them elsewhere. As soon as you lost the eyeball, you abandoned the op. A few hours working with Mike Bolt again and she'd already broken a cardinal rule.

'He's got a gun in the house,' she said quickly. 'It might be best to get some armed response, just as back-up?'

'Is it loaded?'

'Yes.'

'Then you'd better unload it quickly because he's out of the car now and on his way to the front door. Christ, Tina, why do you always do this to me?' She could hear the anger in his voice as she switched off the radio.

She heard the key turn in the lock downstairs. There was no way she could go down to the living room and unload the gun without Brozi being alerted to her presence. She looked round quickly for a place to hide, and settled for the double wardrobe opposite the bed. She climbed inside, noticing that the PC hadn't yet gone into screensaver mode, so if Brozi came up here in the next few minutes, he was going to know someone had been tampering with it. Silently, she cursed herself for the self-destructive streak that constantly seemed to haunt her.

Yet, even then, she couldn't help feeling that little twinge of excitement.

Twenty-four

15.00

The journalist on the Sky News desk sounded bored and irritated as he answered the phone.

'This is Islamic Command, responsible for the attacks on the Crusader forces and those who support them,' said Cain through the voice disguiser. 'We are still waiting for a response from the British government to our demands. Do they not think their people are worth protecting?'

'And can you repeat your demands?'

Cain was pleased by the note of panic that had now crept into the journalist's voice. 'If they do not comply by eight p.m. tonight, we promise to launch an attack so ferocious it will make your Godless country quake.'

The journalist started to speak again but Cain had already ended the call. He switched off the phone, removed the SIM card, and threw it into a bush, before walking a few yards further through the copse of trees and chucking the phone into a tangle of brambles.

The trees opened up in front of him, and he stood at the top of Hampstead Heath, looking down past the rolling parkland to the city that stretched out as far as the eye could see below him, its iconic structures – the Gherkin, the London Eye, the Shard – all clearly visible as they rose up from the mass of buildings around them. Up here it all looked so peaceful, but down there he knew it was chaos as the security forces desperately tried to hunt down the men behind the terrorist attacks that morning.

So far, the government's only reaction to the attacks was to condemn them utterly, send their sympathies to the victims and their families, and repeat their standard mantras that the British government never negotiated with terrorists, and that Londoners should carry on regardless, not allowing the terrorists to disrupt their lives. Although the Prime Minister was supposedly chairing a meeting of Cobra – the government's emergency reaction committee – he'd left it to the Commissioner of the Met to field questions from the nation's media.

So, they were reacting in exactly the way Cain had predicted they would. In other words, everything was going according to plan.

He took out another of his phones. It was time to call Brozi and set up the meeting.

Twenty-five

15.01

Jetmir Brozi clearly didn't invest a huge amount of money in clothes. There were barely a dozen items of clothing hanging up, and a few pairs of shoes cluttered round the floor, but nothing that gave Tina any real cover as she crouched in the half-light of the closed wardrobe.

She could hear him speaking on the phone, his voice faint and guttural. He was getting closer. A stair creaked, then another.

He was coming up.

Jesus, why did she let herself get in this situation? Why couldn't she just do her job properly?

For the first time, fear replaced excitement. If Brozi discovered her, she was trapped, and with no weapon. She wasn't even carrying pepper spray, for Christ's sake.

The bedroom door opened and he walked inside,

finishing up his conversation on the phone. He was talking in English but his voice was low and she wondered if what he was saying was being picked up on the audio.

She looked through the wardrobe's narrow keyhole and saw him walking round with his back to her. From this angle, it was impossible to tell whether or not the screensaver on the PC had kicked in.

Brozi stopped talking, and Tina's whole body tensed. She could hear her heartbeat – a rapid-fire tattoo that she would swear was audible from outside the wardrobe. He was standing still and looking over towards the PC. Slowly, he replaced the phone in the pocket of his trousers and exited the room, his movements unhurried. A few seconds later she heard him going down the stairs.

Tina waited, trying to work out what to do. She couldn't stay in there for ever. At some point, Brozi was going to want to get something out of, or put something into, his wardrobe. He might go out again, of course, in which case she'd be fine. But if he didn't, she was going to have to try to sneak out past him.

The staircase was creaking again. He was coming back up, and his movements were slower, more purposeful, this time.

She stared out of the keyhole, keeping as still as possible, watching the doorway.

Brozi reappeared, and this time he was holding the gun in front of him.

And he was looking right at her.

Tina held her breath.

After looking round the room again, he walked slowly towards the wardrobe.

Tina leaned back, clenched her fists, preparing. Her mobile phone vibrated in her jeans pocket, but she didn't have time to wonder who it was. It was irrelevant now. She was on her own, and none of her new colleagues could help her.

He was right outside the wardrobe now. She could hear his slightly forced breathing. Any second now he'd open the door, take a step back so he was out of range of an attack, and there she'd be. Defenceless and totally vulnerable.

She exploded out of the wardrobe's double doors, leaping straight into him, grabbing for his gun hand.

Caught completely by surprise, Brozi stumbled backwards as Tina yanked his arm upwards, and the gun went off with a deafening bang, the bullet striking the ceiling. They landed on the unmade double bed in a violent embrace with Tina on top. Brozi snarled, showing yellowed teeth, and, as he lifted his head, Tina butted him hard on the bridge of the nose, knocking him back.

But he was strong, and with a grunt of exertion he rolled over, knocking her off him, the gun swinging wildly as he tried to point it at her. Tina kept her grip but allowed herself to be pushed off the bed, landing on her feet and bringing Brozi with her. He spat in her face, and tried to butt her back, but she dodged the blow, and drove her knee into his groin.

Immediately, Brozi's grip weakened and he yelped in pain. Tina gave him a hard shove that sent him tumbling, then turned and ran for the door, slamming it shut behind her. She took the stairs two at a time, going so fast she almost stumbled and lost her balance.

As she hit the first floor, she heard the bedroom door open and the sound of rapid footfalls on the staircase, and then she was on the last flight of stairs down to the ground floor, the front door and freedom only feet in front of her. She reached the door, pulled both handles, saw that he'd put the chain across, slammed it back shut, pulled back the chain, went to open it again—

'Hands up or I shoot!' came the angry, heavily accented shout from the top of the stairs.

Tina didn't know if he was bluffing or not but she made the split-second decision not to stay and find out. Yanking the door open in one movement, she dived on to the steps, rolling down on to the pathway, trying to make herself as difficult a target as possible, before jumping to her feet and vaulting over the gate, noticing with relief that Brozi still hadn't pulled the trigger.

Bolt was already running across the road to meet her, holding his warrant card in one hand, the tension etched all over his face. 'Are you all right?' he shouted, grabbing her by the arm.

'Yeah, I'm fine,' she panted. 'Let's get out of here. He's armed.'

But at that moment Jetmir Brozi came striding down the steps, holding the Glock in both hands in front of him. 'Who the fuck are you?' he yelled.

Tina and Bolt retreated, backing away from each other at the same time, hands in the air in non-confrontational poses as he bore down on them in this quiet little street that suddenly felt like the loneliest spot in the world rather than the middle of an immense and bustling city.

But Brozi kept coming. He was heading for Tina, the gun pointed straight at her head, the end of the barrel barely ten feet away now. His eyes were wild and he looked coked up, which probably explained why he was pursuing her on to the street armed with an illegal Glock 17 in broad daylight.

'What were you doing in my house?' he demanded. 'Tell me now or I shoot you fucking dead! Understand? And stop moving.'

Tina was in the middle of the road now, and she did as she was told, keeping her arms firmly in the air.

'Mr Brozi,' said Bolt firmly, 'we are police officers. If you shoot either of us, you'll go to prison for the rest of your life.'

Brozi stopped, and the first flicker of doubt crossed his face, although he kept the gun pointed firmly at Tina.

'Put the gun down, Mr Brozi,' Bolt continued. 'Then

we can talk about this.' He edged forward ever so slightly as he spoke. 'Armed officers are on the way here right now.'

'Shooting us isn't going to help you,' said Tina, noticing Bolt's forward movement.

Brozi suddenly turned the gun on Bolt. 'Stay where you are.'

Tina had a flash of fear that he might shoot him and it would all be her fault. She thought about rushing him but it was too risky. He was too far away and she'd seen the damage that a bullet could do.

From somewhere to the south of them came the steady wail of a siren getting closer, and Brozi seemed to realize what an exposed position he was in, standing in the middle of the street. Fifty yards away, Tina could see two teenage girls in school uniform standing outside a corner shop at the end of the road, watching. Twin beads of sweat ran down her forehead and into an eye, but she didn't dare move her hand to rub them away.

'Put the gun down, Mr Brozi,' she said with a calmness she wasn't feeling. 'This is not helping anyone.'

'Fuck you, pig,' spat Brozi, retreating up the street away from them. 'Fuck both of you.' Still keeping the gun trained on the two of them, he climbed into his car, a big Lexus saloon, and started the engine, pulling out in front of them.

Seeing the opportunity to get out of the line of fire,

Tina and Bolt rushed over to their own car and jumped inside as Brozi roared past them.

'We're going after him, right?' shouted Tina.

Bolt didn't answer. He didn't even look at Tina. Instead he yanked the key in the ignition and tore away from the kerb.

Tina started talking rapidly into the radio. 'Alpha One to all units, shots have been fired inside Target One home and we are pursuing Target One now in his blue Lexus, licence plate Alpha Freddie Ten Alpha November Charlie, north on Roman Road. Target One is armed with a fully loaded Glock. I repeat, Target One is armed. Approach with extreme caution. Over.'

Bolt was driving fast, his face etched with concentration, and he was barely twenty yards behind Brozi as the Lexus headed for the junction. But then the Lexus's brake lights came on, and Brozi leaned out of the driver's-side window, pointed the gun at them, and started firing.

'Shit!' yelled Bolt, slamming on the brakes and coming to a halt in a screech of tyres, and ducking his head as bullets flew past, one pinging off the car roof with a high-pitched whistle, another blowing a hole in the driver's-side wing mirror.

Tina ducked too, her heart pumping like a steam train, completely caught up in the thrill of the moment. When she looked back up, Brozi and the gun had disappeared back inside the car, and he was driving again.

But before he could reach the junction, a marked squad car appeared round the corner, and turned into the street, driving up it the wrong way and blocking Brozi's path, forcing him to reverse.

'He's coming back!' shouted Tina as the Lexus shot back towards them.

Bolt cursed, and they just had time to take up crash positions before the Lexus hit them with a loud bang, knocking their car several yards backwards, but not doing enough to shunt it out of the way completely.

Knowing there was no way out with the car, Brozi flung open the door and took off back up the street, running along the pavement, and keeping low behind the line of parked cars, still waving the gun around.

With the Lexus in the way, Tina couldn't see whether or not the occupants of the squad car were an armed response unit, and she didn't wait to find out, leaping out of their car and running along the road after Brozi. She was a lot fitter than he was, and within a few seconds she was drawing level with him.

He saw her and waved his gun but didn't attempt to fire, still maybe thinking he could outrun her, even though he was panting heavily and looking like he might collapse at any moment.

Operating entirely on instinct – if she'd thought about it there was no way she would have done it – Tina abruptly changed direction and ran over the bonnet of one of the parked cars, before leaping off the other side and, as Brozi turned to meet her, diving into him and knocking him and the gun flying.

He went down hard, badly winded, the gun well out of reach underneath another parked car. Tina wriggled into position so she was squatting on top of him, her knees holding down his arms. Brozi tried to struggle but then his eyes widened as he saw Tina's expression.

She punched him hard in the face, three times in rapid succession, ignoring the blood flying out of his nose, and the fact that he was no longer resisting arrest. She would have punched him a fourth time too, but she felt her arm being grabbed firmly from behind and looked back to see Bolt standing there.

'Leave him, Tina, or you'll be done for assault,' he told her.

Behind Bolt, she could see two unarmed male uniforms jogging, rather than running, towards her, neither of them looking like they'd have done too much faced with a gunman, and she nodded and turned back to the man who just moments earlier had tried to kill her.

'Jetmir Brozi, I'm arresting you for attempted murder,' she said, as Bolt stepped forward and the two of them hauled him to his feet.

Twenty-six

15.15

Fox sat in his cell, watching events unfold on Sky News. The breaking news was that the Sky newsroom had just received a phone call from a spokesman for Islamic Command, the previously unknown group who'd already claimed responsibility for the bombings. The caller had reiterated his warning that a third, much bigger, attack would take place if their demands weren't met.

The female anchor was now discussing the ramifications of this with one of Sky's reporters who was standing outside 10 Downing Street, while on the bottom of the screen the news ticker gave the latest on the casualty toll: seventeen dead, including four police officers and a civilian killed in the second attack, and sixty-eight injured. A separate breaking news headline stated that there would be a press conference at Downing Street at 3.30.

Watching it reminded Fox of the chaos he and the other terrorists had inflicted on London fifteen months earlier. He'd felt like the king of the world then, an all-powerful lord of life and death, knowing that the whole world was watching him.

And now he was caged like an animal in a shitty little prison cell with lime-green walls, and his moment of glory was little more than a faded dream from another life.

With a sigh, he got up from the bunk and walked out of the cell. He'd petitioned the governor earlier to release him from solitary confinement and, surprisingly, permission had been given. It was recreation time in the wing now, and he was free to come and go as he pleased for the next two hours. The governor liked the prisoners to be able to mingle. He felt it made them less likely to be aggressive if they weren't cooped up in their cells the whole time, and in this, Fox had to admit, he was right. He appreciated the small pleasure of being able to stretch his legs – to walk, and think – even if it was in a confined space. This was the first day since the attack by Eric Hughes that he'd been allowed to do it. Hughes, meanwhile, was still locked up in a separate wing as he'd been the one armed with the shank.

A table-tennis table in the central atrium surrounded by a cluster of tables and chairs provided the focal point for the prisoners when they were given the chance to socialize. Devereaux was already sitting at one of the tables, furthest away from the two screws who stood keeping an eye on things. Muscular and intense, with big staring eyes, and a tattoo of a grinning black skull covering most of his face, Devereaux looked like something out of a horror film, and gave off the air of a man only ever one step away from exploding. With a lot of prisoners, this kind of posturing was just show, but Devereaux was different. He was, as the judge who'd sentenced him put it, 'pure, unadulterated evil'. Currently serving a whole-life tariff for the double murder of two underage prostitutes he'd kidnapped, raped and partly eaten a decade earlier, both screws and prisoners tended to give him a wide berth.

Fox nodded at one of the prisoners playing table tennis, a huge former white supremacist known as Lenny who was one of the softest men in there, and approached the table where Devereaux sat alone, an unlit cigarette sticking out of his mouth.

'Got a smoke?' asked Fox, who'd taken up a ten-a-day habit out of boredom since arriving in prison.

'Sure,' grunted Devereaux, both the skull's mouth and his own mouth moving in perfect time as he pulled a tin of roll-ups from his pocket and put it down on the table.

Fox leaned forward to take one. 'Everything ready?' he whispered.

'Sorted,' answered Devereaux. 'What time, again?'

'Six forty-five exactly,' said Fox, his lips hardly moving.

He got up and walked away, putting the roll-up in his mouth, thinking that it was ironic that at a time when smoking inside public buildings was banned, prisoners could still smoke in their cells. The moment he got out of this place, though, he'd give up on the spot.

Which, if all went according to plan, was now only a matter of hours away.

Twenty-seven

15.29

'What the hell do you think you were doing in there?' demanded Bolt, staring at Tina in exasperation rather than anger. They were standing out on the pavement, just down from Brozi's house, and out of earshot of the dozen or so officers who were in the process of sealing off the street in both directions, while Brozi sat in the back of an arrest van. 'I told you to get out of the house. It was one simple request, and you ignored it.'

Tina took a deep breath, dragging air into her lungs. Her heart was still banging away in her chest, the adrenalin yet to dissipate, and she was experiencing the occasional wave of nausea. She wiped sweat from her brow, hoping she wasn't going into shock. Having a gun pointed at you at point-blank range, knowing that if the person pointing it pulled the trigger you'd almost certainly die, was a truly terrifying experience, even for someone like Tina who'd been on the wrong end of too many guns in her time, and who'd actually been shot twice. There'd been times in her life when she'd been so angry and disillusioned with everything that she'd wanted to die – when she'd taken major risks because, in the end, the consequences hadn't scared her – but now wasn't one of those times.

'Are you all right?' asked Bolt, putting a hand on her shoulder, his exasperation turning to concern.

'I'm fine.' She brushed his hand aside, not wanting his pity. She knew she was the one in the wrong. 'I just wanted to check his PC, that's all, and fit a keystroke tracker.'

'Well, you almost got us killed, Tina. Don't you understand that? Or do you just not care?'

'Of course I care. I was doing my job.' She pulled a crumpled pack of cigarettes from her jeans pocket and lit one, conscious that her hands were still shaking.

'But you weren't. That's your problem. You don't do your job. You do what you think's right, and ignore the consequences, and the rules.'

'I'm sorry.'

'Christ, I wish I'd never taken you on.'

His words stung. 'I found a lead on his PC,' she said with a calmness she wasn't feeling. 'It was an email in the drafts section written in Albanian.'

'How do you know it's a lead if it's in Albanian?'

'Because it was in the drafts section of an anonymous hotmail account. That's how these guys communicate when they don't want people listening in, isn't it?'

'Not good enough, Tina.'

'Come on, Mike. We've got plenty to charge Brozi with now. He's just shot at us, and he's obviously up to his neck in illegal stuff, so he'll almost certainly cooperate. This is the guy who Fox said organized the weaponry for the Stanhope attacks, remember? Who therefore has access to PETN, the explosive used in the bombs this morning.'

Bolt sighed. 'We'll just have to wait and see what the investigating officers say, won't we?'

'What do you mean?'

'I mean we're going to have to bring in another team from CTC to interview him. We can't talk to him now. Not after he shot at us. Now, instead of trying to find the people behind the bombs this morning, we're going to be stuck at the local nick making statements.' He looked at her with a mixture of irritation and sadness, and shook his head. 'I'm going to Islington so I can start getting things moving, just in case he does want to cooperate.'

'What do you want me to do?'

'Stay here and make sure no one goes inside the house until SOCO arrive.'

'You're putting me on guard duty?'

'Just be thankful you're still on duty at all,' he said, and with that he turned and walked away, leaving Tina wondering once again whether she'd messed up everything.

Twenty-eight

15.55

Of all the things I lost on the day I attacked Alfonse Webber, the worst, by far, was my family.

My marriage hadn't been the best in the world, but then whose is when you've got a young child and a stressful, time-consuming job? But up until that moment, we were still doing OK. I loved my wife; I loved my daughter. I think they both loved me.

But clearly the bond between Gina and me wasn't as strong as I'd thought because our marriage didn't survive my prison sentence. Six months in, she said she wanted to end it, and no amount of pleading from me changed her mind. I think there was someone else – at least for a while. She never admitted it, and if there was someone on the scene, he was gone by the time they released me from prison, but there were plenty of nights when I was lying alone in my cell staring at the ceiling, torturing myself about what the woman I loved was up to, and who she was up to it with.

The clouds were beginning to gather behind me and the wind was picking up as I walked up the narrow overgrown path to the front door of my old house in Stamford Hill and rang the doorbell – a process that never felt quite right.

Gina appeared behind the frosted glass a few seconds later. I'd called to say I was coming because I had something for her, and she opened the door straight away.

She was wearing track pants and a T-shirt, and had no make-up on, but she still looked fantastic. Gina might have been a single mother struggling to make ends meet, but the years had treated her well.

'Hey,' she said, with a forced smile. 'You said you had something for me.'

In the pantheon of enthusiastic welcomes it didn't score particularly highly, but then I could hardly blame her. I hadn't been round much lately, not since I'd fallen behind on the child support payments and she'd threatened to call in the CSA to hunt me down.

How the mighty have fallen, eh?

'Can I come in?'

She nodded suspiciously and stepped aside to let me in. The TV was on in the kitchen showing BBC News. The Prime Minister was on screen saying that there would be no negotiations with terrorists, and that Britain would never bow down to blackmail. He advised all citizens to go about their business as usual, but to be on their guard against further attacks. Which of course was easy for him to say.

'God, have you seen all this?' she said, picking up a mug of coffee from the sideboard. 'The terrorists have said there's going to be another attack later today.'

'They would say that. They want to scare people.'

'And it's working,' said Gina quietly, running a hand through her thick curly hair as she stared at the TV screen. 'I can't believe this is happening again.'

I fought the urge to put a protective hand on her shoulder and pull her to me, but it was hard. Very hard.

'Wasn't our involvement in Afghanistan meant to have protected us from this? I remember Gordon Brown saying that once while you were out there.' She looked at me like it was somehow my fault, her body language instinctively defensive.

'Politicians say a lot of things. Most of them are lies.' I realized as I spoke that I sounded a lot like Cecil. Or the mysterious Mr Cain.

She took a sip from her coffee – she hadn't bothered to offer me one – and abruptly changed the subject, which was an old habit of Gina's. She didn't dwell on things. 'So what is it that can't wait?'

'This,' I said, producing a wad of cash secured by an elastic band and handing it to her. 'There's two grand there, in lieu of all my missed payments.'

She frowned, looking down at the wad as if it was

tainted. 'Wow. That's a lot of money. Where did you get it?'

I committed an armed robbery. I shot up a police car containing people I used to work with.

'I've been doing a lot of doorwork, and some bodyguarding too.'

'It obviously pays well.'

'Not particularly, but I've been saving up.'

'You're not doing anything illegal, are you, Jones? Because if you are, I don't want this money.'

'I'm not a criminal, Gina.'

Her expression softened. 'No,' she said. 'I know you're not.'

I am. I'm a violent thug. I'm worse than the men I used to put behind bars.

'Thanks. I appreciate this. But it doesn't mean I'm going to call off the CSA. I need regular payments, Jones.'

'I know. And you'll get them, I promise.'

For a moment we just stared at each other, and I felt a lump rise in my throat. I'd never stopped loving her, and it hurt to look at her now, knowing she didn't feel remotely the same way. When I'd come back from that last tour, she'd been there waiting for me at the air-force base. She'd touched the scar on my forehead – fresh then – and taken me in her arms and held me, sobbing against my shoulder, repeating over and over again that she'd never stop loving me, but that it was time for me to stay home for good and leave the army.

So I'd left the army, knowing it was the only way of keeping my marriage intact. But in the end it had made no difference because she *had* stopped loving me. It had happened slowly, and I know it was my fault rather than Gina's. I'd had mood swings; I was distant; I had bad dreams – dreams of murder and men dying; and the pressures of my new job as a cop kept pushing me closer and closer to the edge, until that final, bitter incident with Webber. The truth was that even before I was sent down, I could see that our marriage was over. The time inside just sealed it.

'Where's Maddie?' I asked, looking around.

'She's having a nap. She's got a bit of a cold at the moment. I think it's the time of year.'

'Can I go up and see her?'

'I don't want you disturbing her.'

'I'll just look in on her. That's all I want to do.' I hadn't seen Maddie in close to two weeks and there was no way I was leaving without seeing her.

Gina sighed. 'OK. But if you wake her . . .'

'I won't. I promise.'

I made my way up the narrow staircase, remembering when this had been my home. It was the first place we'd bought together, almost ten years back now. The house wasn't much, nor was the area, but for the most part my memories of it were good which, to be honest, just made the situation feel worse.

Maddie was fast asleep on her side on top of the

covers, wearing jeans and the Dora the Explorer top I'd bought her the day I was released. A small lamp in the corner cast a dim glow over the room, showing the posters covering the walls and the toys that littered the floor.

I approached the bed and looked down at my daughter. Gently, I lifted a lock of blonde hair from her forehead and touched a finger to her face. I wondered what the future held for this four-year-old girl. Was she really going to become like a foreigner in her own country, as Cain had suggested, or was she going to go on to do great things? Become a doctor or an architect? I didn't honestly care so long as she was happy. And so long as she wasn't ashamed of her father, which made it essential that she never found out what I'd done today.

I mouthed the words 'I love you', and kissed Maddie once on the head, half-hoping she'd stir and smile up at me like she'd done when she was a toddler, so we could share a few snatched words before she fell asleep again.

But she didn't move, and reluctantly I turned away and went back downstairs.

'You didn't wake her, did you?' asked Gina. She was still watching the news. The Prime Minister had been replaced by an aerial view of the block of flats in Bayswater where the second and third explosions had occurred. The death toll from these two was now five police officers and a civilian.

'Don't worry,' I said, 'she's fine. A pack of hyenas wouldn't wake her right now.'

'Good.' She gave me a lopsided smile. 'Thanks for the money, Jones. It's a real help.'

'Look,' I said, feeling a sudden flash of hope, 'do you fancy going out for a bite to eat one night? Somewhere nice. You could get a babysitter.'

The smile disappeared, and her expression saddened. 'I don't think that's a good idea.' It looked like she was going to elaborate but she stopped herself, and I was reminded of something she'd said to me during one of the few infrequent prison visits she'd made: 'When the light goes out, it doesn't come back.'

'Sure,' I said, turning away, conscious of an unfamiliar ringtone coming from my pocket.

It was the phone Cain had given me.

'Where are you?' asked Cecil as I let myself out of the house. He sounded excited.

'Visiting my kid,' I told him.

'Stay where you are. I'll be with you in five minutes.'

'What's going on?'

'You know that meeting Cain was telling you about? It's on. Now.'

He ended the call before I had a chance to reply, leaving me staring at the phone and wondering how he could only be five minutes away, unless he'd followed me here.

I put the phone back in my pocket and zipped up my jacket against the cold. I thought about calling Mike Bolt but something stopped me. I wasn't sure what. Maybe it was just instinct.

Either way, it turned out to be one of the best moves of my life.

Twenty-nine

16.10

Tina stood in the doorway of Brozi's house smoking another cigarette and stamping her feet in an effort to keep out the cold.

About two dozen uniforms had now arrived at the scene, their vehicles blocking both ends of the street as they milled about, waiting for orders. Brozi's Lexus and the Land Rover Freelander she and Bolt had been in earlier were still in the middle of the road where they'd collided, waiting for the photographer to turn up and take some evidence shots of the dramatic scene. So far there was no sign of anyone from CTC or Islington CID. Tina wondered if, when the Islington guys did turn up, she'd see anyone she used to know. She hadn't done a good job of keeping in touch with her old colleagues, which was a habit of hers. When she moved on, she tended to leave her past behind completely, as if it was something best expunged.

She turned and caught her reflection in the glass of Brozi's front window. She was slimmer than she'd been in a while, courtesy of her obsession with the gym. Her hair looked different too. She'd dyed it jet black and had it cut short like it had been a few years ago – more to differentiate her from the woman whose photo had appeared all over the media after the Stanhope siege than because she liked the look, although it had begun to grow on her. She still looked attractive, but there was a hardness about her that seemed to become more pronounced year on year, as if it represented an accumulation of all the bad things that had ever happened to her. And Jesus, there'd been plenty of those.

A thought suddenly struck her just as she was about to start feeling sorry for herself. When Brozi had been threatening her and Bolt on the street with the gun, he'd had a mobile phone sticking out of his front pocket. But she didn't remember seeing it when they'd arrested him. She hadn't seen him drop it either, but then he could easily have done so when he'd been running away from her down the street.

Stubbing her cigarette underfoot, she called Mike Bolt, but he wasn't answering, which she supposed was no great surprise under the circumstances. She left a message asking him to find out if Brozi had had a phone in his possession when he'd been nicked, then walked back down to the area where she'd wrestled him to the ground. A single drop of blood on the pavement marked the spot, and she wondered whether Brozi would try to press charges against her for assault.

If he'd thrown away the phone when he was running, it would be round here somewhere. He'd had the gun in his left hand the whole time so he'd have to have thrown the phone away with his right, meaning it would most likely be in the road or under one of the parked cars. She crouched down and looked beneath the nearest one. There was nothing there, so she looked under the next one, then the next, slowly retracing Brozi's steps, pleased at least that she now had something to do, however mundane it was.

She'd been absorbed in this activity for several minutes when, out of the corner of her eye, she saw a group of uniforms looking across at her. One said something and the others laughed, although they all looked away fast enough when she returned their gaze. She ignored them and continued her careful search, almost level with Bolt's Freelander now, beginning to lose hope of finding anything.

Then she saw it. A newish-looking black iPhone, identical to the one Brozi had been using in his bedroom. It was on the tarmac beneath the bumper of a stationary van, about a foot from the kerb. Not exactly well hidden, but then Jetmir Brozi had been a man in a hurry.

Feeling a rush of vindication, she picked it up and switched it on. There was no password lock, as was often the case with criminals who were constantly changing their mobiles, and it was clear that Brozi hadn't had it long because there were only six calls in the call log, all of them made in the past four days to different mobile numbers. The last call was the one Brozi had been making in the bedroom. He'd been speaking English then, even though she hadn't been able to hear what was being said, but Tina had a feeling that the conversation might have been important. She checked the email section but it was blank, then almost as an afterthought, she opened the photos section.

There were two grainy shots of a man in profile coming out of a house. They weren't the best photos in the world but Tina felt her heart jump, because she recognized the man in them instantly.

It was the man she'd seen run over by a lorry only a few hours ago.

The terrorist who'd bombed the coffee shop.

Thirty

16.25

Tina was still staring at the photo of the bomber when her mobile phone rang. It was Mike Bolt.

Briefly she explained to him what she'd found.

'And are you absolutely sure it's him?' he asked when she'd finished.

'I won't forget his face as long as I live,' Tina said, suddenly feeling vindicated. 'So now we've got a direct link between Brozi and the bombers.'

'That's brilliant, Tina. Well done.'

'You're pleased with me now then, are you?' she said, unable to resist having a dig.

He sighed down the other end of the phone. 'It still doesn't detract from the fact that your actions almost got us both killed, but it's a great lead, there's no question about that.'

'We need to lean on Brozi fast.' She glanced at her watch. 'There's only three and a half hours until the terrorists' deadline, and I'd bet anything that he knows their identities.'

'But we can't. You know that. First of all, he's going to deny the phone's anything to do with him. We didn't even see him drop it. And secondly, after what happened with him shooting at us, I'm not even allowed to see him in case it prejudices future proceedings. We've got a team from HQ coming over to interview him but they haven't arrived yet, and nor has Brozi's lawyer.'

'So we're just going to hang around until Brozi's lawyer and the interview team decide to show their faces? Hoping that he might deign to cooperate with us?'

'This isn't *24*, Tina. We can't torture the information out of him. Just like we can't torture it out of Fox either.' He sighed. 'Listen, it's obvious from all this that Fox knows what's going on. I need you to talk to him again.'

'You're not going to send me back to the prison, are you?'

She could hear the smile in Bolt's voice as he answered. 'It wouldn't do any harm to have you out of the way, but no, I'm not. We're going to set up a secure line at Islington and you can call him from there.'

'I need to offer him something. Otherwise he's got no incentive to help us.'

Bolt was silent as he thought about this. 'Tell him

we're organizing moving him to a secure safehouse, but that it's going to take another day or so to sort the paperwork.'

'He won't fall for that, Mike. He's no fool. Let's try to be a bit creative here. It's clear from what's happened that his info's good. This isn't a set-up.'

'Right now, I haven't got the authority to offer him anything else. I'll speak to the commander but I doubt they'll even contemplate moving him. It would be political suicide. Use your charm, Tina. You've got a name out of him already. See if you can get something else.'

Politics, thought Tina. Policework, like everything else, was all politics, and covering your arse. She sighed. 'OK, I'm on my way.'

Thirty-one

16.35

Voorhess's target, Azim Butt, was bound tightly with bungee rope to a leather armchair in his spacious first-floor living room, and wearing wrist and ankle chains. A ball gag had been placed in his mouth, making it impossible for him to talk, and a blindfold covered his eyes. He'd been conscious for several hours now and after a lot of initial moaning beneath the gag, he'd long ago fallen silent.

Voorhess sat down on a chair next to him with a bowl of hot noodles and removed the gag. 'I'm going to feed you now, Mr Butt. Open your mouth.'

'I'm not hungry. Please, can you not just take what you want and leave?'

'I'm afraid not. I may need to stay for a little while.'

'But why? What do you want? I haven't done anything.' There was a note of pleading in his voice.

'I know it's early to be having supper, Mr Butt, but there may be a delay until your next meal, and these are very tasty noodles. I've just eaten a bowl myself. I stir-fried some spring onions, ginger and chicken thighs in with them, then added soy sauce, rice wine and a splash of sesame oil. So I would appreciate it if you would do as you're told.'

Mr Butt wisely decided to acquiesce, and allowed himself to be fed from the bowl, chewing in a manner that suggested that, actually, he was quite hungry. When he'd finished, Voorhess put a bottle of water to his mouth and let him drink.

'Am I some kind of hostage?' asked Mr Butt, looking up at him from behind the blindfold.

Voorhess put the bowl and the water down on the coffee table. 'In a manner of speaking, yes. All I can say is that if you cooperate, you'll come to no harm. As you can see from the fact that you've just been fed, I'm not here to hurt you.'

'I don't want to die,' said Mr Butt quietly.

'And you won't,' Voorhess told him, putting a reassuring hand on his shoulder. 'Just sit tight, stay calm, and I'll be gone later this evening. I promise.' His words had a soothing effect, but then Voorhess was good at that. He'd once been told by a nurse he'd gone out with back in Cape Town that he would have made an excellent doctor, because he had the perfect bedside manner, his voice exuding a potent mixture of confidence and kindness. It was, he thought almost ruefully, ironic that he did the job that he did.

The downstairs buzzer sounded, reverberating round the whole house.

Voorhess saw Mr Butt stiffen.

'Who could that be?' he asked.

'I don't know.'

Mr Butt's voice was quavering now, which made Voorhess suspicious.

'Are you expecting anyone?'

'It might be my girlfriend. What's the time?'

'It's quarter to five.'

'It's a bit early, and I wasn't expecting her. But it might be her.'

The buzzer sounded again.

'Will she go away if there's no answer?'

Mr Butt didn't reply. He looked scared.

'Mr Butt,' said Voorhess slowly, the bedside manner gone now, replaced by a cold, businesslike tone, 'will she go away?'

Mr Butt swallowed. 'She has a key.'

Ach, thought Voorhess, always complications.

As if appearing to read his mind, Mr Butt looked up at him imploringly from behind the blindfold. 'Please don't hurt her. She's everything to me. We're getting married.'

He would have said more too but Voorhess replaced the ball gag in his mouth and tightened it, before leaning down so that he was close to the other man's ear. 'Don't make a sound, Mr Butt, because if you do, you will put your girlfriend in mortal danger. Nod once if you understand.'

Mr Butt nodded once.

Voorhess had already taken possession of his phone, and he picked it up now. The phone vibrated and a text appeared. It was the girlfriend asking where he was, with lots of question marks. She finished the message by saying she was extremely horny and was coming in to wait for him.

Oh dear, thought Voorhess, walking out on to the first-floor landing.

Darkness was beginning to fall and he made his way through the unlit gloom to the bathroom, grabbed a towel, then started down the stairs as a key turned in the lock.

She had just closed the door behind her and switched on the lights when Voorhess reached the bottom of the staircase. It was the girl from the photo in the downstairs toilet. She turned round with a bright, sexy smile that vanished when she saw that it wasn't her boyfriend but a big man in overalls, holding a gun in one hand and a towel in the other.

In the flesh, she was even more attractive – a tall, willowy blonde with golden skin, wearing a short red dress that showed off her long shapely legs, and high-heeled red court shoes that Voorhess reckoned she probably wore when she was having sex. A short red leather jacket completed the ensemble.

'Oh God,' she said, her mouth dropping open in shock.

'It's OK,' he said calmly, lifting the gun. 'I'm not going to hurt you. Put your hands in the air for me.'

As she raised them uncertainly, he shot her once through her left eye, catching her as she stumbled, and simultaneously wrapping the towel round her head to stem the bleeding. The gun he'd used was the one he'd requested from the client, a .22 calibre with low-velocity bullets, designed to take people out at close range without making much noise or mess. He'd hoped he wouldn't have to use it, but he knew from experience that it was always best to plan for any eventuality.

She was still moving, clearly not dead yet, and he brought her slowly down to the carpet, placing her in a sitting position so that she was leaning back against him, her body juddering in the crook of his shoulder, the warmth of her skin giving him an unpleasant feeling. He didn't like this kind of thing. Putting the gun down on the carpet, he produced a lock knife from his overalls, flicked open the blade and drove it deep into her heart to finish her off and stop it pumping blood, holding her while she died in his arms.

When he was sure she was gone, Voorhess tied a knot in the towel, impressed at how little blood had been spilt, threw the body over one shoulder, and carried her into the adjoining garage. Mr Butt didn't drive, preferring to take taxis everywhere, and Voorhess had parked his Shogun in there. He thought about putting the body in the Shogun's boot, but that would just complicate matters. Instead he laid her down at the back of the garage, trying not to look as her dress rode up to reveal a bright red lacy thong with a black flower in the centre. It seemed such a terrible waste, destroying something so beautiful, and at such close quarters too, and he gave a sigh of relief as he covered her with a sheet of dusty tarpaulin, glad he didn't have to look at his handiwork any more.

Mr Butt didn't make a sound as Voorhess walked back into the room where he sat bound to the chair, but tears were streaming down his face. It was obvious he knew what had happened. The .22's retort hadn't been loud, but he would still have heard it.

Voorhess found a tissue and wiped away his tears.

This was the cue for Mr Butt to make a long keening sound beneath the gag, like a wounded animal, and Voorhess turned away, having no desire to watch the other man's pain. At the same time, there was a bleep from the mobile phone the client had provided him with.

He slipped it from his overalls and checked the message. It read simply: GOODS READY FOR COLLECTION TWO HOURS. FOR USE 8 P.M.

Voorhess nodded slowly, looking over at the holdall

on the sofa. The black explosives vest was poking out and he picked it up, along with the medical kit containing the diazepam.

It was time to make the final preparations.

Thirty-two

16.52

Islington nick held plenty of memories for Tina Boyd. She'd done two stints there as a detective – the first for four years, the second for two. It was the place where she'd fallen in love for the first and only time in her life. DI John Gallan had been her boss, a good-looking, good-hearted man who'd been snatched away from her far too quickly.

She didn't miss the place. It was a big ugly building next door to an even uglier Sainsbury's superstore, and most of the memories only made her unhappy on those few occasions she chose to dwell on them. It was, after all, events that had happened there that had driven her to alcoholism and the steady decline into darkness that had followed.

So it was with a hint of trepidation that she stepped through the doors, nodding briefly to a couple of civilian workers she didn't recognize who were smoking just outside, and went into the reception area. The first thing she noticed was that there was no sense of urgency as a result of the bombs that morning and the terrorists' ultimatum that had followed. The custody sergeant, an old timer called Barnes, was booking in a smiling drunk who appeared to have forgotten his own name and who was having to be held up by two PCSOs, while a second prisoner – young and feral – was arguing loudly with his escort as they tried to get him through the door to the cells. Other people – the lawyers, the civilian workers and the civilians caught up in the police system – wandered in and out, ignoring the dramas going on around them.

Mike Bolt was already in reception. 'The interview team should be here in the next fifteen minutes,' he said as they took the stairs to the second floor of the building. 'But Brozi's refusing to say a word without his lawyer present, and we're not expecting him until five thirty. Plus he wants an Albanian translator, and we're still trying to sort one out.'

'He spoke English well enough to me,' said Tina.

Bolt frowned. 'The problem is, he's not acting like a man who's scared. I think his experience of the British justice system has made him pretty complacent.'

'I'd have thought the fact that he's being charged with the attempted murder of two police officers would have concentrated his mind.'

'You know what it's like, Tina. In this business, nothing's cut and dried.'

And it wasn't. A clever lawyer could easily twist the facts to suit his client's case, particularly as none of the bullets Brozi had fired had come anywhere near hitting either her or Bolt. Ironically, it would have been a lot better for the case, and for scaring Brozi into cooperating, if one of them had actually been shot.

'Listen, Mike,' she said as they walked out of the lift and turned in the direction of the CID offices, 'that message on Brozi's PC might be a clue to something. Can you run it by the Albanian translator whenever he turns up?' She took out her mobile. 'I photographed it on here.'

'Text me the photo and I'll see what I can do,' he said, not sounding particularly interested.

By now they were in an empty office where two phones sat on a desk with chairs at either end. 'We've set up the secure line so you can talk to Fox from here.' His expression was tense as he looked at her. 'If he knows the names of the people involved in the attacks today, and he wants to help himself, then he's got to tell us now, because we're running short on time.'

'Let's get on with it then,' said Tina, picking up one of the phones, while Bolt picked up the other so he could listen in.

After being patched through to the prison governor's office, and given a short lecture from Governor Goodman on how talking to a prisoner like this was highly unorthodox, she was re-routed to the office where Fox had been taken along with his escort to receive the call.

'So the lead I gave you this morning was useful?' said Fox calmly as he came on the line.

'We have Mr Brozi in custody, yes.'

'Would that have anything to do with the events in Islington this afternoon?'

'How do you know about them?'

'I've got a TV in my cell, and I like to keep up with current affairs. It's all over the news that two police officers were shot at by an armed man, who was arrested at the scene. It was Brozi, wasn't it?'

Tina could tell he was trying to knock her off balance, as he'd done that morning. It was working too. The speed with which the media covered events, and Fox's own access to their coverage, meant that even in prison he was only a few steps behind them. Briefly, she told him what had happened.

'I'm impressed,' he said when Tina had finished. 'You get shot at by a suspect and still you stay on duty. I admire you. I really do.'

Tina ignored him. 'We've found evidence that links Brozi to the attacks this morning. Which links them to what happened at the Stanhope.'

'Exactly as I predicted.'

'But we still need the names of the people involved.'

'I know you do,' said Fox, a hard edge to his voice. 'But you need to help me first.'

'We're already in the process of organizing your move to a safehouse but it requires approval at the highest level. We can't move you before tomorrow.' Tina glanced across at Bolt as she said this, and he gave her an approving nod. 'If you give me another name, you'll put yourself in a very advantageous position ahead of your trial.'

Fox grunted dismissively. 'Surely you can do better than that, Tina. You've got a reputation for getting things done. That's why I chose to see you and not some patsy in a cheap suit bound by all the rules.'

'Like I said, the authorities are prepared to cut a deal with you, I can guarantee that. And you *will* be moved to a safehouse.'

'And when I've got that in writing, and I'm in this safehouse, then I'll help you. But not until then.'

Tina felt her frustration building. She pictured Fox on the other end of the phone, a smug expression on his face. A man with an ordinary demeanour but who'd been responsible for dozens of murders and felt not a moment's remorse. She wanted to grab him by his short, thinning hair and drive his head into the table again and again. To make him spill his guts and tell her everything he knew.

But she couldn't.

And he knew it.

'Get me out of here and we'll talk,' he said quietly.

'I can't get you out of there tonight. I've just told you that.'

'Then put me on to someone who can. Or as far as I'm concerned, this conversation's over.'

Tina was aware of Bolt shaking his head beside her, warning her to take it easy. But she no longer cared.

'If people die because you won't help—'

'Then what?' he said. 'What'll you do exactly?'

'I'll fuck you up. I don't care how long it takes, I don't know how I'll do it, but make no mistake, I will.'

Fox let out a dismissive sigh. 'You won't have to. If you leave me in here, other people will do it for you. And then it'll be too late. For both of us.'

Thirty-three

17.25

Night was closing in fast as the car headed south through Bermondsey, passing through a series of featureless industrial estates and retail parks in the direction of the Old Kent Road.

Since Cecil had picked me up at the old family home over an hour earlier, we'd followed a round-about U-turn-filled route across north-east London, before detouring through the grand, ostentatious wealth of the City of London, and crossing the river at Tower Bridge. We'd met Cain a few minutes after that on a back street lined with trendy apartments near Jamaica Road, and it was there that we'd changed cars. We were now in an Audi A5 estate I hadn't seen before. If anything, traffic had been lighter than usual and I wondered whether a lot of people had left work early as a result of the bomb threat that hung over the city like a black, menacing cloud.

Once again Cecil had run the bug finder over me, and made me turn off my phone. I'd protested, but he wasn't taking no for an answer. Not that it mattered. Bolt had been right. The bug finder hadn't picked up the two GPS devices in my wallet, but it had still been a nerve-racking few seconds.

Cain was driving now, with me in the front passenger seat next to him. Cecil was on his own in the back, sitting directly behind me, which was making me paranoid. We turned on to a quiet, poorly lit back road, flanked on one side by empty-looking warehouses, and on the other by a row of immense gas towers that stretched up into the cold dark sky behind a high brick wall. A car came past the other way, but otherwise the road was empty and there was a bleakness about the place that made it difficult to believe we were in the middle of a city. I suddenly wondered whether they'd somehow found out I'd met up with Bolt and concluded, quite rightly, that I was working for the cops. If they had, this would be as good a place as any to kill me. All Cecil had to do was put a gun against the back of my headrest and pull the trigger, and that would be that. It only takes half a second to die. I've seen it happen in war zones. A single explosion; a sniper's bullet. Bang, it's all over. Just like that. It took all my willpower to stop myself from turning round to see what Cecil was doing.

Don't panic, I told myself. They don't know. They can't. Mike Bolt's the only man who knows my identity. If they suspected me, they'd drop me like a stone, not lure me into the middle of nowhere.

Cain slowed the car and turned it into a short dead-end road with a high fence at the end and scrubland behind it. He turned to face us. 'OK, these people we're going to see. I've dealt with them before, and they've been reliable, but this is the biggest deal we've done together. I'm buying some contraband from them – contraband that's going to be passed on very quickly, so neither of you needs to know what it is.' He looked at us both in turn. 'But I can guarantee you this. It's going to be used to strike a real blow against the establishment, which is what we all want. I'm using the bulk of the money the two of you earned this morning as payment, which is why we've got to be careful. Men can do stupid things where big money's involved – we all know that.'

'Who are we dealing with?' I asked him.

'Albanians from Kosovo. Ex-members of the KLA. They're not nice people but, as I said, they've been reliable in the past. The meeting place is a scrapyard down a road off here. I reccied the place yesterday. There was no one around and the place was locked up, which means it's probably not used much. There's nothing wrong with that, of course. We don't want any unwanted attention, but it also means that if anything goes wrong, we're on our own. Which is why we're going in armed. Cecil, can you do the honours?'

Cecil leaned down behind the driver's seat and brought up the battered Lonsdale holdall that LeShawn Lambden had been using to carry his crack takings before we'd taken it from him. He opened it up to reveal two pistols and an MP5, all sitting on a huge wedge of cash.

'I'm sure everything's going to be fine,' said Cain, taking one of the pistols and handing me the other. 'We're businessmen, and no one wants a bloodbath. But I'm also not the kind of man who takes chances.'

I ejected the magazine, checked that it was loaded, then slipped the pistol into the back of my jeans where it couldn't be seen beneath my jacket.

'Jones, you and me are going to go in the front. I'll do the talking. You're just there for back-up. Follow my orders the whole time, OK?'

I nodded.

'What about me?' asked Cecil.

Cain pulled a sheet of A4 paper from his jacket pocket and unfolded it, revealing a Google aerial-view map of the area. 'You get out here and take the holdall and the MP5 with you, but keep the gun hidden just in case you run into anyone. Cut through the fence at the end of the road and turn left. There's a dirt path that leads behind the buildings. Follow it round until you come to the scrapyard, here.' He tapped his gloved finger on a building near the top of the map, which he'd marked with a cross. 'When you're level with the main building, you'll see a small hole in the fence. I made it yesterday and there'll be just enough room for you to get through with the holdall. Text me on today's number as soon as you're inside the perimeter, then stay within earshot of the main building but out of sight. There are wrecked cars everywhere, so there'll be plenty of hiding places. Don't move until you hear me call you. Understood?'

'Understood.'

'But if you hear either me or Jones shout the words "This whole thing's wrong", you come in straight away with your finger on the trigger because that means we're in trouble. And you take out anyone who gets in your way.'

Cecil repeated the phrase and grinned. Those were just the kind of instructions he liked. 'Got it.'

The way Cain was talking left me in no doubt that I was about to cross a major line. If this meeting turned violent and I ended up pulling the trigger, I knew Mike Bolt wouldn't be able to protect me.

To be honest, I was sorely tempted to jump out of the car then and there, but there were way too many things stopping me, not least the fact that I might end up getting a bullet in the back of the head the moment I opened the door.

Behind me, Cecil finished checking the MP5 before replacing it in the holdall, and slinging it over one shoulder. He gave Cain and me a nod then disappeared into the night.

We watched him jog down to the end of the road

and disappear into the scrub. Above the trees and the flat roofs of the buildings, the tower at Canary Wharf rose up like a glowing finger in the distance, probably not much more than a mile away.

'You know,' said Cain after a couple of minutes, 'the biggest robbers in the country work in there.' He pointed at the tower. 'Every day they steal thousands of times what you took from those crack dealers today. And they get away with it. Just like the MPs who fiddle their expenses and line their pockets. Or the pondscum like Alfonse Webber who laugh at the law and the justice system, and get stronger every day because no one's able to stop them.' He looked at me, something in his expression asking me for understanding. 'All I want to do is create a fairer society. One that promotes hard work and decent values. Where the bad guys get punished and the good guys get rewarded. And you've got to fight for that. Sometimes it's a lonely battle, but that doesn't mean it's not worth fighting. Remember that.'

The frightening thing was, he was right. If you wanted to change the world, you had to stand up and be counted. But that didn't mean you had to kill civilians. Cain was a twisted individual – a typical extremist, who believed totally in the rightness of his cause, even if it meant killing hundreds of innocent people.

Right then, he sickened me. But I didn't show it. Instead, I just nodded and told him I agreed.

A phone made an annoying doorbell sound somewhere on Cain's person. He didn't even bother taking it out to check it. Instead, he turned on the engine and put the car into gear.

'You ready?'

I could feel the warm metal of the gun pushing against the small of my back.

'Always,' I told him.

Thirty-four

17.35

Gina Burnham-Jones didn't like the position she'd found herself in.

For a long time, she'd truly loved her husband. The fact that he was a soldier had never been ideal. Gina had never fancied herself as an army wife. She'd grown up in a loving family home within the same small Bedfordshire town, with both parents present, and had wanted the same for herself. But you can't choose who you fall in love with. It just happens. And Jones had just happened. She'd met him in a wine bar in the West End while he'd been on leave and out with friends, and things had just clicked. He was tall and rangy, with model good looks, and eyes that were alive with promise. Even her mum, who'd never been keen on her previous boyfriends, announced that Jones had a really positive aura about him.

In the end, it wouldn't have mattered what her

mother had said. Gina had been besotted, and she and Jones were married within six months. That had been back in 2002, in the summer before the Allied invasion of Iraq. Gina had known that her husband would have to serve away from home sometimes, but at that time it never occurred to her that he'd end up fighting two wars, and that the tall, handsome, laughing man from her wedding day would change irreversibly.

The change had begun after his tour in Iraq, where he'd lost a friend to an IED. After the first tour of Afghanistan, it became even more marked. He stopped laughing. Occasionally Gina would come into a room and find him staring off into space, as if he was on drugs. He had bad dreams where he'd wake up either screaming in fear or shouting with rage. She tried to get him to leave the army, but he'd said it was his life, and that he couldn't imagine doing any other job. Gina had reluctantly accepted his decision but had also decided she wanted a child to fill the void that was opening up in her life.

Maddie had been born just before Jones went off to Afghanistan on his second tour. It had been a hard time for Gina. She'd suffered from post-natal depression, and her own mum, who would have helped lighten the load, was diagnosed with breast cancer. And with the TV news filled with reports of young soldiers dying in the dusty killing fields of Helmand Province, Gina was in constant fear that her own husband might not be coming back.

When he did, she gave him an ultimatum. Leave the army or lose her.

He left, but things were never the same between them, and their marriage had begun its steady disintegration, shattering completely when he'd been sent to prison.

Even after she'd told Jones it was over, Gina hadn't dated for a long time. She'd felt too guilty. After all, it wasn't his fault that he'd become the dark, violent man he now was.

But the fact remained that she no longer loved him, and as a healthy thirty-five-year-old woman she longed for companionship, and a chance to start again.

She'd met Matt on the internet. He was a solid, serious man, ten years older, and very different in personality from how Jones had been in the good old days. But he cared for her, and he made her feel wanted, and she suspected she was beginning to fall in love with him. They'd been seeing each other for six months now, and had kept things very low-key, but Gina knew that soon she was going to have to tell Jones, because she wanted to make things official and have Matt meet Maddie. She'd almost said something to him when she'd seen him earlier, but it hadn't felt like the right moment. It would have to happen soon, though.

Gina looked at herself in the mirror. The face that looked back at her was still pretty. There were a few lines round the eyes, and crossing her forehead, but nothing that a little foundation couldn't cure, and she wore the toughness of the last few years well. She wondered whether or not to put on lipstick. She was seeing Matt tonight. He was taking her out to a surprise destination for dinner and had asked her to dress up. She had no idea where it was, but it had been in the diary for weeks and Matt had begged her to keep the night free, and had promised that she'd enjoy it. Thankfully Maddie was feeling better now, and downstairs watching TV, otherwise Gina would have had to cancel it.

In truth, she'd rather not go out, especially if it was into central London, what with the terrorists threatening another bomb attack, but she felt foolish, and maybe even a little cowardly, saying that to Matt. Gina knew how important tonight was for him and, not for the first time, she wondered if he was planning to propose. They'd talked more than once about living together, and the previous week when they'd been lying in each other's arms in his bed, he'd told her he loved her, and she'd smiled and said 'I love you' back. It had felt good saying it too.

She reached for her red lipstick, wondering whether she'd say yes if he asked her to marry him tonight, and smiled to herself, because she knew that she would.

Thirty-five

17.37

The place we were meeting was as deserted as anywhere you were going to get in London. You reached it down a winding side road right at the end of the industrial estate, which finished at a pair of heavily padlocked high-mesh gates with a large CLOSED sign stuck on one of them. A light glowed dimly in a Portakabin just inside the entrance but that was the only sign of life.

We waited for a few seconds, and then a shifty-looking, unshaven guy smoking a cigarette appeared in the headlights on the other side of the gate as he checked out the car. He wore a heavy donkey jacket with bright green illumination strips that may or may not have concealed a gun.

'Recognize him?' I asked Cain.

'Never seen him before. He'll just be muscle.' Cain

got out and went to speak to the guy, leaving the engine running.

I knew this was my last chance. I could jump in the driver's seat and drive off before either of them had a chance to react.

But I didn't. I just sat there waiting as the guy silently unlocked the gates and Cain came back to the car.

We drove slowly inside and I watched in the wing mirror as the gates were shut and locked again, effectively trapping us inside. A potholed track led through a graveyard of burnt-out vehicles and huge tangled heaps of crushed metal, rising up on each side of us.

'Have you been here before?' I asked Cain, my words breaking the silence.

'No,' he answered, without looking at me, and I could see that, although he was trying to hide it, he was uneasy too.

The track stopped in front of a large single-storey building with its double doors open and light flooding out from inside. Cain parked next to a Ford Transit van, which looked to be the only driveable vehicle in the whole yard, and we got out. There was a strong odour of acetylene, engine oil, and something else too – similar to chip-shop fat – that made me want to gag. I looked around, searching for a glimpse of Cecil and his MP5 amid all the crap, but there was no sign of him. In fact there was no sign of anyone.

Somewhere off in the distance I could hear the rhythmic rumble of a commuter train as it gathered speed, and once again I had this uneasy feeling that this could all be a trap, and that the whole point of bringing me here was to kill me.

I pulled my jacket down to conceal the gun, and joined Cain at the front of the car.

'OK, let's go,' he said. 'And remember, I do the talking. You just do the strong, silent routine.'

We walked side by side through the building's double doors, moving carefully as if we were back on patrol in the wilds of Afghanistan, and stopped just inside. The room was big and windowless, one side lined with floor-to-ceiling shelving containing everything from copper piping to car radios, the other side dotted with newly arrived cars, some up on raised platforms, and various bits of machinery. An ancient-looking desk and chairs sat at the far end of the room, beyond which was an open door; and it was through this door that two men now emerged, both dressed in leather jackets and jeans – one small, the other large and powerfully built.

'Hey, Mr Cain, glad you could make it,' the small one called out as he and his friend started towards us. His accent was eastern European.

'Good to see you, Dav,' said Cain. 'Have you got what we've come for?'

'I have,' answered Dav. 'Have you got our payment?'

Cain grinned. 'Course I have. You know me. I'm a man of my word.'

The two men, both Albanians by the look of them, stopped in front of us. Dav was somewhere in his forties, with a pinched, heavily lined face and long, straggly hair that had been dyed black by someone who didn't care much about the quality of his work. He was grinning, showing teeth that looked like they needed some serious investment, and there was the malevolent gleam of the sadist in his eyes. Straight away I was on my guard. The other man, who looked like he was about to burst out of his leather jacket, was a lot younger, and by the way he was standing back, he was Dav's bodyguard.

Dav and Cain shook hands.

'If you're holding two hundred K, you're hiding it well,' said Dav, still grinning.

'It's near here. You can have it as soon as I've checked out the goods.'

Dav nodded. 'Sure. Come this way then, guys.'

He motioned for us to follow him, and I'd just started to relax a little when a mobile phone started ringing. It was Dav's, and he pulled it out of his leather jacket, frowning down at the screen. 'Excuse me for a second, Mr Cain. I need to take this.' He walked away from us, talking quietly on the phone in Albanian, while the rest of us stood in vaguely uncomfortable silence.

'Everything all right?' asked Cain when Dav had ended the call.

'Sure,' said Dav, but something in his tone didn't ring true. 'Business problems. I just need to make one more call.'

I exchanged glances with Cain as Dav walked further away, his back to us. Cain shrugged, as if there was nothing to worry about. And maybe there wasn't, but I could feel a tingling in the base of my spine that reminded me of the feeling I used to get out on patrol in Helmand, where danger lurked round every corner.

Dav finished the call and replaced the phone in his leather jacket. 'Sorry about that,' he said, coming back over. This time he was staring at me. 'So who's your friend, Mr Cain? I've never seen him before.'

'He's one of my people. He's good.'

'Yeah? Is that right? How long you known him?'

I saw that Cain was frowning, and the tingling in my spine suddenly got a whole lot worse. 'Long enough. Why?'

'Look, what the hell is this?' I demanded. 'If you've got a problem with me, you ask me about it. Not him.'

Dav's eyes narrowed. 'Yeah, I got a problem. A real problem.'

'What's happened?' asked Cain, sounding confused.

But before Dav could answer, I heard movement to my left. I swung round, instinctively going for my gun, as a guy holding a pump-action shotgun appeared in the gap between two of the shelf units, while at the same time the guy who'd let us in at the gates appeared at the double doors behind us. He too was holding a shotgun.

'Don't even think about it,' Dav told me, taking a step back so he was out of the shotguns' line of fire.

My fingers were touching the pistol in my waistband, but right away I knew I was never going to be able to hit both gunmen before one of them blew a very large hole in me. Even if they were crap shots, they'd be hard pushed to miss from the range they were at, and I couldn't rely on Cain, a man I'd only known for a few hours. I moved my hand away from the gun.

'What the hell's going on, Dav?' demanded Cain, who'd also made the sensible decision not to go for his own gun.

'That call I just had was from a good friend of mine,' said Dav, bringing out a pistol from under his jacket, which he pointed at us. 'The man we deal with over here, a guy called Brozi, has been arrested. You know anything about that?'

Cain looked completely caught out by this revelation. 'Of course not. We're here to buy the merchandise we talked about.'

'Brozi's a careful guy. The only way he gets caught is if someone set him up.'

'Look, I only ever deal with him by phone. I couldn't even tell you what he looks like. And I only spoke to him to confirm this meeting a couple of hours ago.' There was a long silence as both men sized each other up. Then Cain spoke again. 'We've done business before. You know you can trust me.'

'We have. But him.' Dav flicked his head dismissively in my direction. 'Him I don't fucking trust.'

I felt the adrenalin building inside me, but I knew my best bet was to stay calm and go on the attack. 'What are you accusing me of?'

I took a step towards Dav, who lowered his pistol and pointed it at my groin with a hand that was way too steady. 'Don't move, or I'll blow your balls off.' His eyes blazed with anger and his finger tightened on the trigger.

He barked something in Albanian to the big bodyguard who produced a thin-cord garrotte from under his jacket, and walked round behind me.

'What the hell's he doing?' I snapped, my hand hovering over the gun, knowing I was already too late. At the same time, the shotgun-wielding thug who'd been hiding behind the shelves walked towards me until the end of his barrel was only a few feet from my gut. His face was blank and I knew he'd kill me without a second's thought.

'Don't go for that gun,' said Dav quietly. 'You won't make it.'

'I'm not a cop,' I answered, looking him right in the eye, working hard to keep my voice steady. I felt the gun being removed from the waistband of my jeans, leaving me completely unarmed.

'Maybe you're not. But we're going to find out one way or another. And you, Mr Cain, get your gun out and drop it on the floor.'

'Look, Dav,' said Cain, raising his hands, palms outwards, in the universal gesture of reconciliation, 'I can vouch for him. He's definitely no cop.'

'Drop your gun, or I get my friend to shoot you.'

'This whole thing's wrong,' Cain called out, using the agreed code to tell Cecil we were in trouble.

'Drop it. Now.'

Reluctantly, Cain pulled out his gun and laid it down on the floor. He was scared now too, but he glanced at me briefly, his expression saying: Don't worry, it's going to be all right. This is just a misunderstanding.

But it wasn't. Someone, somewhere, had betrayed their contact, and the grim irony of it all was that it had absolutely nothing to do with me. I couldn't see how Mike Bolt could be responsible, but if he was, then I'd tear him apart with my bare hands.

But right now that was the least of my problems, because if Dav searched me, then there was a good chance he'd find the GPS units in my wallet, and that would be as good as a death sentence.

And then suddenly I was being yanked backwards as the garrotte Dav's bodyguard was carrying was whipped over my head and tightened round my neck. My breath was cut off like a light switch, and spots of light danced in front of my eyes as I was lifted up on to my toes. And all I could think was that this was it, the end, that I was about to die without saying goodbye to my daughter, and that they'd never find my body.

'This whole thing's wrong!' shouted Cain, using the code for a second time, his voice echoing round the room. 'This whole thing's wrong! Let him go!'

Dav said something else in Albanian and the cord was loosened enough for me to breathe again, but I was still unable to move and panting wildly for breath. The big guy was patting me down now, looking for more weapons. He found the mobile phone and lobbed it over to Dav, who caught it with his free hand and inspected it. Seeing that it was switched off, he lost interest and lobbed it away, ignoring my gasps for mercy.

Next came the wallet, and Dav put his gun away so he could use both hands to check through it more carefully.

Jesus, I'd messed up. My whole life was in that wallet, not just the two GPS units Bolt had given me. My address.

My family.

'This whole thing's wrong!' yelled Cain again.

But there was no movement outside the door. No Cecil. No nothing.

'Shut the fuck up, Cain!' snapped Dav.

He shouted something in Albanian and one of the other gunmen came forward and searched Cain from behind. Cain tensed, and for a moment I thought he might go for the gun on the floor, but he didn't resist as it was kicked away, out of reach.

'This isn't the way we do business in this country,' he said angrily. 'You treat your customers properly.'

Dav's expression was like stone. 'Someone betrayed Brozi. It wasn't any of us. So it has to be you, or someone close to you. How long have you known this guy for? Uh?' He waved an arm at me. 'How long?'

Cain hesitated. For just one second, but it was one second too long. 'Long enough.'

Dav shook his head emphatically. 'Not long enough.' He pulled a crumpled photo from the wallet. It was an old one my mum had taken of Gina and Maddie, when Maddie was about a year old, and we'd still been a family. 'Nice picture.' He grinned, showing his nicotine-stained teeth. 'This your wife and kid?'

I swallowed hard, which with the thin cord round my neck was no easy feat, the anger rising in me at the thought of this arsehole holding such a precious photo. I thought about elbowing the big guy in the ribs and making a break for it, grabbing Dav's gun and shoving it against his head, but there was no way I'd make it.

'Put it back,' I hissed, as the big guy tightened the garrotte once again.

Jesus, I was scared now. More scared than I'd ever been. And angry with myself too for getting involved in this. I should have turned Bolt down flat. Instead, here I was, trapped with a bunch of madmen, with Cecil, the one man I trusted in this whole thing, nowhere to be seen.

Dav slipped the photo back in the wallet, then pulled out my driving licence. I stiffened. It had my old address on it. The family home where my wife and daughter still lived. I couldn't believe I'd made such a basic error as to keep my real ID on my person. But I had.

Dav stared at the licence, then back at me. 'So, Richard Burnham-Jones. How did you meet Mr Cain here?'

'He's part of our organization,' Cain insisted, his voice steady. 'And we really don't like people treating us this way. So I'd advise you to let him go so we can continue our deal.'

'Don't advise me, Mr Cain,' said Dav, putting my wallet in his back pocket. He barked something in Albanian and the shotgun-wielding thug who'd searched Cain lifted his weapon and pointed it at the back of his head.

For a single terrifying moment I thought he was going to pull the trigger and blow Cain's brains all over the dirty floor, but nothing happened, and I was impressed at how calm Cain kept as he looked slowly over his left shoulder at the gunman.

'Put your hands in the air, Mr Cain, and don't say another word. Understand?'

Cain nodded once.

'So, I ask you again, Richard Burnham-Jones. How did you meet Mr Cain?'

It wasn't easy for me to talk with a garrotte round my neck, but I made the effort. 'I did some work with one of his guys,' I gasped. 'I proved myself. And now I work for him.'

'I don't like you, Richard Burnham-Jones.' Dav spat my name out like it was contagious. 'There's something about you that's not quite right. I can smell it, you know. I've always been able to smell trouble.' He came closer now, his face only inches from mine, and I could smell the stale smoke on his breath. 'You know what we used to do back home to guys who fucked with us? We killed their whole fucking family. Wife, mother, father. Even their baby children. All of them.'

He turned away and walked over to one of the shelf units, bending down to pick something up. It was only when he turned back round that I saw what it was.

A bloodstained meat cleaver with a steel blade that gleamed in the light.

I started struggling again but I was powerless against the garrotte, and every time I moved it bit deeper into my neck. Jesus, where the hell was Cecil?

'Where's the money?' Dav demanded, resting the cleaver against his shoulder, flat side up. The question was aimed at Cain.

'I told you,' said Cain. 'Near here.'

Dav motioned towards the big guy holding me, and the next second my legs were kicked from under me and I was forced to the floor so I was lying back with my head resting in the big guy's lap, the cord still biting into my neck. I started choking and it loosened just a little. At the same time, Dav came over and knelt on my legs just above the knees, holding them in place before putting the cleaver's blade against my shin. I could feel the sharpness of the blade pushing hard on the skin.

'Tell me where the money is or I'll cut off his fucking leg! You think I'm bullshitting, yeah? You think I'm bullshitting?'

'I didn't take you for a thief,' said Cain, still keeping his voice even. 'I thought you were a businessman.'

Dav glared at him. 'I am a businessman, but I'm no fucking sucker. Someone took down our middleman and now you turn up here without your money. I want to know what's going on.'

'So do I. This whole thing's wrong!' Cain shouted these last words so loudly that Cecil would have heard him if he'd been chewing popcorn at the top of the London Eye.

But where was he? For Christ's sake, where was he?

'The money, Cain. You tell me where it is, or I take his leg. Then yours.' He raised the cleaver high above his head, his thin feral features alive with excitement.

And in that moment I knew he was going to do it.

Channelling all my strength, I flung myself upwards, ignoring the tightening of the cord, and knocked Dav off me.

He yelled out in anger and lashed out with the cleaver, slicing the material of my jeans. I felt a flash of sharp pain as the blade cut into my leg, and then he was back sitting on my legs again. I could no longer breathe, and my vision was blurring as he raised the cleaver for a second time.

And then the whole room erupted in a hail of gunfire, and suddenly the cord went slack.

Everything now happened incredibly fast. Dav was staring towards the door, and I went for him, fuelled by a potent mix of anger, adrenalin and fear, grabbing his cleaver arm in one hand as he scrabbled wildly for the gun in the holster beneath his leather jacket.

He wasn't fast enough. With my free hand I punched him twice in the face, before swatting his other arm to one side and yanking out the gun as he rolled backwards across the floor, still holding the cleaver.

There was another burst of gunfire and I hit the deck, rolling across the floor before swinging round with the gun in my hand as bullets sprayed round the room, ricocheting in all directions.

Both the shotgun-wielding Albanians were on the floor. The one who'd been covering Cain lay sprawled out, not moving, while the other was down on his knees pointing his shotgun unsteadily at Cecil who was standing in the doorway, holding the MP5 in front of him. Cecil fired again, at exactly the same time that the Albanian pulled the trigger. The Albanian took a burst of fire to the chest but stayed upright, while Cecil was forced to dive out of the way to avoid the shotgun blast, which struck the wall behind him, puncturing a hole in the brickwork.

Meanwhile the big guy who'd had the garrotte round my neck fired a shot in Cecil's direction, then swung round towards me, firing wildly as he went. The two of us were only ten feet apart and I took rapid aim at his torso and pulled the trigger.

But nothing happened. The safety was on.

I flicked at it with my forefinger but now the big guy was aiming right at me and I could smell the cordite from his weapon.

For a tenth of a second the whole world stopped. I was too late. I was going to die.

And then the side of my assailant's head exploded in a shower of blood and brain matter as a bullet slammed into it, and he went down hard, firing off a last shot that flew up into the ceiling, before dropping the gun.

I turned and saw Cain kneeling in a firing position, holding the pistol he'd come here with, his face grimly determined as he continued firing, hitting the surviving guy with the shotgun who, though he'd been hit by Cecil, was still trying to get to his feet, and sending him sprawling into the shelf units.

Now that only left Dav. I jerked round just in time to see him running wildly for the door at the back of the building. I didn't even hesitate. Holding the gun two-handed and finally flicking off the safety, I took aim and opened fire, missing with the first two bullets, but bringing him down with the third and the fourth.

He stumbled forward into the desk, dropping the cleaver in the process, before slipping on to his knees.

I stood up, still pretty unsteady on my feet after what had just happened, and walked towards him, gun outstretched.

Dav gave me a defiant look as I stopped and pointed the gun at his head.

'Don't shoot him,' barked Cain, coming over with Cecil. 'We need to know where the weapon is we're buying.'

'Fuck you,' hissed Dav through gritted teeth. He was clutching at his stomach, blood oozing through the gaps in his fingers.

'You're not the only one who knows how to use a cleaver,' said Cain, reaching down and picking it up from the floor. He grabbed the hand that Dav was using to stem the blood from his wound and slammed it down hard on the desk. 'Tell me where the weapon is or I'll start on your fingers and by the time I reach your head you'll have told me every secret you've ever had.'

Dav looked up at him, saw the cold look in his pale eyes, and his expression weakened. 'It's out the back. We were always going to give it to you. I just didn't trust this bastard. I still don't.'

'Cecil. Check it's there.'

Cecil disappeared through the door.

'You know I trust you, Cain,' said Dav as they waited, trying unsuccessfully to hide the desperation in his voice. 'I wouldn't have fucked you up. You let me go, yeah, and no one'll ever mention this again. I'll get rid of the bodies of my friends.'

Cain didn't say anything. He was still holding the cleaver above Dav's hand.

Cecil came back into the room. 'It's there, and it's still in the box.'

Cain nodded. 'Good.' He turned to me. 'He's all yours. Prove to him you're no cop.'

Dav's eyes widened. 'I believe you! Please!'

I pushed the end of the barrel into his forehead, while he wriggled beneath it. It was only a minute since he'd been threatening to cripple me for life and yet my anger had dissipated. I almost felt sorry for him.

A bead of sweat rolled down my temple and suddenly I was back in Afghanistan on that single terrible day when I'd killed in cold blood for the only time in my life. Strength. I needed strength. Because if I didn't shoot him, there was no way I was walking away from here.

Out of the corner of my eye, I saw Cecil staring at me, his face taut with tension.

For a long, drawn-out second we all waited.

Then I pulled the trigger.

Thirty-six

17.45

I watched the body slide slowly to the floor, then dropped Dav's gun into his lap and pulled my wallet from his pocket before turning away, having no desire to look at what I'd just done. For a few seconds the room was silent, bar the incessant ringing in my ears. I rubbed my neck where the cord had bitten into it and fought down a rising nausea.

'Where the hell were you?' I asked Cecil.

'It's a good question,' said Cain. 'We almost ended up dead in here.'

'They had another guard posted near the fence. I had to get past him.'

'Where's he now?'

'I was waiting for him to move. Then I heard you shout from inside, so I took him out with a knife, then came over as fast as I could.' He was bouncing on his toes like a flyweight boxer as he talked, the adrenalin from the firefight making him hyper. He looked round at the bodies littering the room. 'What the hell happened in here?'

Cain sighed as he looked down at Dav's body. 'This one got a phone call to say that Brozi, the guy who set up this deal, had been arrested, and because they didn't know Jones, they thought he might have had something to do with it. It's a pain. These guys were useful suppliers. But at least we've got what we came for. And if they're dead, they can't talk. I'm sorry about what happened, Jones. I wasn't expecting that.'

'Neither was I,' I grunted, not wanting to let him off the hook easily. I'd come far too close to dying, and it had scared me.

There was a pool of blood forming round Dav's head and I tried to ignore it. I inspected the cut on my leg where Dav had caught me with the cleaver, but it was only a minor flesh wound and would stop bleeding soon enough.

Cain turned to Cecil. 'Let's grab the box and get out of here. Jones, make sure you've got everything. At some point, this place is going to be a major crime scene, and if any of us have left any trace we were ever here, wc're in real trouble.'

I nodded, but I was suddenly filled with an intense curiosity. Five men had just died, all for a single weapon. I was also damn sure that whatever the weapon was, it was going to be used against the people of this city. Cain clearly didn't give a shit about taking innocent lives, so I needed to make sure that it wasn't something that was going to affect my family.

I was following them into the back room when Cain turned round.

'Where are you going?' he snapped.

'I want to see what I almost got killed for.'

Cain seemed to think about this for a moment, then exchanged glances with Cecil who was standing inside the sparsely furnished back room where an open six-foot-by-three-foot wooden crate rested on a metal table. From the angle I was standing at, I couldn't see what was inside.

'Jones is one of us now, sir,' said Cecil. 'We need to trust him.'

Cain paused, clearly not convinced, before finally he nodded.

We approached the crate and looked down.

And straight away I realized why they'd wanted to keep its contents a secret so badly.

Thirty-seven

17.48

After a twenty-minute argument with Islington nick's chief superintendent, Mike Bolt finally managed to get out of his office with his job and his position still intact. The chief super was furious at the way an op on his patch had degenerated into a hail of gunfire in broad daylight, and that the captured suspect was now claiming he'd been violently assaulted by one of his arresting officers, and had injuries that appeared to back up his claim. The fact that the arresting officer was Tina Boyd had only added to his fury. It seemed the chief super didn't have particularly fond memories of Tina's tenure at the station.

On one hand, Bolt could see his point of view: the whole thing had almost ended in disaster thanks to Tina staying in Broni's house after she'd been told to leave. Yet the fact remained that the photos she'd found on his phone represented a hugely important lead. They linked that day's bombings with Fox, and with the Stanhope attacks that Bolt had spent the previous fifteen months investigating. Fox might not be cooperating, but if Brozi talked, they might be able to break the case wide open before the terrorists' eight p.m. deadline.

It frustrated Bolt that he couldn't question Brozi himself, but at least now the CTC team had arrived at Islington and were fully aware of how urgent their task was. He took a deep breath. He needed a coffee. In fact, he needed a couple of cold pints and a whisky chaser to settle his nerves after what he'd been through that day. But a coffee was going to have to suffice because it was going to be a while yet before he'd be getting off duty.

That didn't matter, though. He might have come within a few feet of getting shot, but for the first time in a long time, he actually felt good. Months of tedious detective work and repeated dead ends had been swept aside, and suddenly he was seeing action again, just like in those long-ago days when he'd been part of the Flying Squad, chasing down armed robbers in adrenalin-fuelled ambushes. And, whichever way he cared to look at it, most of what had happened today was down to Tina Boyd. An hour ago he'd been furious with her for taking the kind of extreme risks she always did, but now that fury was subsiding.

He was en route to the canteen when Tina appeared in the corridor up ahead talking to a very tall, gangly young man in an ill-fitting suit.

She smiled when she saw him. 'Mike, this is Mr Ridic, the Albanian translator. He's going to be assisting CTC with the Brozi interview.'

'Good to meet you,' said Bolt, shaking hands. He turned to Tina as Ridic excused himself. 'I thought you were meant to be giving a statement.'

'I've made it. It didn't take long. I mean, the shooting was all over in a few seconds, wasn't it?' She gave him a look that suggested there hadn't been any problems. 'They want to see you now.'

'Anything I should know?'

'Only that I told them that Brozi was resisting arrest, and I only struck him once to make sure he released the gun.'

'I heard Brozi's claiming you assaulted him.'

Tina shrugged. 'Well, he would do, wouldn't he? But you know better, right?'

Bolt sighed. 'Don't worry, Tina, I've got your back.' Then he remembered something. 'Did you speak to Mr Ridic about the email message on Brozi's PC?'

She nodded. 'He translated it for me but I don't know how much use it is.'

'What did it say?'

'Hold on a second.' She pulled a scuffed notebook from the back of her jeans. 'The exact wording was "Collection confirmed. Place and time as agreed." But

I've no idea what it means. Maybe Brozi will enlighten us.'

'Let's hope so,' said Bolt, and moved to go past her, wanting to get his statement over and done with.

And then it hit him. Jones had told him earlier that he was needed as security for a meeting during which something was going to be handed over. Could this be something to do with the collection in Brozi's email? He needed to talk to Jones as soon as possible.

Bolt was always extremely careful about calling his informant unless it was an emergency, in order to minimize the risk of compromising him, but he decided that this was one. Excusing himself, he called Jones's number, but only got an automatic message saying the phone was switched off.

He immediately called Nikki Donohoe in the Special Operations office.

She answered on the first ring. 'Glad to hear you're still alive, boss. Sounds like you're getting all the action out there.'

Bolt chuckled. He liked Nikki. She didn't let things faze her. 'Luckily Brozi was a crap shot.'

'I heard your Miss Boyd gave him a bit of a kicking.'

'He resisted arrest. Listen, Nikki. Those two GPS units I signed out for our informant this morning – I need you to switch them on right now, and tell me where they are.'

Bolt paced the corridor while he waited for her to

input the data. There was still no absolute proof that today's bombs were linked to the Stanhope attacks, but the fact that Fox had fingered Brozi, and that Brozi himself was linked to the café bomber, meant that it was extremely likely. Again, that didn't necessarily mean that Cecil Boorman and his mysterious boss, Cain, were also involved. But with barely two hours to go until the terrorists' ultimatum expired, it was something they needed to find out fast.

After a few seconds, Nikki came back on the line. 'Both units are together in Bermondsey about three quarters of a mile south of the river.'

Bolt thought about this. He'd told Jones to call him if Cain or Cecil had made contact with him, and he hadn't. 'OK, keep me posted of their movements.'

'Does this mean I'm going to be needed late tonight, Mike? If I am, I need to let the old man know so he can get back from work and sort out the kids.'

'Yeah, you are. Sorry about that.'

He felt for Nikki. Unlike him, she had a family life to juggle. But right now that wasn't his top priority.

Suddenly Jones was. What the hell was he doing?

Thirty-eight

17.50

The Stinger is an extremely accurate shoulder-launched surface-to-air missile. It has one major battlefield purpose: to bring down enemy aircraft. They're sought after by terrorist groups because of their ability to take down passenger jets if they're fired by a trained operative.

I swallowed. This was big.

'What the hell are you going to use it for?' I asked Cain.

'It's going to be used for a targeted attack. There may be civilian casualties, but they're not the primary purpose of the attack. That's all I can tell you.'

That was when I knew that Cain was responsible for the bomb attacks earlier that day. All over the news they'd been talking about the third attack that the terrorists had scheduled for later that night. This was no coincidence.

I stared at both Cecil and Cain in turn. 'Are you telling me you two were behind the attacks this morning?'

They exchanged glances, and I wondered if I'd gone too far.

'Am I a part of this organization or not? Because if I am, I need to know what's going on.'

'Yeah, of course you are,' Cain said eventually. 'And everything will become clear soon enough. But right now, we need to get out of here. Grab your stuff.'

I walked over to where Dav had chucked my mobile, trying hard to ignore the dead bodies strewn round the room. I had a real dilemma now. If I let on to Bolt about the Stinger, then eventually I was going to have to give up the details of what had happened here, and the fact that I'd killed someone. Bolt had promised to do all he could to protect me, and I knew he'd do his best. But in the end he didn't have the power to grant me immunity from prosecution for murder. At the same time, though, I couldn't just stand back and allow a Stinger missile to go into circulation. The point was, you didn't buy one of those things unless you were planning some sort of terrorist spectacular, and if I let matters take their course, I'd be responsible for hundreds of deaths, and there was no way I'd be able to live with that.

As I bent down to pick up my mobile, I glanced over my shoulder and, seeing that the other two were still in the back room, I pulled the two GPS units from my wallet and slipped them into my back pocket. I had no idea if Bolt had switched them on remotely or not. If he had, I was already in trouble, because he could use them to trace me here. But I'd worry about that later. Right now, I had to make sure that I didn't lose the missile.

I looked down at the mobile and cursed. The screen was cracked and it wouldn't turn on. So I couldn't even warn Bolt about what was happening.

'What are you doing?' snapped Cain as he came back into the room carrying one end of the crate.

'He broke my mobile.' I held it up for him to see.

'Never mind that. Get moving, and get the boot open.'

I walked out of the double doors and into the crisp evening air. There was no sound of approaching sirens. It was as if the bloody events here had never even happened. I could hear the distant sounds of traffic and commuter trains and, as I looked up to the sky, I saw the red lights of aircraft coming in from the Channel towards London and the final approach into Heathrow. The earlier clouds had blown away and it was a clear night. You could even make out a few stars amid the light pollution. Perfect for a missile operator to target a plane and shoot it out of the sky above the city so that, as it broke up, it could rain down debris on the streets and houses below. And the thought that kept rattling through my head was that it could be *my* street. It could be *my* wife and child torn apart by jagged, smoking lumps of steel.

I slipped one of the GPS units out of my back pocket and pulled open the hatchback boot as the other two manoeuvred the crate round so that it could slide inside. Stepping out of the way, I put a hand on the crate to help steer it on its way, affixing the unit to its underside as I did so, keeping my expression as neutral as possible even though my heart was hammering away in my chest, knowing that if it fell off, I'd be dead.

But it didn't. The other two finished pushing the crate inside, and a minute later we were driving through the scrapyard entrance.

I'd survived. But I had a terrible feeling that this could change at any time.

Thirty-nine

18.05

'Are you sure you should be going out tonight?'

Gina Burnham-Jones's babysitter and neighbour, Sue, was a big maternal woman in her late sixties who'd decided to take Gina under her wing after Jones had left, and who worried about her constantly.

Gina smiled. 'Of course I'm sure. You can't let people like that dictate your life.' She avoided using the word 'terrorist' so as not to worry Maddie, who was currently playing with her Sylvanians on the lounge floor.

'What are you sure about, Mummy?' she asked, looking up from her game.

'Nothing that concerns you, young lady,' said Gina with a wink.

'Ears like a hawk, that one,' whispered Sue.

The doorbell rang. That would be Matt. Gina got up from the sofa, conscious of the fact that there was no frisson of excitement like there had been with Jones in the early days.

'Who's at the door, Mummy?'

'A friend of mine. We're going out.'

Maddie jumped up from her game and wrapped her arms round Gina's waist. 'You're coming back, aren't you?'

Gina felt a surge of guilt. Maddie missed her dad badly, and the experience of him leaving had made her insecure. 'Of course I'm coming back, darling,' she said, kissing her daughter on the forehead and exchanging glances with Sue, who was pulling an irritatingly sympathetic face.

She wondered how Maddie was going to react when she met Matt, and knew it wasn't going to be instant happy families. Jesus, why did life have to be so complicated?

Gently extricating herself from Maddie's arms, Gina said her goodbyes and went to the door, checking herself in the mirror en route and feeling pretty satisfied with her reflection.

Matt took a step back when he saw her, a look of admiration in his eyes. 'Wow, Gina, you look beautiful.'

'You look pretty good yourself,' she said, and he did. He was wearing a neatly pressed dark suit and three-quarter-length Crombie coat which, coupled with his well-groomed silver hair and strong bearing, gave him an air of comforting sophistication. His aftershave was strong but smelled good.

'So, are you going to finally tell me where we're going?' she asked as he put an arm round her waist and led her to his car.

'Well, we're going into the centre of town, I can tell you that much. But the final destination remains a surprise.'

Gina felt a twinge of irritation. She liked a surprise as much as the next person but the whole cloak-and-dagger aspect of this evening seemed a bit much.

'I don't mean to be a pain,' he said with a rueful smile, reading her thoughts. 'But when you do find out, you'll be pleased that it was a surprise.' He leaned forward and kissed her lightly on the lips. 'I promise.'

'OK,' she said, intrigued once again. 'I'll give you the benefit of the doubt.'

The funny thing was that Matt wasn't the type for surprises. A police officer with twenty-nine years' service, he was a typically logical and pragmatic detective who, by his own admission, had no imagination whatsoever. He tried to be romantic – he was clearly trying to be romantic now – but he could never quite pull it off.

'I'm surprised you got the night off,' she said as they got in the car, 'what with all this terrorism stuff going on.'

'There's only so much we can do,' he answered, 'and there are plenty of people better qualified than me out there looking for them.'

'Do you think the terrorists will do something when their eight p.m. deadline runs out?' Whatever Gina might have said to Sue back in the house, she was still nervous.

'If they do, it'll be something small-scale. Whatever the media might say, these people bark a lot louder than they bite. And it's not something you need to worry about.' He smiled at her as he pulled the car away from the kerb, and there was a gleam in his eyes. 'Tonight we're going to enjoy ourselves.'

Forty

18.15

The street was quiet when Cain dropped us back where we'd parked Cecil's car earlier, near Jamaica Road. The journey had been largely made in silence. All of us I think, even Cain, were shocked by the ferocity of what had just happened, and the fact that we'd left behind so many bodies.

In my left hand, unseen by the others, I clutched the second GPS device Bolt had given me. I didn't know whether the Audi we were in belonged to Cain or not – I suspected not – or how long he was going to hold on to it for, but as I sat there next to him I decided to leave the GPS unit in it. It was a high-risk move but I no longer cared. The important thing was to stop him, and any attack he was planning on carrying out. I'd worry about everything else later.

Cain was talking again now. 'You did well today, gentlemen,' he said, as if he was giving us a pep talk at school. 'Remember that. We had a challenge and we overcame it. There'll be an extra bonus for this as well, Jones.' He gave me a nod as he said this, as if this somehow made up for the fact that I'd been only seconds away from having my leg cut off and was now an accessory to mass murder.

'Thanks,' I said. I mean, what else could I say? The important thing was to get out of there and warn Bolt about what was happening.

As I got out of the car, I stuck the GPS unit on the underside of the passenger seat, well out of sight, and pictured a scene where Cain was spreadeagled against the Audi, surrounded by armed cops, while they took the Stinger out of the back.

Game, set and match, you arsehole.

A minute later, Cecil and I were standing on the pavement watching as Cain drove away into the night, taking the missile with him.

'Is he going to be the one firing that thing?' I asked Cecil as we got into his car and pulled away from the kerb going in the opposite direction.

'I don't want to think about it.' Cecil looked at me. 'You shouldn't either.'

'Do you have any idea of what the target is?'

Cecil shook his head, keeping his eye on the road. 'No, but we're doing it for the right reasons, you and me. We've got to make the people angry. We've got to make them rise up against all this multicultural shit, and if we manage that, it'll have been worth it. Won't it?'

I nodded, acting like I agreed with him, even though I found it hard to believe what I was hearing. I'd known Cecil a long time. He'd been a good soldier. A bit of a loose cannon, yes, but I'd always thought his heart was in the right place. And now here he was talking about committing mass murder on an industrial scale.

'You look like you need a drink,' he said. 'And I know I do. Let's grab one somewhere.'

I was horribly conscious of the terrorists' eight p.m. deadline. 'Just drop me home, can you?' I said wearily.

Cecil gave me a suspicious sideways glance. 'You're not going to do anything stupid, are you?'

'Look, the fact is I almost got killed back there, so I just want to be alone for a while, all right? And let's go the direct route. Because I think it's pretty obvious now that we're not being followed.'

'Sure,' he said, apparently mollified, and fell silent.

I counted the minutes in my head as we drove. The flat I called home was at the top end of Stoke Newington, a good twenty minutes away if the traffic wasn't bad, which thank God it wasn't. My head felt like it was going to explode. I needed to piss, I needed to stop this missile being fired and, more than anything, I needed to work out my next move. If either Cecil or Cain were arrested, they could testify against me in a court of law over the murder of Dav, and it was almost certain I'd be convicted and sent down for life. There was no way round that.

It was just after 6.30 when we pulled off the A10 at Stoke Newington, opposite the Abney Park Cemetery, still a good half mile from where I lived. The traffic had suddenly snarled up, but I knew there was a pub just round the corner.

'Drop me here, I'll walk the rest of the way.' Cecil tried to protest but I cut him off with a look. 'Like I said, I want to be alone.'

He seemed to accept what I'd said, and we shook hands and said our goodbyes. I heard him do a U-turn in the traffic and turn south, and I counted to ten, then sprinted for the pub, counting down in my head the minutes that the Stinger had been on the streets. Knowing that the moment I made the call I'd be setting in motion a chain of events that would either put me in the ground, or behind bars for the rest of my life.

Forty-one

18.41

Bolt and Tina watched the interview with Jetmir Brozi unfold through the one-way mirror that looked into the interview room.

It didn't make for riveting viewing.

On one side of the table sat the two officers from CTC, a man and a woman in power suits, who'd only finished taking Bolt's statement ten minutes earlier. They'd come across as competent and businesslike, and were treating the situation with the urgency it needed. Alongside them was Ridic, the Albanian translator. At the opposite end sat Brozi wearing a defiant, slightly bored expression. He had his own translator next to him, who was there to pass messages from his lawyer, a bald-headed Englishman with a moustache and an expensive suit who looked like he charged more by the hour than Bolt and Tina earned together in a day, and who was several feet back from the table, with his legs crossed and a notebook on his lap.

Brozi was adopting the professional criminal's method of dealing with police interviews and answering every question with a heavily accented 'No comment'. Bolt often wondered why criminals persisted with this line of defence. It might save them the effort of having to think up lies, or contradicting themselves, but it invariably made them look guilty in the eyes of a jury when the transcripts of the interviews were read out in court.

Bolt would have liked to be the one leading the interview but, to be fair, it didn't look like it would have done much good anyway. Brozi was sticking to his routine, clearly unfazed by the scale of the charges facing him, or the prospect of spending the next ten years in prison. His arrogance was frustrating, but the interviewing officers were continuing regardless in the hope that he might weaken, or his lawyer might talk some sense into him.

It wasn't working.

Bolt shook his head in frustration. 'He's not going to talk.'

Tina sighed. 'So where does that leave us? Brozi won't talk. Fox won't talk. And we're running low on time.'

'I've got an informant out in the field, who I saw this morning. He has a connection to someone who's been of interest to us for some time. He told me that he was providing security for a meeting today.'

Tina raised an eyebrow. 'You never told me about this. Is that why you were so interested when I told you about the message on Brozi's PC?'

'Only the core members of the team know the guy exists. I shouldn't even be discussing him with you.'

'Come on, Mike. I've helped you today. I know we had a lucky escape, but don't shut me out. We make a good team. You know that.'

She was right and, even after what had happened earlier with Brozi, it still felt good to Bolt to be working with Tina again.

He gave her a brief rundown of what Jones had been doing, without divulging his ID or any details that might help her put a name to him. 'I gave him two GPS units this morning and I got Nikki to switch them on three quarters of an hour ago. Last time I spoke to her they were both still together.'

'So why don't we get surveillance units on to them?'

'On what grounds? I don't know who the units are with, and I won't know until I get hold of the informant, but he's not answering his phone. I called HQ and the commander told me to hold back until we know more. There's not much else we can do.'

He took a gulp of freezing cold coffee and pulled a face.

'Want another one?' asked Tina, pointing to his cup.

'Please,' he said, aching for something stronger.

As she left the room, Bolt stared back through the mirror to where Brozi was answering 'No comment' to yet another question. It was at times like this, he thought, that even something as extreme as torture would be justified. It wouldn't take long. A man like Brozi would break in minutes. Bolt had seen his kind before, full of bravado when faced with police officers forced to abide by stringent rules, but a coward at heart. It upset him that he could even countenance a thought like this, but he was exhausted and frustrated.

His mobile rang, and he checked the caller ID. It was a landline he didn't recognize, but he picked up anyway, more in hope than expectation.

Jones's voice came on the line, tense and breathless. 'There's a Stinger missile in circulation. Cain's got it.'

Bolt took an instinctive breath. The shock was immense but he knew he had to stay calm. 'Where is he now?'

'I don't know. He left us about twenty minutes ago, but I left a GPS in the front of his car, and another on the box with the Stinger in it. So you should be able to track it.'

'How come you waited so long to call?'

'It would take too long to explain now.'

'Christ . . . Whereabouts are you?'

'In a pub in Stoke Newington, not far from home.'

'Do you have any idea how he's planning to use it?'

'No, but I can give you the make and registration of

the car Cain's driving, in case the GPS batteries run out.'

Bolt pulled a notebook and pen from his back pocket. There were a hundred other questions he wanted to ask Jones but there was no time for any of them. He needed to get off the phone and find that missile.

'OK. Stay where you are. I'll call you back as soon as I can.'

'I need protection, Mike. If Cain finds out I talked to you, I'm a dead man.'

'Don't worry, there's no way we're going to be going public with this. By the time things start to happen, I'll have pulled you out and sorted protection. I've got to go.'

He ended the call, and immediately called Nikki Donohoe back at the office. She picked up on the second ring.

'Where are the GPS units right now?' he asked her.

There was a short pause while she checked. 'They've split up. One's just passed through the Elephant and Castle roundabout and is heading north on St George's Road towards Lambeth and Westminster Bridge.'

'Jesus. Towards Parliament?'

'In that direction, yes.'

'What about the other?'

'It's in Bermondsey. On a place called Gowland Street, just off Tower Bridge Road. And it appears to be stationary. It looks from Google Earth like there's a set of lock-up garages running parallel to the street, and it's in one of them. I'm just checking but I don't think the area's covered by CCTV.'

Bolt's heart was racing. Finally they were in the game, but the problem was, he had no idea which of the two GPS units was with the Stinger.

'Get on to HQ straight away, Nikki, and tell them the exact locations of the two units. One of them, and I don't know which one it is, is stuck to a box containing a Stinger missile. We need to scramble arrest teams and ARV units. I don't care what it takes. We've got to get hold of this thing and take it out of circulation. I'll call the commander.'

'I'm on it,' she said with the calm tone he'd learned to expect from her.

'What's up?' asked Tina, coming back into the room with the coffees.

'Leave the coffee, we're out of here,' said Bolt, checking the location of Gowland Street on his phone. 'I'll tell you about it in the car.'

Forty-two

18.45

The Central Atrium of HMP Westmoor's Central Wing was busy with prisoners enjoying the chance to socialize for an hour after supper before they were locked in their cells for the night, as Devereaux approached the table-tennis table, head down, flanked by two other lifers.

One of the lifers bumped shoulders with another prisoner, and as he turned round to remonstrate, the lifer slammed him bodily into the table-tennis table, knocking it on to its side. One of the other prisoners who'd been playing yelled something and Devereaux went for him, throwing a punch that sent him sprawling into another group of prisoners sitting at a table playing cards. They were up on their feet in an instant, charging into the fray as the aggression that always simmered beneath the surface in closed male environments suddenly erupted.

That was all it took. A single nudge, and within seconds more than a dozen prisoners were involved in a messy, swirling brawl, while three dozen more either tried to get out of the way or closed in to watch.

Such was the speed with which everything happened that the two closest prison officers were caught completely by surprise. For a few seconds they simply stared at the scene erupting in front of them. Then they blew their whistles in unison and moved to break things up.

Two things stopped them before they'd reached the mêlée. First, Devereaux – a man who scared the shit out of all but the hardest of the screws at the best of times – yanked one of the legs free from the table-tennis table and screamed an unintelligible but bloodcurdling battle cry. Then, waving the table leg above his head, he ran at the screws, a look of such intense fury beneath the skull tattoo that it looked as if his eyes were going to pop out of his head.

Second, Wahid Khan, a convicted drug dealer and gangland torturer with anger management issues, emerged from his cell on the first floor carrying a flaming mattress which, with a roar, he sent hurtling into the safety netting below. Afterwards he would state that he was simply caught up in the moment, but the fact that he'd managed to set fire to his bedding within seconds of the violence starting meant his claim was treated with scepticism during the subsequent investigation.

Most of the screws, unused to such a general challenge to their authority but recognizing the volatility of the situation, ran for their lives, an act that immediately sent the prisoners into a euphoric frenzy as they saw how easy it was to take charge. The TV was smashed, as was the table-tennis table, and chairs that had been screwed to the floor to prevent them being used in just such a disturbance were ripped from their fittings and flung at the two screws who were still in their midst, and who'd been joined by two more from the other end of the wing. But only four strong, they were hopelessly outnumbered by the prisoners and they too retreated rapidly, shouting into their radios, as the alarm sounded across the prison.

Fox saw all this from the door of his cell twenty yards down from Khan's. The noise was incredible, as was the sense of animal excitement in the air. He watched as Khan stood on the walkway beating his chest and screaming abuse at the guards, the other prisoners, and the whole world in general. He was a big man, overweight, with a gut that hung over his waist like a jutting upper lip, but when he turned and ran at Fox, he moved with real pace.

'Nazi bastard!' he screamed, his voice unnaturally high as it echoed across the landing.

Which was when Fox saw the sharpened spoon he was clutching in his hand, its tip glinting in the strip lights.

As the four guards raced to the main door so they could seal off the wing, Fox raced away from Khan, hurtling down the metal steps two and three at a time, yelling at the guards for help.

One looked his way and slowed down, but only momentarily.

Fox could hear Khan coming down the steps behind him, yelling obscenities, his voice breathless and angry. But Fox had kept himself fit during his time inside, and his current injuries didn't stop him from running fast. Even so, as he hit the ground floor and sprinted towards the guards, his face was a mask of pure fear.

Two more guards had appeared on the other side of the main door and were in the process of unlocking it. Fox knew that the policy in prison riots was to seal off the wing where the disturbance was occurring to prevent its spread to other areas of the prison, while reinforcements were brought in to bring it under control.

'Help me, for Christ's sake!' shouted Fox, joining the four guards at the door.

Twenty yards behind them, the main bulk of the prisoners were advancing steadily like an unruly football crowd, several of them unleashing missiles in the direction of the door but making no effort to charge it, while from the side Khan was continuing to advance on Fox, the improvised knife in his hand now visible to all the guards.

'Hurry the fuck up!' screamed the most senior of them as the door was finally opened and they raced through. Fox went with them, and no one tried to stop him. They were all too keen to save their own skins.

It was only when the door had been thrown closed safely behind them that one of the guards grabbed Fox's arm and slammed him against the wall, demanding to know where he thought he was going.

But by that point it didn't matter.

The first stage of the op had been 100 per cent successful.

Forty-three

18.58

Cain parked the car at a meter in the shadows of Westminster Abbey. He was right in the heart of the establishment here, barely a stone's throw from the Houses of Parliament where, right now, politicians of every shade were debating the attacks that he'd helped mastermind today. And doubtless spouting the usual load of hot air. It was a pity, he thought, that the Stinger couldn't be used against them, but he no longer had the missile. It had safely been dropped off at a lock-up garage, where it should already have been collected by the mercenary they'd hired, the mysterious but reliable South African Voorhess, who'd be firing it in about an hour's time, when the deadline they'd given the government ran out.

The air was turning cold as Cain started off down the quiet night street on foot, pulling his cap down and his collars up to make sure that any cameras only got a very limited shot of him. He didn't feed the meter as he wouldn't be using the car again. It had been bought in cash at auction three months earlier and there was no way of tracing it back either to him or Cecil. As always, he'd planned everything down to a tee. The only fly in the ointment so far was his weapons contact, Jetmir Brozi, whose arrest had turned the arms deal in the scrapyard into a bloodbath and come close to getting them all killed. Brozi knew very little about Cain but, if he decided to talk, he could still provide information that might lead them in his direction.

But right now Cain wasn't unduly worried about what might happen to him, and the reason for this was simple enough.

He was dying.

The doctors had diagnosed terminal lung cancer three weeks earlier. If he sought treatment, he had as long as a year. If he didn't, he had half that, possibly less. So far, the symptoms – a persistent cough, and severe abdominal pains – were sporadic at best, but lately he'd noticed them getting worse. For a long time he'd never feared death, even in the midst of battle, but the events today at the scrapyard had made him realize how much he'd miss life when it was finally snatched away from him.

This made it even more important for him to bring his work to a conclusion. His aim was to bring down the government. Once this had been achieved, his hope was that the country's native population would rise up and turn on the immigrants flooding the country and the intellectual elite who supported them. This had been his goal ever since he'd joined the shadowy group of individuals who called themselves The Brotherhood more than three years ago. Most of their footsoldiers had been killed during the Stanhope siege, which was why their numbers were now so small, but this no longer mattered. After today, the campaign of violence would give way to a new strategy as Garth Crossman, their leader and the man who bankrolled their activities, rode the wave of revulsion over today's attacks, and the loss of his own wife in them, to enter politics for the first time at the head of a new political party promising radical change.

Cain smiled to himself. Crossman cut an impressive figure. He came across like a nice guy. He could really change things, given the chance, and by the time people realized what he was really like, it would be far too late.

Only two people knew Crossman's real identity. One was Cain himself. The other was William Garrett, codenamed Fox.

And he'd be dealt with soon enough.

A marked police patrol car turned into the street fifty yards ahead of Cain, moving slowly, as if its occupants were looking for something.

Cain ducked down behind a parked van and

watched as the police car drove past him down the street, coming to a halt in the middle of the road next to the Audi estate he'd been driving only a couple of minutes before. It then moved on about ten yards, but pulled into an empty parking bay, with its engine still running. At the same time, a second police car drove in from the opposite end, slowing up as it drew level with the first one.

Knowing this was no coincidence, Cain jogged in a low crouch, using the parked cars as cover, before ducking into a narrow back alley and breaking into a sprint.

They'd been betrayed.

And it could only have been by one man.

Forty-four

19.07

I'd spoken to Bolt twice in the last half hour, after each call nodding a thanks to the landlord.

The conversations had been brief, and slightly surreal. He'd asked me a lot of questions about the Stinger, and I'd had to answer him while standing at the corner of a bar talking on a pub phone, shouting occasionally to make myself heard above the din of booze-fuelled conversation coming from all around. Hardly secure, but then desperate times call for desperate measures. Thankfully, Bolt had been more interested in minor details than in how we'd come to be in possession of it. What did the box the Stinger was being carried in look like? How big was it? Where in Cain's car had I planted the GPS unit? That type of thing.

He'd finished the last call by telling me he'd send officers from CTC to collect me from the pub as soon as some were available. But I was getting restless. The bar was busy with a mixture of after-work groups and wrinkled locals, and the two TVs on opposite walls were both on Sky News, which was endlessly regurgitating the same material about the bomb attacks earlier. The confirmed death toll from the earlier bombs was now twenty, including five police officers, and it made me wonder what the hell Cain and Cecil were hoping to achieve. They'd killed a whole load of innocent people, and ripped apart the lives of hundreds of others. Just as they'd done in the Stanhope siege. And all for what? A few hours of constant network coverage.

What struck me looking round was that I could see that only a handful of the pub's clientele were even watching the TVs. Most were engaged in conversation. People were laughing, exchanging gossip. Getting on with their lives. Already the bombs were old news. But this was just the way it was in the era of the internet and twenty-four-hour news. Attention spans had shortened dramatically. Even the terrorists' threat of a third attack was no longer appearing to have the desired effect – on these people, at least.

I knew better. They should be afraid. A Stinger missile would take the slaughter to a whole new level, and unless Bolt and his people acted fast, there could be a massacre on the scale of Lockerbie within hours.

I thought about phoning Gina to warn her, but what the hell would I say? That there was a missile in circulation capable of bringing down a plane, and that she should grab Maddie and leave the city as soon as possible? It would be pointless. In the end they were better off where they were. And what if Gina asked me how I knew about it? I could hardly tell her the truth. That while working undercover for the people who'd sacked me and helped put me in prison, I'd helped acquire it for the terrorists, one of whom was an old colleague of mine, while simultaneously committing cold-blooded murder.

As I snaked my way slowly through the pub's customers towards the exit, I realized I was shaking. I hated myself for my part in all this, but self-preservation was also kicking in. I needed to think, to settle down in my own home, down a beer, and work out the story I was going to tell Bolt's colleagues. One that was somehow going to avoid mention of a gang of dead Albanians.

I'd been in worse situations before, I told myself as I walked back out on to the street, breathing in the cold air. But at that moment I couldn't honestly remember when.

Forty-five

19.09

'OK, we're here,' Bolt said into the radio as he and Tina pulled into Gowland Street, a narrow road flanked on both sides by new-build townhouses, which ran parallel to the lane of lock-up garages from where the stationary GPS unit was sending its signal. They were only a couple of hundred yards south of the river here and very close to the overhead railway lines heading into nearby London Bridge Station. The street was deserted as Bolt drove the Islington pool car he'd signed out earlier, a battered Ford Focus, past the turning to the lock-up garages, before parking further down. 'We've got a visual on the entrance to the lock-ups,' he continued, as he flicked on the car's hazard lights and looked in the rearview mirror, suddenly feeling very alone, even with Tina beside him. 'There doesn't appear to be much activity at the moment. What do you want us to do? Over.'

He was talking to the control room at New Scotland Yard, where responsibility for the operation to retrieve the Stinger safely had now been handed.

'Stay where you are,' said Commander Thomas Ingrams, Bolt's boss and the head of CTC, who was at the other end. 'The GPS unit is still in place, and armed response vehicles are on the scene. They're currently being held back on Druid Street, and the armed surveillance team are en route. We've been on to the owner of the lock-ups and he rented out number five six weeks ago to a man identifying himself as Vincent Cain. Over.'

'That's our man. Did he get a description? Over.'

'No. It was all done over the phone. The owner's coming down to you with the keys to number five. What's your exact location? Over.'

Bolt gave him the details, before asking if they'd located the other GPS unit.

'Affirmative,' answered Ingrams, an edge to his voice. 'It's in an Audi A5 parked in Westminster, less than half a mile from the Houses of Parliament. We're currently throwing a secure cordon round the whole area, but there's no sign of the occupants, and according to the officers at the scene, no sign of a box in the back of the car either.'

'That means the device must be in the lock-up here. Over.'

'That seems the most likely scenario. We need to get it out as soon as possible.' There was an edge to

Commander Ingrams's voice. 'As soon as you have the keys, I want you to go in with the armed back-up, do a brief risk assessment to make sure the immediate area's clear. It's unlikely the unit's going to be booby-trapped, but if you see anything suspicious pull back and let us know. Then we'll have to consider evacuating the buildings nearby and blowing the door. Over.'

'Understood,' said Bolt, and signed off.

'You're going to be the golden boy if this all works out,' Tina told him.

He shook his head. 'No, I'm not. I should have had more control over my informant and kept him on a tighter rein. God knows what happened at that meeting, but I didn't like the way he sounded.'

'Is he likely to have done something bad?'

Bolt thought about it for a moment. 'You know, deep down I believe he's a good man, but he's got a pretty chequered record. He's an ex-squaddie, an ex-cop, and an ex-con. In that order.'

Tina chuckled. 'He sounds like an interesting guy.'

Bolt turned and smiled at her. 'You'd probably like him. But I've got a feeling he's in a lot of trouble.'

Realizing there was no point in holding things back from her now that Jones's work was effectively over, he told her about how they'd used him to get close to Fox in prison, before using him for a second time on the outside to get close to Cecil Boorman. 'I think because everyone was so keen to get the people behind the Stanhope attacks, no one was too worried about how we went about doing it. But I feel like we've left Jones on his own for far too long, and I'm the one responsible.'

'Where is he now?'

'In a pub near where he lives, waiting for CTC to bring him in. I wanted him to avoid going home while Cecil and Cain are still out there. Just in case.'

As Bolt spoke, headlights appeared in the rearview mirror and a big people carrier pulled up behind them. 'I think this might be the owner of the lock-ups.' He got out of the car and went over to the people carrier's driver's-side window, where a harassed-looking middle-aged man badly in need of a shave was fiddling with a set of keys.

He asked Bolt what was going on.

'I can't comment right now, sir,' said Bolt. 'I just need the keys to number five.'

'Is it a body?' The guy looked excited now, but Bolt gave him a withering look and turned away.

'Are we ready to go?' asked Tina, when he was back in the car. She sounded excited too, but for different reasons. Tina loved the action. And if truth were told, he loved it too.

He handed her the key. 'Ready when you are.'

He put in a quick call to the control room to give them a status update, then drove towards the turning to the lock-ups' entrance, slowing up to wait for the two armed response vehicles that were providing cover to pull into position behind him. As soon as they were in place, he swung the wheel hard and drove into the narrow lane where half a dozen single-storey lock-up garages lined both sides.

A security light came on, bathing the area in an orange glow as they pulled up halfway along, giving the two ARVs space to come in behind. One of the garage doors up ahead was open, with a light coming from inside, and a man poked his head out, and poked it straight back in again.

For a second, Bolt thought that the man might be in number five and that they'd disturbed him picking up the Stinger, but then he realized that they'd stopped right next to five, and that its door was firmly shut.

They exited the car and walked over as a crowded commuter train rumbled along the overhead track fifty yards away, heading out towards the suburbs. Conscious of Commander Ingrams's warning that the door could be booby-trapped, Bolt examined the frame, in case anything was out of place.

'What do you think?' said Tina. She had the key in her hand. Armed cops were standing behind her, their weapons at the ready.

Bolt knew the people they were dealing with had access to explosives and sophisticated bomb-making resources. They'd set a booby-trapped bomb for the security forces earlier in the day. If he made the wrong call, whoever opened the door would be killed instantly.

A strange thought occurred to him then. Would it really be so bad if he died? It would all be over in an instant. One big bang and that would be it: the end of everything. The worry, the pressure, and, if he was honest, the unrelenting loneliness of his life. It was almost ten years since his wife Mikaela had died in a car crash. He'd been the one driving the car, and he still had her photo by his bed. Jesus, he missed her, just as much as if it had happened yesterday, and in that moment he knew that whatever happened, he'd be haunted by her ghost for the rest of his life.

He turned to Tina. 'Let's make sure we clear the area, then I'll open it.'

Tina frowned. 'Are you sure? I don't want you dying on me, Mike Bolt.' It was as if she'd read his mind.

'Excuse me,' said a voice behind them, and Bolt turned round to see the man whose head they'd just seen emerge from the open lock-up. He was in his sixties, and wearing overalls, and he was looking with a mixture of concern and interest at the armed cops. 'Are you interested in that garage?' He motioned towards number five.

'Yes,' said Bolt, showing his warrant card.

'It's just, someone was in there about ten minutes ago. A man I haven't seen before. He was getting something out, I think. I saw him load a holdall into his boot.'

'Can you describe him?'

The man thought about it for a moment. 'I didn't get much of a look at him, I'm afraid. He was quite a big bloke, though, and he was driving a big black four-wheel-drive. I think it might have been a Shogun.'

Taking the key from Tina, Bolt told everyone to move well back. He was pretty certain that the man wouldn't have had time to booby-trap the place, but even so, he still held his breath as he unlocked the door.

The door opened and he stepped inside and switched on the light, feeling a palpable sense of relief.

A large wooden crate, just like the one Jones had described, was on the floor in the middle of the room. The lid was off and, as Bolt approached it, he knew it was going to be empty.

And it was.

They were too late. The missile was in circulation and, with less than an hour to go before the terrorists' ultimatum, they had no idea where it was, who had it, or what its target was going to be.

Forty-six

19.12

Voorhess had seriously considered killing the old man who'd seen him earlier at the lock-up garages.

He'd almost done it too, when the man had given him a shock by poking his head out of the garage slightly further up, just as he'd been putting the Stinger in the back of his Shogun. It wouldn't have been difficult. There was no one else around, and there was no way the old man would have been expecting it. Voorhess might have been a big man but he had the kind of friendly face and open, natural smile that set people immediately at ease. He was also obsessive about no one seeing his face when he was on a job. It was the sole reason he'd insisted on collecting the missile from a quiet, neutral location. So that the client never saw him. The irony of then being spotted by someone else was not lost on him.

Even so, he'd made the snap decision to leave the

old man alive on the basis that it was highly unlikely he'd ever connect him to the day's terrorist attacks. Instead, he'd given the man a friendly wave and a grin, keeping his body language as natural as possible, before getting in the driver's seat and pulling out of there.

Now, as he reversed the Shogun into Mr Butt's ground-floor garage, careful not to run over his girlfriend's body, Voorhess was pleased that he'd spared the old man. He didn't like unnecessary killing, especially when it was at such close quarters, as it had been with Mr Butt's girlfriend earlier. The old man had looked a cheerful fellow, and it amused Voorhess to think that he would never know quite how close he'd come to death.

But for Mr Butt himself, it was unfortunately going to be a different story.

Forty-seven

19.15

'Get in there,' grunted the screw, manhandling Fox into the cell.

'They tried to kill me again,' said Fox, as the screw went to shut the cell door. 'You saw them. I'm not safe in this place.'

'You're a lot safer than we are right now,' replied the screw. He was one of the young ones, an ex-squaddie who'd told Fox when they'd first met a couple of months earlier that he was a disgrace to the armed forces and his regiment. The screw looked scared and confused now, though. This was clearly his first riot. He gave Fox another shove and slammed the door shut.

The decor was better in here, thought Fox, as the key turned in the lock. They'd had a refurbishment on this wing recently, and the walls had been painted a soothing cream. The bed was new too, but he didn't sit on it, even though he was tired from his recent exertions.

The whole prison was in lockdown now, with Fox's wing completely sealed off with the prisoners inside. It was, he thought, amazing how easy it had been for the inmates to seize control. Hopelessly outnumbered, the screws had been thrown into panic, and in their haste to ensure the disturbance didn't spread to the other wings they'd neglected to search him properly. Which was a mistake on their parts.

Fox took the mobile phone from his pocket. He'd bought it from another inmate two days previously. There were always plenty of mobiles inside prisons, smuggled in during visits when physical contact was permissible, or by the guards themselves who sold them on for profit. Fox had always considered the British penal system far too liberal, but it was certainly working in his favour now.

He sent a text to a number he'd memorized. It was only three words long, and it said simply: SWITCH IT ON. When he'd got confirmation that it had sent, he deleted the message and turned off the phone, removing the SIM card and flushing it down the toilet, before shoving the handset under the mattress on the bed.

He leaned back against the wall. Now it was just a matter of waiting.

Forty-eight

19.28

'They're clearing all the airspace above Greater London,' said Bolt, coming off the radio to Scotland Yard. 'Apparently it's a huge inconvenience.'

Tina lit a cigarette and took a much-needed drag as she walked over to where he was standing at the entrance to the lock-ups. 'It's a lot better than having a plane shot down.'

'The problem is, we've only got the word of one informant that this missile even exists, and the transport system's in enough of a mess as it is after what happened earlier.'

'We know that the guy who collected the weapon came here at around seven o'clock, and that he was driving a black four-wheel-drive, probably a Shogun,' said Tina, who'd just been talking to the old man who'd seen him. 'If we can get some footage from any CCTV cameras around here, we can get the registration and track the suspect that way.'

'I've just been on to Control to get them to check all the available footage. Did the witness get any of the number plate?'

Tina shook her head. 'Nothing. He said the guy wasn't acting suspiciously so there was no reason for him to check it. We're lucky he can almost certainly ID the model.'

'I'll make sure they know the time we're looking at. It'll narrow it down a bit.'

He went back to the car to radio in again, and Tina took another drag on the cigarette. The night was cold and clear and above her head she saw the lights of an approaching plane, less than a thousand feet up. Someone might be aiming the Stinger at it right now, preparing to fire. As she watched, the plane banked sharply and made a sweeping U-turn until it was heading east and away from the centre of the city, and she gave a sigh of relief. It was good to be back at the sharp end of the fight against crime but, as always, it felt like a losing battle. You put down one person, two more appeared to take his place. The key, though, was to keep fighting. That had always been Tina's philosophy. Never give up. And, even though there'd been times when she'd come close, she never had.

'I think we might have a break,' said Bolt, hurrying back over. 'Control says a black Mitsubishi Shogun passed through the camera at the entrance to Crucifix Lane heading south at six fifty-eight. That's about three minutes' drive from here so the timings fit perfectly. They've got the Shogun's registration number so they're pulling out all the stops to track its route.'

'That's got to be our man, Mike, and he's got to be the one who's going to be using the missile as well.'

Tina stubbed her cigarette out underfoot and looked at her watch. It had just turned 7.30. Less than half an hour to the terrorists' deadline.

She took a deep breath. She hated waiting around, especially when time was so short. She just wanted to get out there, chase down the Shogun and its driver. Nicking the bastard before he had a chance to fire his missile. But just because they'd got his registration didn't mean they were going to get him.

Knowing she wouldn't be able to smoke in Bolt's car, Tina decided to live dangerously and light another cigarette. The pressure was beginning to get to her. It had been a long and intense day, yet they'd made real progress. Now, with the sky cleared of planes, they'd taken away the terrorists' targets, and although she knew that would only put off an attack rather than stop one altogether, it was still something.

An armed cop in one of the two ARVs parked a few feet away gave her a disapproving look as she dragged hard on the cigarette, savouring the dirty taste, and she gave him a far harder look back, pleased to see him drop his gaze.

She smiled to herself as she turned away, pacing the

row of lock-ups, shivering against the cold.

And that was when she saw it. Over in the distance.

Her heart lurched in shock as the grim and terrifying possibility occurred to her.

The terrorists might not be after a plane at all.

Forty-nine

19.31

Voorhess stood amid the lush foliage of Mr Butt's roof garden staring up at the dark sky. Although it was a clear night, he could see only two stars, the light pollution obscuring the rest. It made him think once again of home, where even close to Cape Town the stars would swarm like bright dust across the night sky.

There was a biting chill in the air, and he was pleased that, if everything worked out, he would be leaving this country first thing the following morning. He didn't like crowds, and he didn't like bad weather, and the UK could be relied upon for both. He was staying in a hotel in Heathrow tonight, then after flying to Bangkok he was off on a well-deserved week's holiday down south on the isolated island of Ko Pida near the Malaysian border, away from all the backpackers and the boorish Russians, before returning to Cape Town via Singapore – a million dollars richer.

The money was being paid into an account in the name of a consultancy company based in Bermuda. From there it would go via Panama to the Cayman Islands before being transferred in small increments back into South Africa as and when he needed it. It was a complicated procedure, and it cost him a great deal of money to set up the shell companies and keep the accounts active, but Voorhess knew it was worth the investment. With this new money his retirement fund would stand at almost two million dollars. Not enough to quit work just yet, but five more years of earning and careful spending and he'd be able to realize his dream of opening a small guesthouse on the shores of the Western Cape, hopefully with a handsome young boyfriend in tow.

As he stared skywards, he frowned. When he'd first come out here a couple of hours earlier, the sky had been criss-crossed with vapour trails and the lights of planes coming in and out of Heathrow ten miles to the west of him. Now it was empty. Was it a coincidence or had someone somewhere found out about the Stinger? He couldn't see how they could have done, but then he knew very little about the client who'd hired him to fire it. Usually, this was an advantage. The less he had to deal with his clients the better. But the problem was, he had to trust the fact that they were reliable and efficient. He told himself not to become too paranoid. It might simply be that the planes had been moved as a precaution after the bombs earlier in the day.

He removed the missile launcher from the holdall at his feet. The last time he'd fired a Stinger he'd brought down a helicopter in the Western Congo containing a high-ranking mining executive. They were extremely simple to use and very accurate if you knew what you were doing, which Voorhess did. He gave the launcher a quick inspection. It looked new, and appeared to be in perfect working order. But he still had a nagging feeling that something wasn't right.

Putting the missile back down on the ground, he walked over to the edge of the garden and looked down at the empty street below. Lights were on in most of the houses on the opposite side, and in one of the windows he could see two boys of about twelve, faces pressed to a single PC screen, looks of intense concentration on their pale, round faces. Voorhess felt sorry for them. When he'd been their age he was out exploring the dusty hills and wooded creeks round his parents' farm, hunting deer and fishing for trout, enjoying the sunshine and the fresh air.

And then, out of the corner of his eye, he saw it. A marked police car cruising past the end of the street, sirens off. Moving slowly.

For Voorhess, this and the absence of planes in the night sky was too much of a coincidence. He knew all about the client's ultimatum, the fact that he had to fire the missile at eight p.m., but to stay put much longer was simply too risky. He looked at his watch. Just after 7.30. Not enough time to void the contract.

He'd have to get this thing over and done with soon. With a deep breath, he turned round and looked towards his target.

Fifty

19.32

Bolt was sitting in the car waiting for an update on the suspect Shogun's route from the control room at Scotland Yard when Tina yanked open the driver's-side door and leaned in, her eyes alight with excitement. 'I think I know what their target is. Look.' She grabbed him by the arm and almost pulled him out of the car, pointing up into the distance over the lock-up garages.

Bolt followed her arm to where London's newest architectural masterpiece, the Shard, stretched up a thousand feet into the sky, barely half a mile distant. It was swathed almost completely in darkness except for a thin strip of light round the observation deck.

'Isn't tonight the official opening?' continued Tina.

'I don't know,' Bolt replied. 'If it is, surely they'd have cancelled it after everything that's happened today?'

'But the lights are on up there and the last I heard the Prime Minister was telling everyone to keep calm and carry on as usual. They've got all sorts of dignitaries attending. It's a great target, Mike. Look at it. The party's right there on the observation deck. This can't be a coincidence.'

'Shit. We need to find out if that Shogun's still moving. If it is, then it's unlikely the Shard's the target.' But even as he spoke the words, he didn't believe them.

Clutching the radio to his ear, he immediately re-established contact with the control room at Scotland Yard.

'Have we got a line on what's happening with the suspect vehicle, over?' he asked, staring up at the Shard, wondering how on earth he'd overlooked it as a potential target.

'Control to Car One,' said the female controller, 'we can now confirm that the suspect vehicle went through a camera on the A2198 Long Lane at 19.09, and there have been no further sightings. Over.'

Bolt felt his heart sink. 'So the Shogun's stationary? Can you triangulate an approximate location for it, over?'

'We're just waiting for Hendon to get back to us with that, over,' answered the controller, referring to the police Data Centre where all the data from the UK's vast network of CCTV and ANPR cameras was kept.

'We need to know urgently if it's within missile range of the Shard,' Bolt told her. 'We believe the Shard may be the terrorists' target. Can you confirm whether tonight is the opening-night party? Over.'

There was a commotion and the sound of raised voices at the other end of the radio as the people in the control room at Scotland Yard processed this new information. In the background, he could hear Commander Ingrams shouting to someone to find out.

Half a minute later, Ingrams's voice came over the radio. 'Mike, I can confirm it is the opening-night party tonight. It started at seven. We're going to warn the owners and get the building evacuated immediately. We've also just got confirmation from Hendon that the Shogun's somewhere in an area of Bermondsey bordered by Long Lane in the north and the New Kent Road in the south. It's about eight hundred by eight hundred yards.'

'Jesus. That's a hell of a wide area to cover.'

'I know. We're going to flood it with officers. Hopefully it'll put the shooter off firing if he sees police everywhere, and we've still got twenty minutes until the deadline. We're going to need you, and the ARV units with you, down there to help right away. We'll send you the exact coordinates now. Over and out.'

Bolt gestured to let the two ARV drivers know they were on the move, and he and Tina jumped back into

Islington nick's battered Ford Focus.

'It looks like you were right,' he told her as he did a rapid three-point turn and drove back out on to Gowland Street in a screech of tyres.

'That's only an achievement if we stop him,' she said as Bolt hurtled down the street, with the ARVs following.

Fifty-one

19.41

Gina Burnham-Jones felt like she was on top of the world as she stared through the huge floor-to-ceiling glass windows, more than thirty feet high, at the carpet of lights spread below her. She could see the arc of the Thames as it did a sweeping right turn past the Gherkin and the NatWest Tower, snaked under Tower Bridge, with the Tower of London just beyond it, and then alongside Canary Wharf, before its dark waters slipped away into the distance, towards the sea.

'It's beautiful, isn't it?' she whispered, squeezing Matt's hand.

He smiled. 'So it was worth the surprise, then?'

She smiled back. 'It was well worth it. A few hours ago I was washing Maddie's clothes and cleaning the bathroom. And now here I am, drinking champagne and hobnobbing with the rich and famous.'

The observation deck of the Shard ran right round

the building on three floors. Number 69, the central floor, where she and Matt now stood, was crowded with guests attending the opening-night party. Above their heads, and beyond the open-air observation deck on the seventy-second floor, Gina could see the shards of glass that made up the top of the tower as they disappeared into the night sky like icy, stretching fingers.

The whole thing was incredible. For the first time in her life, Gina really didn't know where to look. She'd already recognized several TV personalities, a well-known businessman, and at least two gold medallists from London 2012, all milling about in groups as immaculately turned-out young waiters and waitresses moved among them dispensing a never-ending flow of expensive-looking canapés, and even more expensive-looking drinks. No one seemed to be talking about the bombs, which made Gina feel a little foolish for worrying so much. Thankfully, security coming into the building had been extremely tight. All the guests had passed through metal scanners and had had their bags searched before getting into the lifts, and she was pleased to see that everyone looked like they belonged.

She noticed a TV cameraman filming proceedings while a female reporter stalked the area with a mike in her hand, clearly prowling for someone to interview. Gina turned away quickly, having no desire to embarrass herself on TV.

'No offence,' she said, putting her arm through Matt's and moving close to him, 'but how did you get an invite to a swanky do like this?'

'Because I'm handsome, debonair and popular,' he answered.

Gina raised a sceptical eyebrow, and he lowered his eyes and gave a sheepish smile.

'A few of us ordinary Joes got an invite if we'd done something for the community. I won a bravery award once. I guess it qualified me.'

'You never told me about that.'

He shrugged. 'You never asked.'

She loved Matt's modesty, and the fact that he never felt the need to brag, and she leaned forward and kissed him on the lips.

He kissed her back, hard, and when they pulled away a second later he must have seen something in her expression because he held her tightly, looked into her eyes and said, 'I've been meaning to ask you something.'

Gina smiled at him. She felt giddy, light-headed, and it wasn't the alcohol. She suddenly felt good about her life for the first time in a long while.

At that moment there was a commotion over by the lifts, and Gina turned to see half a dozen uniformed security officials emerge, a sense of urgency about them. 'Ladies and gentlemen, I'm afraid we're going to have to bring the party to a temporary halt,' the most senior of them announced, shouting to make himself heard above the noise of conversation, as the other officials fanned out into the room. 'We need to evacuate the observation deck.'

There was a sudden silence, and then, almost as one, everyone moved rapidly towards the lifts, the noise level rising again as fear spread round the room. 'Please don't worry, this is purely precautionary,' shouted the official. 'If you can just form an orderly queue at the lifts, we can get everyone down far quicker.' But there was an edge to his voice as he spoke, and Gina could see he was nervous. So was everyone else, as it rapidly became clear to them how exposed they were up there, almost a thousand feet above London. They crowded around the lift doors, everyone wanting to be on the first lift down.

Matt, though, remained perfectly calm. 'Don't worry, Gina, everything will be fine.' He pulled out his warrant card, and stopped one of the officials. 'I'm a police officer. Can you tell me what's going on?'

'We've had intelligence that there might be an attack on the building,' said the official as quietly as possible.

'What kind of attack?'

'We don't know, but we need to get everyone out as soon as possible.'

Matt nodded. 'I'll get up to the top deck and bring people down.' He turned to Gina, giving her a reassuring smile as he took her firmly by the arm. 'Go over to the lifts and try and stay as far away from the windows as possible. I'll be with you in a minute.'

And before she had a chance to say another word to him, he turned and disappeared into the crowd.

Fifty-two

19.45

On the roof half a mile away, Voorhess slipped on a pair of earphones, having finished his inspection of the Stinger. Then he inserted the battery coolant unit into the launcher's hand guard, shooting a stream of argon gas into the system, along with a chemical energy charge that gave the missile the power it needed to reach its target.

It was now ready to fire.

Getting down on one knee, with his back to the southern edge of the roof to allow for backdraft, and camouflaged by all the pot plants, he rested the missile on his shoulder and slowly lifted the launcher until it was pointed at the lights on the main observation deck of the Shard, sixty-nine storeys up. It really was a beautiful building, thought Voorhess, who'd always had an admiration for original architecture, and it seemed a pity to put a hole in it.

But he comforted himself in the knowledge that the physical damage would be cleared up soon enough, leaving it looking as good as new in no time. Those inside weren't going to be so lucky, though. The three-kilo warhead on the end of the missile would wreak havoc in the enclosed, crowded space, and the beauty of the whole thing was that he couldn't miss. Unlike the helicopter he'd shot down, this wasn't a moving target, and as the only real heat source in the whole building, and with no other heat sources in the immediate vicinity, the missile would lock straight on to it.

The observation deck was now in the launcher's sights. He couldn't see inside and had no idea who was in there, but this no longer concerned him. His target was the building. Right then, it was all he was interested in.

For a long moment he paused for reflection, knowing that what he was about to do would be seen and talked about all over the world. A satisfied smile passed across his face as he pressed his finger down on the trigger mechanism and, with an angry shriek, the missile took flight.

They'd just turned off Long Lane and on to a residential road, having just split from the two ARVs to maximize the ground they could cover in the hunt for the Shogun, when Tina heard a high-pitched whoosh – the sound rockets made when they were shot up into the air in firework displays – and saw a thin plume of smoke shoot across the top of buildings no more than two hundred yards to the south-west.

She opened her mouth to say something, her eyes fixed to the missile as it seemed to sit perfectly still in the air for a half a heartbeat before suddenly accelerating upwards, leaving a long, perfectly straight vapour trail like an arrow pointed straight at the Shard.

As Bolt did an emergency stop, Tina jumped out of the car and watched, dumbstruck, as the missile raced towards its target. It seemed to travel for a long time, but in reality it must have been barely seconds. And then it struck the observation deck with an audible bang, followed by a flash of bright light.

They'd been too late.

Fifty-three

19.46

When the missile struck, Gina was standing against the wall at the edge of the scrum of nervous guests near the lift entrance.

She saw something bright hurtling towards them from outside the window and then, before she had time to react or properly process the information, there was a loud explosion, followed by an immense, almost deafening sound of shattering glass.

Instinctively, she threw herself to the floor. She heard a single piercing scream of panic coming from somewhere very close, which stopped as abruptly as it had begun. And then there was a deathly silence, broken only by the howling wind as it gusted in through the broken glass. Nothing moved. No one cried out.

Slowly, unsteadily, Gina got to her feet. And witnessed a scene of total devastation. There was a huge hole in one of the floor-to-ceiling window panes at the southern end of the observation deck, about twenty yards from where she was standing. A blazing fire next to it ran almost the entire width of the room, its plumes of thick black smoke slowly advancing on her like an army of ghosts. All around Gina, guests staggered to their feet, their faces white with shock. Many had deep cuts. Some were covered in blood. One young woman still had a drink in her hand as she wandered round aimlessly, seemingly oblivious to the four-inch piece of glass sticking out of her stomach, which was staining her white cocktail dress a deep red.

Gina turned away from her, too shocked even to feel nauseous, which was when she saw the five or six bodies lying close to the fire. One was in the uniform of the security guards; another had a TV camera next to him, a blackened hand resting on top of it. There was a man in a dinner suit lying on top of a woman, who may or may not have been the TV reporter Gina had seen only a couple of minutes earlier.

Gina stifled a gasp. The man in the dinner suit looked like it might be Matt.

Oh God, no. Please. Not him.

Filled with a sudden sense of urgency, she made her way through the ranks of shocked, bloodied guests, ignoring the heat from the fire and the carnage all around her. She moved aside as a large, middle-aged man stumbled towards her, one cheek literally hanging off his face, blood gushing from the wound, his mouth gaping open. She didn't even look at him. She was too busy staring through the thickening smoke at the body of the man in the dinner suit.

It was difficult to tell but it looked like his hair was the same colour as Matt's.

The heat from the fire was becoming more intense now, and was burning her face. Behind her, people were beginning to talk again, several of them trying to take charge. Gina was only feet away now, and she could see that the woman lying beneath the man in the suit was the TV reporter. It looked like she was asleep except for the huge gash that had split open her skull, exposing the bone. The man in the suit had his face buried in her shoulder as if they were locked in an embrace.

Blinking against the smoke, Gina bent down next to him, feeling a terrible sense of dread. He wasn't moving, and the back of his suit was shredded where the material had been torn open by hundreds of shards of glass. Gina had never seen a dead body before tonight, but even so, she could tell that he was dead. She heard herself begin to sob. To have been given a taste of hope and then, in the next instant, have it snatched away was too cruel a blow.

And then she felt a firm hand on her arm, pulling her away. She turned round to see Matt standing there, his tie askew, his lip bleeding, and a look of sheer relief on his face.

'Come on,' he said. 'Let's go.'

Tina stood staring up at the flames and smoke angrily swirling out of the Shard's windows as she listened to Bolt talking into the radio, his voice cracking with the shock of what they'd just witnessed. 'Missile has just hit the Shard observation deck!' he was shouting. 'I repeat: missile has just hit the Shard observation deck! There's a fire burning up there!'

Tina thought she could just make out figures moving behind the huge wall of glass as the fire billowed through the observation deck, obscuring the view. The sight made her guts wrench. All their efforts to stop the Stinger had been in vain. Had it been fired at eight p.m., on the deadline the terrorists had given them, they might have prevented the attack, but by launching it a quarter of an hour early, the terrorists had shown a breathtaking callousness. Tina felt gutted and galvanized at the same time. Because they could still catch the perpetrator if they moved fast enough, although the smoke trail from the Stinger that would lead them to him was already dissipating above the rooftops around them.

She jumped back in the car, slamming the door shut. 'Drive! We need to catch the bastard!'

For a moment, Bolt didn't say anything. He looked utterly shell-shocked. Tina had never seen him like this before.

She grabbed his arm and physically shook him,

fully prepared to kick him out of the car and drive herself. 'Mike, drive, for Christ's sake! We can still find the shooter!'

'All right! All right!' he shouted back, snapping out of his trance. 'But for once, do not do anything stupid, understand?'

'Just fucking go!'

Giving her a glare of intense anger, he yanked the car into gear and accelerated down the street.

Fifty-four

19.47

Voorhess knew he had to move fast.

After putting his balaclava back on, he strode down into the living room and crouched down beside Azim Butt, who was literally shaking with fear in his seat. The reason for his distress was that he'd seen the heavy black explosives vest he was wearing, which Voorhess had fitted to him earlier while he'd been unconscious from the dose of diazepam. Although the actual explosives themselves weren't visible, as they were sewn into the lining, both the vest's weight and the exposed wires running between the pockets made it obvious to even the most naive of civilians what it was.

'I'm going to untie you now, Mr Butt,' Voorhess explained as he removed his gag, 'but I must warn you: the jacket you're wearing contains explosives, and it's connected to a pressure pad beneath your seat. If you try to remove the jacket or leave the seat, you'll set off the bomb and blow yourself to pieces.' As he spoke, he untied each of Mr Butt's ankles in turn. 'What I want you to do is remain exactly where you are until help arrives. It won't be long, I can promise you that.'

'Please don't kill me. Please.'

Voorhess started on the left wrist. 'No one's going to kill you if you do as you're told. When help arrives, they'll come through your front door. When you hear them, you call out and tell them that you're wired to a bomb. They'll send in the experts and deal with the device.'

'I don't believe you.'

'I just want to slow them down, Mr Butt,' Voorhess told him, putting on his most reassuring voice as he released the final bond. 'And remember, don't tell them anything about me that could be of use. I don't want to have to kill your young son in Cobham.'

Mr Butt's eyes widened. After everything else he'd been through, this was clearly the biggest shock of all.

'Yes,' said Voorhess calmly, 'I know about him. Now give a poor description and he's safe. A good one and he dies. Understand?'

Mr Butt nodded frantically. 'Yes, yes. I understand.'

Beneath the balaclava, Voorhess smiled. 'Good.'

He stood up and left the room, moving quickly. He'd fitted an electronic sensor to the front door of Mr Butt's house earlier: as soon as the door opened, the sensor would activate, automatically sending a text message to Voorhess's phone. This would be his cue to set off the bomb.

Afterwards, the conclusion would be that Mr Butt himself had been the man who'd fired the missile, and had then lain in wait to ambush the police when they arrived, trying to take as many of them with him as possible. Given the power of the bomb, there wouldn't be enough left of Mr Butt to uncover any evidence of his incarceration; and, anyway, Voorhess had been very careful not to leave marks on him. A background check would show no obvious links between Mr Butt and Islamic fundamentalism, but the physical proof of his involvement would be more than enough.

It was, thought Voorhess, a near-perfect plan, which was just the way he liked it.

Fifty-five

19.49

'Slow down!' Tina yelled as they drove on to the residential road of modern townhouses where a thinning pall of smoke still hung over the rooftops. 'It was fired from down here somewhere.'

The road was too narrow for on-street parking, and all the houses had attached garages, and car ports, but there was no sign of a black Shogun anywhere as they drew level with the properties directly beneath the smoke. But now that it was drifting on the breeze, it was impossible to pinpoint the exact place from where the missile had been fired.

Tina opened her window, looking for some kind of reference point. The sirens were coming from everywhere now, their sound almost deafening, and the car's radio was alive with rapid-fire chatter as officers converged on the area from all sides. No one, it seemed, could believe what had just happened. She was still in shock herself. They both were, although thankfully Bolt had calmed down.

'It had to have been fired from one of this group of three or four houses here,' she said, pointing out of the window, her heart still pumping hard from the tension.

Bolt gave their location to Control and stopped the car as the door to one of the suspect houses opened. A middle-aged woman in a tracksuit stepped outside, looking round with a puzzled expression on her face. Her gaze then fell on the battered Ford Focus that Bolt was driving, and she gave him a suspicious glare.

Bolt opened the window and flashed his warrant. 'Police,' he hissed, not wanting to alert any suspects. 'Get back inside.'

The woman pulled a face and shook her head as if she didn't believe him.

'Leave her to me,' said Tina, getting out of the car.

But she was only halfway across the road when she heard an automatic garage door opening to her left. 'Get inside!' she urged the woman. Bolt was gesturing at her to get back in the car but Tina was already walking towards the house next door, wanting to get a look at the car coming out of the garage.

Suddenly she was blinded by headlights as a black Shogun drove out.

Tina's next move was utterly instinctive. She sprinted over and went for the front door handle.

There was a single shadowy figure in the driver's

seat. He gave her a brief half-second glance, and their eyes met.

Tina grabbed the handle and the Shogun accelerated on to the road, taking her with it. She tried to yank the door open but the damn thing was locked. She saw Bolt drive towards the Shogun, trying to cut it off, and then she let go, hitting the tarmac with a painful thud and rolling over and over.

Looking up, she just had time to see the Shogun slam into the Ford Focus side-on, shunting it round ninety degrees in a crunch of metal, before it reversed back just as suddenly, forcing her to scrabble out of the way on her hands and knees. Tina thought he was trying to kill her, but he wasn't. He was just getting some extra purchase so he could drive into the back of the Focus and force it off the road. Once again he slammed against it, and as Tina got to her feet, the Shogun made a hard right and sped down to the end of the road. Hopelessly, pointlessly, Tina chased after it, ignoring the pain that seemed to come from every part of her body, as the Shogun made another right at the junction and disappeared in an angry screech of tyres.

Behind her she saw two marked patrol cars drive on to the road, sirens blaring. Turning round, she ran towards them, holding up her warrant card, yelling at the cops in the lead car to continue the chase. And then, as they manoeuvred around the battered Focus and accelerated away after the Shogun, she ran over to where Bolt still sat in the driver's seat, looking dazed.

'Mike, are you OK?' she asked. They may have been on the verge of a real row a few minutes earlier, but the fact was she cared about him far more than she liked to admit.

'Yeah, I'm fine,' he grunted, just managing to open the crumpled driver's-side door and get out.

'The other cars are on his tail but he's got a bit of a head start.'

'Shit,' he said, leaning against the car and rubbing the back of his head, still unsteady on his feet. 'We can't let him get away. Not after what he's done. I just heard on the radio that they'd already started the evacuation of the observation deck, but that they took a hell of a lot of casualties.' He glared at her. 'I thought I told you not to do anything stupid.'

'I didn't. And before you start giving me a load more crap, remember this: I got a look at him.'

Bolt's expression brightened just a little. 'Would you recognize him if you saw him again?'

'Absolutely,' said Tina with a cold certainty in her voice. 'And if I ever do, I'll kill him.'

Fifty-six

20.00

Garth Crossman held his seventeen-year-old daughter and stroked her soft blonde hair as they sat together on the chaise longue. Lucy was a beautiful girl in so many different ways, and she'd taken the death of her mother earlier that morning in the first of the day's attacks extremely hard, as was only to be expected.

On the TV, the news was showing the flames pouring out of the upper reaches of the Shard, and the male voiceover was reporting on the third of the day's terrorist attacks in a tone that was coming close to panic.

No one yet knew the extent of the casualties, but many of the guests from the opening-night party, which not only included leading politicians, businesspeople and celebrities but even, it was rumoured, at least two minor royals, were carrying injuries as they were led from the building. There were also a number of bodies visible behind the glass on the observation deck, even though the camera was trying to avoid them, focusing instead on the first of the fire crews that were now desperately tackling the blaze. But what was obvious to everyone watching was the sheer scale of the disaster, and the ease with which the terrorists had been able to strike at the heart of London, and at one of its most iconic landmarks.

It was like the Stanhope siege all over again, and Crossman felt an elation so pure and ferocious it made him want to shake. Not only had he got rid of his wife, who'd found out far too many of his secrets for her own good, but the attacks that he'd masterminded and invested in – attacks he hoped would push the UK to the brink of social breakdown – had been carried out with near-perfect precision. The missile had hit the Shard before the ultimatum they'd given the government, but it didn't matter. Crossman had always known that the government would never agree to the demands they'd made. In fact, he'd banked on the fact that they wouldn't, and that the Prime Minister would refuse to negotiate. Now that the third attack had taken place, he looked weak and ineffective, a spent force.

Garth Crossman loved his country. He loved the fact that it had pioneered the industrial revolution, colonized half the world with its armies, its culture and its ideals, and had stood proud and stable for generations while the hurricanes of change battered the nations around it. *That* had been the land of his grandfathers. But like the other members of The Brotherhood, he hated what it had become, and it was this feeling of anger, combined with the cold ruthlessness that had served him so well in his business dealings, that had pushed him on to the path he was following now, a path that was littered with death and destruction.

There was another reason too. Garth Crossman would never forget the day when as a twelve-year-old boy he'd been mugged and beaten by a group of local youths after leaving school one day. There'd been four of them – two black, two white. They hadn't just robbed him. They'd tormented him, cutting up his blazer and cap with a Stanley knife, putting the knife up against his face, laughing as he wept and begged for mercy. They'd threatened to scar him for life. They'd made him take off his trousers, and thrown them into the river. They'd laughed at his tears.

Bastards.

Crossman lived with that ordeal every day of his life. It simmered beneath the surface, filling him with hatred and anger and a constant desire for revenge. Not just against the four thugs who'd put him through that humiliation, but against every piece of lowlife scum that walked the streets, as well as the weak-kneed scum in authority who stood up for them.

'Who could be doing something like this, Dad?'

Lucy whispered, her face pressed against his chest for comfort, as the sound of the news presenter's tones reverberated around the room in surround sound.

'People with no conscience, sweet one,' said Crossman in soothing tones, using the pet name for his daughter. 'I'm afraid there are a lot of bad people in the world. But I'm here to protect you. I'll always be here.'

He fumbled for the remote control, enjoying the warmth of his daughter against him, and switched off the TV, knowing he could enjoy the coverage later. Right now, it was his duty to make Lucy feel better, and loved, again.

One of three mobile phones on the coffee table beside him rang, the ringtone immediately identifying it as the phone used only for emergencies. He tensed. Only two people in the world knew that number. He checked the screen. It was an inner London landline. Almost certainly a payphone.

'I'm going to have to take this,' he said apologetically, lifting her head from his chest and getting to his feet. 'I'll be back in a minute, I promise.'

She gave him a small tear-stained smile to show she understood, and Crossman smiled back at her, thinking what a beautiful, charming girl she was.

He took the call in the adjoining room. It was Cain, and when he spoke, his words sent a cold shiver up Crossman's spine.

'We may have a problem.'

Fifty-seven

20.01

Voorhess knew he had to dump the Shogun fast. There was no way he was going to drive it back to the airport now.

Somehow the police had known about the Stinger attack before he'd carried it out. It was the only thing he could think of to explain the way they'd suddenly appeared on Mr Butt's doorstep when he'd driven out. A few seconds later and they'd have had him, and although he'd tried to run them over, that hadn't stopped the plainclothes female police officer – an attractive, if slightly hard-faced, woman – from trying to get into the car to arrest him. More problematic, though, was the fact that she'd seen his face. With the exception of the old man earlier, no one had ever seen him on a job before and lived to tell the tale, which was why he was still working after more than a decade of being a professional killer.

What was really irritating was the fact that none of this was his fault. He'd done his job, just as he'd promised he would. He should have been warned that Mr Butt had a girlfriend with a key, because that too had almost ended in disaster. Voorhess prided himself on his skill and attention to detail, and he expected the same from those who hired him. And they'd let him down.

Now he was on the run with the police coming at him from all directions.

He saw a small hotel up ahead on the right with parking in front of it, and turned in. There were no spaces so he double-parked in front of two cars, blocking them in, then got out and started walking fast, knowing he'd left DNA traces inside the Shogun that the police would be able to recover, but unable to do anything about that now.

As he stepped out on to the pavement, he spotted a police patrol car, its blue lights flashing angrily, hurtling towards him on the other side of the road.

Where others saw problems, Voorhess always saw opportunities – it had been something drummed into him by his father, along with the importance of decisiveness – and he immediately stepped into the road and waved them down. A physical description of him had almost certainly been circulated by now, but it would be basic, and with no reference to his size since he was sitting down when he'd been spotted, and he was banking on the fact that in the heat of the moment it wouldn't occur to the pursuing officers that their target would be trying to attract their attention.

The police car veered across the road and stopped next to him, the driver sticking his head out of the window, a sour, accusatory look on his face. Obviously he wanted to get back to chasing terrorists.

'The hotel! I saw a man!' stammered Voorhess, approaching the car.

When he was only a foot away, he drew the .22 that he'd used to kill Mr Butt's girlfriend from beneath his overalls, pressed the barrel against the surprised officer's forehead, and pulled the trigger. The man gasped and fell back in his seat, and Voorhess leaned down so he had a view of the officer in the passenger seat – a young man in his early twenties with a pallid complexion – and shot him in the face as he went for the door handle, putting a second bullet in his chest for good measure.

Already he could hear another siren coming closer, and he knew he was going to have to move fast. Putting the gun back in his overalls he ran round to the back of the car and opened the trunk, throwing in the holdall containing his possessions. Then, taking a quick look round to check there were no witnesses, he pulled the driver from the seat, hauled him over to the boot and bundled him inside, grabbing his cap in the process.

A second cop car was approaching fast now,

coming the other way, barely a hundred yards distant and closing, and it took all of Voorhess's self-control to put on the cap, jump in the driver's side and pull away from the kerb and back on to the left-hand side of the road.

The approaching cop car slowed as it came closer, which was when Voorhess heard groaning coming from the seat beside him. Out of the corner of his eye he saw the young, pallid-faced cop lean forward in his seat, blood pouring down his face, making a keening sound, and trying to lift an arm, clearly some distance away from being dead.

Slamming his arm into the injured officer's chest and knocking him back in the seat, Voorhess nodded towards the other cops as the two cars passed each other, blocking the view of their injured colleague as he accelerated down the road.

Only when he'd put a bit of distance between them did he let go of the young cop, who was wriggling and gasping in his seat like a zombie from a cheap horror film. Slowing the car, Voorhess pulled the .22 free, shoved it against the cop's temple and pulled the trigger.

Which was the moment the radio crackled into life, the caller asking for the current location of the car Voorhess was driving.

'Bravo Four, do you copy?' asked an anxious male voice. 'We have just heard gunshots. Bravo Four. Please respond. Over.'

With a sigh, Voorhess pulled the unit free from its stand and threw it out of the window, wondering if he was ever going to get out of this Godforsaken city in one piece.

Fifty-eight

20.06

The squad cars were arriving in force now, blocking the road at both ends. The problem was, thought Tina ruefully, they were far too late. It had been at least ten minutes since the black Shogun had disappeared into the night, and so far it hadn't been located, even though dozens of police vehicles and a helicopter had now joined the search, and every minute that passed meant their terrorist was getting further and further away.

Initial reports from Control suggested that there were as many as fifty casualties from the strike on the Shard, including at least two MPs and a well-known TV reporter, but so far there was no word on how many of them were fatalities.

Tina and Bolt were now coordinating the evacuation of all the properties within a fifty-yard radius of the house from where the missile had been fired, in case there were further suspects inside.

'The house belongs to a Mr Azim Butt,' Tina told Bolt as she finished leading a couple and their two young children beyond the thin strip of scene-of-crime tape that acted as the edge of their cordon. 'Thirty-one years old, and keeps himself to himself. According to the neighbours, he's lived here for about eighteen months. They reckon he's got a girlfriend who's often here too.'

Bolt nodded. 'That tallies with what Control have found out about him. He owns a couple of businesses supplying imported goods to the restaurant and retail trades. Makes OK money, but he's got a three-hundred-grand mortgage on the house. He's got no criminal record, and his name doesn't come up on any watchlists, but he *is* a Muslim.'

'He definitely wasn't the man I saw drive out in the Shogun. The man I saw was white, early or possibly mid-forties, weather-beaten features. Big build too, whereas Mr Butt is supposedly only a little guy.'

'So, who the hell is he?' Bolt frowned, the lines on his face looking more pronounced than Tina could remember. He still looked shaken up by everything that had happened, and she could tell that he was trying hard not to show it.

'Whoever he is, he's got to be someone with a military background. You need to be trained to fire a Stinger. Not any idiot can do it. And he didn't panic when we tried to intercept him either.'

'We'll get him,' said Bolt emphatically. 'He won't

get far with half the Met on his back.'

Tina resisted saying that he'd managed pretty well so far. Instead, she turned and walked back through the cordon to carry on helping with the evacuation. Fox had claimed the people behind Islamic Command were homegrown extremists, which would explain why the man leaving the property was white. And they'd already established a link between Fox and Islamic Command via Jetmir Brozi. But she still felt they were missing something. And she wanted to know where the hell the owner, Mr Butt, was.

A uniformed cop was approaching the suspect property, completely against all the rules. As Tina watched, he leaned down and peered in through the letterbox.

'Hey, get back from there,' she called to him, knowing it was hypocritical of her to criticize a fellow cop for breaking the rules, when she'd made a career out of it, but knowing too that the terrorists had left a booby-trapped bomb for the police earlier, and might easily have done so again. 'No one's going in there until bomb disposal arrive.'

The cop turned back to her, his expression anxious. 'But there's someone in there, and he's crying out for help.'

'It doesn't matter,' said Tina, walking down the drive and grabbing him by the arm. 'We've got to be really careful here. It could be a trap.'

'He sounds like he's in trouble, ma'am.'

'OK, but get back.'

She looked over to where Mike Bolt was now talking to a group of CO19 officers who'd just arrived on the scene, then bent down and opened the letterbox.

She heard it immediately: the faint sound of a man calling out from somewhere within the house, the fear in his voice obvious.

'This is the police,' she called out. 'Is that Mr Butt?'

He didn't answer so she repeated herself, louder this time.

There was a pause, and then he shouted back, 'Yes. You've got to help me. I'm trapped.'

'I hear you. We'll be with you very soon.'

She stood up and waved at Bolt to get his attention.

Voorhess pulled up to the entrance of the park, and parked the police car against the fence in the shelter of some trees where it would be difficult to see it from the road. Sirens were still blaring in all directions but he no longer took any notice of them. Instead, he grabbed his holdall from the trunk, and climbed over the fence and into the park. He moved swiftly in the darkness towards the other side, forcing himself to stay calm, even though he felt more than ever like a hunted animal.

He needed to cause a diversion by detonating the bomb at Mr Butt's house. The police would be gathered round it now, making their final preparations for entry, and he was sure to catch a few of them with the explosion. With any luck, he'd also hit the woman who'd seen him.

He pulled the mobile from his pocket and speed-dialled the number of the phone attached to the battery pack inside the bomb, wondering if he'd be able to hear the dull thud of the explosion from where he was now.

'What the hell are you doing? Get back from there!'

Bolt marched towards Tina, waving her away from Butt's front door, thinking that she was like a naughty schoolkid sometimes, always delving into places where she shouldn't be going. He could feel his legs shaking beneath him as he walked. He felt dizzy, and was still having difficulty coming to terms with the fact that he'd almost been crushed to death only a few minutes earlier. Above the buildings in the distance, he could see the thick black plume of smoke pumping out of the upper floors of the Shard into the night sky – a brutal reminder of the attack he hadn't prevented. If only he'd reacted quicker, if only he'd kept a better eye on Jones, and had him followed to the meeting where they'd got the missile. If only he'd worked harder these past few months to catch the people behind the Stanhope siege, then he might not be here. But he'd failed. It was as simple as that, and he only had himself to blame.

'Mr Butt's inside,' said Tina, coming forward to

meet him. 'He's calling out saying he's trapped, and he sounds scared.'

'Just get back from there, and keep going with the evacuation. Bomb disposal are on the way. It's best just to leave it to them now.'

She nodded and turned away, while Bolt looked up at the house. If Butt was involved in the attack, the only reason he'd still be inside would be to ambush them, presumably in some kind of suicide attack when they broke into his house. Yet, how was he connected to Cain and Cecil Boorman? The whole thing didn't make sense.

The explosion that ripped through the first floor of the house in a single blinding roar sent Bolt flying backwards and tumbling over the low wall separating the front of the property from the pavement. He remembered feeling a wave of hot air rush over him, followed by the sound of pieces of masonry falling around him with strangely dull thuds – all in the space of half a second. And then he felt a sharp, sudden pain, and the world seemed to fade out.

Fifty-nine

20.12

Voorhess heard the faint sound of the bomb blast, but took no notice as he ran through the darkness of the park, keeping to the single line of trees that ran alongside the main path, using them for camouflage. In his youth, he'd been a good middle- to long-distance runner, having always been too big to be a sprinter, and he still jogged four times a week round the rugged coastal paths of the Cape close to where he lived. As a result, he was able to keep his tiredness in check. He'd always found that running calmed him, and allowed him to think. But now, for the first time in a long time, he felt the pressure of what was going on around him.

A police helicopter had already passed close to the edge of the park. If it came directly over, which it would do soon enough, its heat-sensing equipment would locate him, and once he was in its sights it would be locked on to him until he was caught. He had to get back among other people where he'd be just one of many heat sources. It was his only option, because he was terrified of small spaces. Of being trapped. Prison represented a worse fate for him than death itself. At least death was quick. Years held in a cell seemed to him to be the most barbaric form of torture.

He decided then that he wouldn't be taken alive.

He heard the helicopter turning somewhere behind him, and then the sound of its rotors drawing closer. The southern boundary of the park was barely thirty yards away, and he could see the lights of a car driving past on the other side. He redoubled his pace, sprinting with every last scrap of energy he had.

The gate was locked but he vaulted straight over it. The helicopter was getting closer now. Soon it would pick up his heat source and that would be it. The end.

Twenty yards to his right, a small hatchback car was stopped at a red light, the heavy beat of mindless music booming out from inside. Two other cars were stopped at the lights on the other side, all waiting for a young couple to cross the road. The hatchback was revving its engine impatiently as Voorhess slowed down and jogged over to the passenger door, trying to look as casual as possible, banking that on an old car like this the door would be unlocked. The lights started flashing orange, just as the helicopter came hurtling over the park, and Voorhess yanked open the door and jumped unceremoniously inside, before the driver had a chance to pull away.

The driver – young, white and pimply – stared at Voorhess with his mouth hanging open.

'Drive,' growled Voorhess, producing the .22 and shoving it in the kid's ribs.

The kid stared at the gun, made a pathetic mewing noise, then did exactly what he was told as the helicopter passed overhead, loud and close.

Sixty

20.13

The whole world sounded muffled to Tina, as if someone had stuffed her ears full of cotton wool. She got to her feet unsteadily and looked around. Everyone seemed to be moving in slow motion, their voices sounding distant and alien as they hurried towards her.

It took her a few seconds to de-scramble her senses and work out what had happened. The bomb blast had come as she'd been crossing the road, its force, and her own instincts, sending her sprawling across the concrete. She looked back to see the first floor of Azim Butt's house completely ablaze, with gouts of flame and thick plumes of smoke pouring out of the blackened window frames. Chunks of masonry of varying sizes, from half bricks to foot-square lumps, some on fire, dotted the road in front of the building, and Tina was immediately relieved she hadn't been hit by one of them.

And then, as her eyes focused on the scene, she saw a body in front of the garden wall.

Shit. Mike.

Feeling a rush of panic, Tina ran over to where he lay and knelt down beside him. His eyes were closed and there was a cut on the back of his head that was leaking blood, but it was difficult to tell how deep it was. She called his name, hardly able to hear the sound of her own voice, still partially deafened by the blast, terrified that something had happened to him, and appreciating at the same time the depth of her feelings for him.

Then his eyes opened and he stared up at her and she had this sudden urge to lean down and kiss him.

'Are you all right?' she asked, trying hard to keep the air of desperation out of her voice.

'I think so.'

He started to get up, but his legs went from under him and he stumbled into Tina, almost knocking her over.

'It's all right, I've got you,' she said, just about managing to hold him up.

Turning round, she shouted for help, and a group of CO19 officers ran over, followed closely by two paramedics with a stretcher.

'Christ, my head hurts,' said Bolt as he was lifted on to the stretcher by the assembled group.

'Don't worry,' said one of the paramedics, 'we'll have you in the hospital in no time.'

Bolt shook his head, squinting against the pain as they carried him away from the blazing building. 'No way. Treat me here. I haven't got time to go to hospital.'

'I'd do as she says, Mike,' said Tina, who was walking alongside the stretcher, wanting to hold his hand, but knowing it wouldn't be right. He didn't look good, though.

'I'm OK,' he said, trying to sit up, but not quite making it.

The paramedic started to say something else but Bolt cut her off by leaning over the side of the stretcher and throwing up, only just missing Tina's feet.

At that moment, his mobile rang inside his jacket. He looked up at Tina, frowning as he tried hard to focus. 'Can you answer my phone?'

She nodded, reached inside his jacket and pulled it out, as the paramedics put him into the back of the ambulance.

'Mike Bolt's phone. Tina Boyd speaking.'

'This is Commander Ingrams, CTC Control. What's happening down there?'

Tina told him about the booby-trap bomb.

'How bad's Mike hurt?' asked Ingrams, sounding genuinely concerned.

'I think he's concussed, but he's conscious and fairly lucid. They've just put him in an ambulance. Have we managed to locate the suspect in the Shogun yet?'

'No. We're throwing a huge security cordon round the whole area, but there's no sign of him.' Ingrams exhaled loudly. 'And we've got another problem too. There's a major riot at the prison where they're holding William Garrett. One wing's been completely taken over by the prisoners and now there's a disturbance in a second one.'

Tina thought back to the conversation she'd had with the prison officer, Thomson. How he'd described the prison as a tinderbox, a place that only functioned because the prisoners allowed it to. And now it seemed they'd decided to stop cooperating.

'Is Fox OK?' she asked.

'It was his wing it started in, but they managed to get him out. Apparently there was a second attempt on his life. It failed and he's unhurt, but it sounds like he was lucky.'

'He told me this would happen. It's not a coincidence.'

'I know it's not,' said Ingrams. 'I understand Garrett told you he'd name the people involved today if he was moved to a safehouse, and offered some kind of deal.'

'That's the gist of it, yes.'

'We're in the process of organizing his move to a safehouse right now, but as you can imagine, it's a very sensitive issue, particularly in light of what's happened today. I want you to stay by your phone tonight because if he's moved, I want you to talk to him again. You've clearly developed some kind of rapport.'

'Thank you, sir.'

'There's something else as well. We've just sent two detectives to the pub where they were meant to meet Mike's informant, but he wasn't there. We need to debrief the informant urgently, as I understand he was the person who told us about the missile. Yet no one seems to have any contact details for him.'

'I'll speak to Mike now.'

Tina ended the call, and looked over the growing throng of emergency services vehicles towards where the Shard stood, dominating the skyline, its austere beauty brutally violated by what had just happened.

The people responsible had won the battle, but she was as determined as she'd ever been that they weren't going to win this particular war.

Sixty-one

20.22

On the TV in the poky front room of my flat, the Shard was burning, but I couldn't bring myself to look at it. I couldn't bring myself to switch channels either. So there it was: a constant reminder of everything I'd done this afternoon.

I took a last slug of the beer and put down the bottle, feeling like a condemned man.

I'd killed a man in cold blood. Shot him while he begged for mercy. I'd killed in cold blood before, back in Afghanistan – two Taliban wounded in a firefight with our patrol whom we could easily have taken alive. I'd stood above them, like I'd stood above Dav, and emptied more than a dozen rounds into each of them in turn. Afterwards I'd felt guilty. I still do. They might have been trying to kill me but, in the end, it was we who were in their country, and what I'd done was barbaric.

The difference was, those killings had been carried out in a dusty, hot war zone thousands of miles from home, and away from the prying eyes of the media.

Today's bloodshed had been right on my doorstep.

So, Bolt and his colleagues hadn't stopped the terrorists' third attack. Like most other people, I hadn't had a clue that the Shard was having an official opening-night party tonight, and it was difficult to believe that it would still have gone ahead after the earlier bomb attacks. Clearly, it was part of the government's strategy of carrying on as normal in the face of the terrorist threat. If so, it hadn't worked.

Cain had got exactly what he wanted, and what he'd predicted – chaos and terror. And with this morning's coffee shop bomber now identified as a thirty-one-year-old Muslim man, it looked like Islamic fundamentalists were going to get the blame. Cain was probably toasting his success right now.

That was unless, of course, the police had already tracked him down using the GPS unit I'd planted. If so, he might actually be under arrest, along with Cecil. I was just going to have to wait to find out.

The huge problem I had was that both men could implicate me in the slaughter at the scrapyard, and Dav's murder, if they chose to testify against me in a court of law. I could go back down for years this time, and never see Gina or Maddie again. It was a bastard of a position to be in. My plan, as much as I had one, was to tell the detectives from CTC that Cain and

Cecil had gone to the meeting without me, and had then shown me the missile at a neutral location, and hope for the best. It wasn't exactly foolproof, but right now I didn't have anything else.

I needed to speak to Bolt to tell him I was at home. There was no point putting off my interrogation any longer, and with a couple of beers inside me, I felt fortified enough to deal with it.

But as I got to my feet, looking round for the phone, the doorbell rang.

I thought about not answering it, but the noise from the TV made it obvious I was in. I went over to the window and pulled back the curtain a few inches.

Cecil stood on my doorstep – small and wiry, bouncing on his feet against the cold – his back to the small communal garden. He gave me a quick wave and nod, motioning for me to open the door. He'd changed from earlier, and was wearing a bomber jacket and jeans, the coat zipped up against the cold.

I didn't like him turning up at my flat out of the blue. It made me uneasy. But he'd seen me now, so to ignore him would arouse suspicion.

'What do you want?' I called through the glass. 'I thought I told you I wanted to be left alone.'

Cecil pulled a face. 'What is this?' he called back, his voice muffled. 'You're going to leave me out here in the cold? We need to talk.'

It was pitch black outside. My flat was on the ground floor, one of four in an old detached house cut off from the road by a high hedge. It was a secluded spot. Too secluded. The old lady directly above me was deaf as a post; the other neighbours were commuters who were out most of the time.

'Come on, what the hell is this, Jones?' Cecil called again, clearly irritated now.

Alarm bells were sounding in my head. I decided then that, old friend or not, I wasn't going to let him in.

A shadow suddenly appeared behind the window to my right, obscured by the curtain, and before I could react Cain was standing in front of me, his pale face ghostly in the moonlight, the vein throbbing obscenely on his cheek. He was holding a pistol with a suppressor attached, the end of the barrel touching the glass.

'Pass the front-door keys through the window, Jones,' he said, loudly and firmly.

'What the hell's going on?' I demanded, putting just the right amount of indignation in my voice, knowing that I was too late to make a move.

Cecil had also brought a pistol with suppressor attached out from beneath his bomber jacket, and I could see that his eyes were alive with anger.

'You've got questions to answer,' announced Cain. 'About who exactly you work for.'

And I knew then that they'd found out about me. Which meant I no longer had to worry about what I said to the police.

Because I was already a dead man.

'I've got a home address for the informant, Richard Burnham-Jones,' said Tina into the phone, shouting to be heard above a helicopter flying overhead, as she walked further down the road away from all the activity surrounding Azim Butt's house. She read out the address, then waited while Commander Ingrams dictated it to someone next to him.

'Right, we'll get officers round there now,' said Ingrams. 'In the meantime, we have authority to move Prisoner Garrett. There's a park two hundred yards south of where you are. A helicopter's going to pick you up there in five minutes and take you up to the prison to sign him out. We're setting up a safe-house about eight miles from the prison. I want you to travel with Garrett and the escort to the safehouse by road.'

'Why not by helicopter?'

'It's too risky. We haven't picked up the Stinger shooter yet. If there are any more Stingers in circulation they could be used against a helicopter, and we really can't afford to lose Garrett.' He paused. 'You're to tell him that if he gives you the full names of everyone involved in the attacks today, and all those involved in the Stanhope siege, he'll be kept in a safehouse until the trial, and we will ask the trial judge to strongly consider his cooperation when passing sentence. In other words, he won't serve a life-term sentence.'

'Are we allowed to do all that, sir?' asked Tina. The idea of giving Fox all he'd asked for, with the Shard still burning barely half a mile from where she stood, stuck in her throat. It wasn't right.

'We're effectively in a state of emergency here, DC Boyd. The attacks today, particularly the last one on the Shard, make the government look weak, and they can't have that. If Garrett is the key – and it looks like he may well be – we have to make him talk. We can't torture him, although God knows there are plenty of people here who would love to do it, so this is the only way. Tell him this, too. If he doesn't talk, if he holds out for a deal that's never going to happen, then he'll be transferred to Belmarsh by car later tonight, held in solitary confinement until his trial, and if necessary for the next fifty years. We're not pussyfooting around here, DC Boyd. You need to make sure he knows that.'

'I'll make sure he knows,' said Tina coldly. 'And I'll make sure he talks.'

Sixty-two

20.24

I retreated down the hall and into the kitchen at the back of the flat, hands in the air, as Cecil walked towards me, gun outstretched. Behind him, Cain quietly closed the front door.

'I don't work for anyone,' I said, still indignant. 'I'd have thought that was pretty obvious after what happened today. I killed a man. And it wasn't self-defence. Or have you forgotten about that?'

It was clear that Cecil hadn't. A flash of doubt crossed his face as I spoke, giving me a chink of hope, although it was quickly counter-balanced by the merciless gleam in Cain's eyes.

I stopped in the middle of the kitchen, my back to the window, and kept talking, knowing it was my best chance of staying alive. 'So who the hell am I meant to be working for?'

Cain and Cecil stopped a few feet in front of me.

Cecil kept the gun pointed at my chest, while Cain kept his gun down by his side as he addressed me like a judge passing sentence. 'The police knew about the Stinger attack before it happened. Our operative was almost caught. And, according to the news reports, the people inside the Shard had received a warning before the missile was fired.'

'How the hell was I meant to have done that? I don't even know who your operative was. Or what happened to the Stinger after you dropped us off.' My tone remained confrontational, but inside I was reeling. The evidence against me was overwhelming, and I cursed myself for coming back here.

'There was a bug in my car,' continued Cain. 'It led the police to me. It could only have been planted by you. That car was clean when I picked you up. I'd never used it before, and if it had been bugged before we went to the scrapyard then we would have been arrested as soon as the shooting started. But we weren't. Which meant it was planted afterwards. So tell us who you're working for, and I promise we'll make it quick.'

'How many times do I have to tell you? I'm not working for anyone. No police force or government agency's going to let me get away with armed robbery or murder, are they? And I've committed both today. And why would I want to work for the authorities after what they've done to me? Come on, Cecil,' I said, knowing he was the weak link, 'you've served with me. You know what I'm like.'

'He might be telling the truth, sir,'. said Cecil uncertainly, still keeping the gun pointed firmly at my chest.

'He's not,' Cain told him, before addressing me again. 'You're working for someone, Jones, otherwise you wouldn't have had access to a bug. And I'm guessing you got cold feet when you saw the Stinger. I told you it would have been better if you hadn't looked in the box.'

'Listen, there's no way—'

'Shut the fuck up!' he snapped, his words cutting through the air like a shard of glass. He turned to Cecil. 'He's obviously not going to talk, and we haven't got time to hang around. Finish it.'

'Don't do it, Cecil. I'm your friend.'

Cain grunted dismissively. 'You're a fool, Jones. That's what you are. You had a chance to become one of us, and you threw it away. Finish it, Cecil. For The Brotherhood.'

I stared at my old army colleague, willing him to believe me, fully aware that this was my last chance.

But it was slipping away.

Cecil's expression hardened. In the end, he was a soldier through and through. And a soldier obeys orders. 'Turn round, Jones,' he said, his harsh Belfast accent amplified in the stillness of the room. The accent of my executioner.

It was over.

I turned round.

Which was when I noticed the kitchen window was slightly ajar, and I remembered opening it earlier to let in some fresh air. In the next second my hand shot out and grabbed a frying pan sitting on the kitchen top, and I ducked suddenly, flinging the pan back in the direction of Cecil.

Even with the suppressors, the shots seemed loud in the confines of the room as I took a running jump at the window, adrenalin coursing through me, and leapt through it as if I was doing a bomb into a swimming pool, sending it flying open with a bang, before landing on the gravel of the residents' car park at the rear of the building.

I rolled over and jumped to my feet, diving behind one of the cars as Cecil appeared at the window and fired a shot at me, just missing my foot. I heard Cain saying something from behind him but couldn't make out what it was, and then Cecil disappeared. A couple of seconds later I heard my front door opening and shutting again, and I knew they were going to come round to cut off my escape.

Knowing I had only seconds to get out on the street and to safety, I got to my feet again.

Which was when all my strength seemed to sap out of me and I realized I'd been hit. I looked down. There was a hole in my gut and another in my chest, both of them pumping blood on to my check shirt – a gift from Gina a couple of Christmases ago. I thought of her then, and Maddie, and knew I had to survive this. For their sakes.

I staggered across the car park, clutching at my wounds, trying to stop the bleeding. But I was going too slowly to reach the street in time. Cain and Cecil would be out here any second and I'd be a sitting duck. I made a snap decision and dived into the bushes that bordered the property, wriggling as far as I could inside, wincing against the pain that was beginning to envelop me.

Just in time. Almost immediately, Cain and Cecil appeared round the side of the house, holding their guns and looking round urgently, only ten yards away.

'He can't be far,' hissed Cain. 'I hit him at least once, and you hit him too. Look, there's blood on the gravel.' He pointed to where I'd originally taken shelter behind the parked car, and I prayed one of my neighbours had heard the commotion and called the police. In the flat above, I could hear the old lady's TV blaring away, drowning everything else out.

I held my breath as Cain approached the bushes, only a couple of yards away now, and bent down, pulling some of the foliage aside with the gun. I stayed absolutely still, knowing that if I made even the tiniest move he'd discover me. My lungs felt close to bursting and all the time I could feel the blood leaking out of me into the earth.

And then there was the sound of tyres on gravel

and the glare of headlights as a car pulled into the car park.

I used the noise to exhale and drag in another lungful of air, peering through the gaps in the bushes as the car parked between two others. It was a BMW, and I recognized it straight away as belonging to the guy on the top floor, a brash City worker called Rupert who was a couple of years younger than me and who never bothered to say hello.

As he got out of the car, briefcase in hand, he looked accusingly towards Cecil and Cain, who'd both hidden their guns. 'Can I help you, gentlemen?' he asked, staring them down. He looked confident and at ease, clearly not expecting trouble, and I wanted to shout out to him to jump back in the car and reverse out of there.

But I didn't say a word as Cain walked towards him, bringing round the gun from behind his back. 'No,' he said simply, and shot Rupert twice in the chest, waiting as his victim fell against the car with a gasp and slid down it, before landing in a heap on the gravel. He then put a third bullet in his head before walking back in the direction of the bushes.

'We need to hurry,' he snapped at Cecil. 'Keep looking for him.'

I held my breath again as Cain stopped less than half a yard from where I was lying and began poking inside the foliage with the gun.

He was going to see me any second.

'Jesus, where the fuck is he?' I heard Cecil curse from a few yards further up. 'He's got to be somewhere.'

At that moment, Cain's face appeared in the bushes just above my head, and I wondered in that instant if he could smell my blood. All he had to do was look down and I was finished.

I clenched my teeth, preparing to die.

Outside on the street, a car slowed down.

And then I heard something bleep loudly, and Cain's head disappeared.

He moved away from the bushes, pulling a mobile phone from his pocket and staring down at the screen. 'We need to move.' He paused, then said something that completely threw me. 'Fox is going to be en route at any moment.'

Fox. The only surviving terrorist from the Stanhope siege. What the hell did Cain mean?

'But we've got to find Jones,' said Cecil anxiously. 'We can't leave him. He's a witness.'

But Cain was having none of it. 'Even if he's still alive, there's nothing he can do to us. He's in this as much as we are. Come on.'

And with that, they turned and walked away across the gravel, quickly disappearing from view.

I was still alive. But only just.

Sixty-three

20.50

Fox sat on the bunk smoking a cigarette and listening to the faint sounds of violence drifting through the prison like music to his ears.

The cell they'd put him in didn't have a TV so he could no longer see what was happening in the outside world, but it didn't matter. He knew it would be bedlam out there as the government tried to show they were in control of a situation when they quite clearly weren't. He smiled. It felt good to experience power again. He knew the police were desperate for any information he could give them – all the more so now that the name he'd given Tina Boyd had produced such dramatic results. But that was the reason he'd chosen Tina. Unlike so many coppers these days, she got things done

Fox had always been a patient person. As a child he'd been able to sit for hours fishing with his father at the lake near their home, knowing that if he waited long enough, a trout would bite, because in the end one always did. It was a trait that had served him well during the long monotonous days he'd spent in prison.

But as he sat there now, he was finding it hard to stay calm. All his months of planning rested on what would happen in the next few hours. There was still so much that could go wrong. And in his heart, he knew that this was his one opportunity. He'd played all his cards. Now he would have to wait and see whether they trumped everyone else's or not.

In his office, Governor Jeremy Goodman stared at the phone on his desk, listening to its high-pitched ringing. At the still very productive age of sixty-four he was actively considering retirement for the first time in his life. He'd worked in the prison system for more than thirty years, the last ten of which had been spent running Westmoor, and he prided himself on the safe, peaceful environment he'd fostered for the prisoners during that time. And now, suddenly, all his good work was being destroyed, as the prisoners repaid his work with a destructive and ultimately pointless riot, which had now spread to two of the prison's wings.

Knowing he could avoid it no longer, he picked up the phone. The person at the other end was the Home Office minister Alan Harris, an irritating little man with a 'hang 'em and flog 'em' approach to criminal behaviour which was entirely unsuited to a modern, progressive society.

After a cursory attempt at pleasantries, Harris got straight down to business. 'We're moving Prisoner William Garrett,' he said in a nasal voice that grated on Goodman every time he heard it.

'On whose authority?'

'The Prime Minister's. The paperwork should already have arrived in your email account. An armed police escort with copies of the paperwork will be arriving at the prison in the next fifteen minutes.'

'Are you sure about this, Minister? Prisoner Garrett is perfectly safe here. He's in protective custody, well away from the disturbance, which we've contained in two wings. We also have Tornado Teams and riot police en route, the first of which should be here any minute.'

'But you've also had two attempts on Garrett's life, Governor, and the last one was less than an hour ago. I'm sorry, but whatever you may think, your facility, for all its *progressive* policies, is simply not secure enough. And we can't afford to lose this prisoner.'

Goodman bristled at the way he was being spoken to by a jumped-up little twit like Harris who was obviously taking real pleasure out of the situation, even though it was clear that with three attacks in London in one day he was hardly on top of things either.

'Prisoner Garrett will be ready,' he said curtly, and ended the call without waiting for a reply.

'Everything all right, sir?' asked Officer Thomson, the most senior of the prison officers on duty, as Goodman put down the receiver. Thomson was stood to attention, with his hands behind his back, looking every inch the military man he'd once been.

Goodman sighed. 'Prisoner Garrett is being removed. You need to go and get him ready. And make sure you give him a full body search. I don't trust him an inch.'

Thomson frowned. 'Where are they taking him, sir?'

'I don't know. And to be perfectly frank, I don't care. He's someone else's problem now.'

Sixty-four

20.55

Mike Bolt's head hurt like hell, but he was feeling a lot better than he had three-quarters of an hour earlier when he'd been hit by whatever it was he'd been hit by.

Since then he'd been sick twice, and ordered to go to hospital by the doctor who'd treated him at the scene, but he'd steadfastly refused. While he could still stand, he wanted to be involved, which was exactly what he was saying now to Commander Ingrams as he paced the street with the phone pushed against the bandage that had been wrapped round his head. 'I've worked this case from the beginning. I've been involved in everything all day. And the fact is, I don't want to stop now.' He was at a crossroads a hundred yards from Azim Butt's ruined townhouse, the sound of it burning still clearly audible. To his left, the Shard stood like a tall, wounded giant breathing smoke and fire, a symbol of his failure.

'Listen, Mike,' said Ingrams in a weary voice that told Bolt he'd already made up his mind, 'we really appreciate all your efforts, and your bravery today, but there's nothing more you can do.'

'Have we caught the shooter yet?'

'No. And we haven't brought in Cecil Boorman yet either. Or the man he's supposed to be working for, Cain.'

'So there's still plenty to do.'

'It's in hand, Mike.'

'You need to talk to Jones. He might be able to help.'

'We would do, but we can't find him. We sent two officers round to his home address, and he wasn't answering the door.'

Bolt tensed. This wasn't good. 'Did they try to get inside?'

'The door was locked and we haven't got a warrant to break it down. I've had to pull the officers away for other duties.'

'Let me go up there. He might be back now. Come on, sir. It's not as if I'm on my deathbed.'

'Sorry, Mike. According to the doctor, you've got concussion. I can't let you carry on. You need to get to a hospital straight away.'

Knowing he wasn't going to win this particular battle, Bolt conceded defeat and ended the call.

He took a deep breath, shivering against the cold. Ingrams and the doctor were right. He needed to go to hospital. But he'd always been a stubborn man, and fiercely competitive too. Tina had been in the firing line just as much as him today, and yet she was the one taking Fox to the safehouse. He was also worried about Jones. There was no reason for him suddenly to go AWOL. Two hours ago he'd been fully prepared to make a statement, and had promised to wait at the pub for the guys from CTC to pick him up. Which meant that either something bad had happened to him or, more likely, he'd turn up again soon.

Bolt might have been officially off duty, but that didn't mean he couldn't go and have a look for him. After all, he was the one who'd got Jones involved in all this in the first place. Maybe he'd stop in at a hospital afterwards if his headache failed to dissipate.

Having made the decision to carry on, and immediately feeling better for it, he walked back up towards the police cordon. It was time to retrieve Islington nick's battered Ford Focus and make himself useful once again.

Sixty-five

21.05

When the knock on the cell door came, Fox had to resist smiling.

'Prisoner 407886,' came the barked command, 'stand up and show yourself, and keep your hands where we can see them.'

Fox got off the bunk and stood a few feet in front of the door, holding up his hands in a gesture of supplication as the guard peered through the inspection hatch. A second later the door was unlocked and four screws stood there, headed by Officer Thomson. All the guards were wearing plastic gloves, which could only mean one thing.

'This looks ominous,' said Fox, as the screws came inside.

'You know the drill, Mr Garrett,' said Thomson. 'Clothes off. We're going to give you a full body search.'

'Any particular reason why?'

'I don't have to give you a fucking reason, Mr Garrett, but since you ask, you're being transferred with immediate effect, and we're making sure you don't take anything that doesn't belong to you.'

'I have to say, I'll feel a lot safer being out of here, sir. For some reason, the other prisoners don't seem to like me. Sounds like they don't like you much either.' He nodded in the direction of the corridor where the sounds of shouting, yelping and banging as the prisoners vented their frustrations were clearly audible.

'I don't know what your game is, Garrett,' hissed Thomson, coming close, 'but whatever it is, remember this: you can be as cocky as you like, but you're never going to taste freedom for as long as you live. And I'll tell you something else. I hope you live a long fucking time.'

Fox didn't say anything. Thomson's words reeked of frustration. In the end, he was a small fish trapped in exactly the same pond as the men he was guarding. All he had were empty threats, and both of them knew it.

The search was thorough and invasive, just as it was supposed to be. Fox stood there and took it in cool silence, ignoring the jibes about how much he enjoyed having fingers rammed up his arse, ignoring the taste of those fingers then being deliberately shoved into his mouth, zoning out of the whole experience by staring unblinkingly at the wall and thinking of what lay ahead of him: the heat and the sunshine, and the sound of waves lapping gently on some distant shore.

It was all over in a couple of minutes and they didn't find anything. Though they tried to hide it, the guards were clearly in a hurry and Fox had hardly got the last of his clothes on before he was pushed up face first against the cell door and his hands cuffed roughly behind his back.

'Come on, you fuck,' said Thomson, grabbing him by the collar and almost lifting him off his feet as he hauled him out of the cell. It was as if he was trying to get as much unpleasantness in as possible while he still had the chance.

Let him, thought Fox. In the end, Thomson was just like everyone else who chose to play by the rules. Impotent. He was probably hoping that Fox would snap and assault him, so that he'd have the justification to give him the kicking he'd doubtless been wanting to ever since the day Fox had first arrived. But there was no way Fox was going to give him the pleasure, and he didn't resist as he was marched down the corridor towards the front of the main building.

En route, they passed a long line of black-clad, helmeted officers heading the other way. This was the Tornado Team, the Prison Service's equivalent of riot police, who were always sent in to deal with prison disturbances. Fox had never seen them before. Westmoor had been remarkably peaceful during his stay, but these guys looked suitably mean and moody behind their flame-retardant masks, and Fox had little doubt that they'd quell the trouble easily enough. Most of the prisoners had little stomach for a fight, not when there was real opposition. But it didn't matter. The violence had achieved what it was supposed to, and now, whatever Officer Thomson might have thought, Fox was going to get his first taste of life outside the prison gates for fifteen months.

There was still much that could go wrong but he felt a real excitement as he was led through various barred doors to the prison's main reception area, and saw Tina Boyd waiting there, flanked by two armed cops carrying MP5s.

This was it. He was finally on his way.

Sixty-six

21.13

Tina signed the last of the papers giving her custody of Fox and handed them back to the worried-looking prison officer behind the reception desk. There was a definite tension in the air. The riot might not have been audible from where Tina was standing, but its effects were etched on the features of all the prison staff.

She felt the fear as much as anybody. She'd seen more than her fair share of destruction today. On her way here in the helicopter she'd had to pass the burning Shard, its base surrounded by emergency services vehicles, and as they'd come in to land a large fire in one of the prison's wings had been clearly visible. It reminded her of the riots of August 2011 as they'd spread across London and the rest of the country like wildfire. It had seemed then as if society was on the verge of complete collapse. In a way, it felt like that now.

But Tina had always been a fighter. Rather than letting the fear overwhelm her, she used it to keep her steadily building exhaustion at bay. She might not have been feeling top of her game but there was no way she was going to show Fox that as he stopped in front of her, flanked by his prison escort.

'Hello, Miss Boyd,' he said, keeping his tone neutral.

'Hello, Mr Garrett,' she answered curtly, once again struck by how insignificant he looked. Barely an inch taller than her, and probably no more than eleven stone at most, his thinning hair making him appear prematurely middle-aged, he stood there with shoulders slumped and his head bent forward. But she knew it was an act. Fox was a dangerous killer, however much he tried to hide it. 'Are you ready?'

'Whenever you are.'

Tina nodded to the prison officer who'd escorted her to the interview with Fox on her first visit, ten hours and a whole lifetime ago. Thomson, she thought his name was. 'Thanks, we'll take him from here.'

'He's all yours,' said Thomson, giving Fox a hard shove in the back. 'He's been given a full body search, but I'd watch him if I were you. He's a slippery bastard.'

'Can I ask a favour, Miss Boyd?' said Fox, as Tina led him by the arm out of the main doors and on to the front steps of the prison, where two police cars and a van waited to take him away. 'Do you mind if I wear the cuffs in front of me rather than behind? They're making the stitches on my arm rub in this position.'

Tina met his eyes. There was none of the cockiness that he'd exhibited earlier, and his request seemed a genuine one, but she wasn't fooled. 'I'm afraid not.' She gave his arm a tug and carried on down the steps.

'That's not getting us off to a very good start.'

'Give me the names of everyone involved in today's attacks and I'll think about it.'

'If I do that, you'll just march me straight back in there. I need some leverage, and there's no way I'm telling you anything until I've got it in writing that you're keeping me in the safehouse until my trial.'

'Then you're going to have to travel in some discomfort.'

'Let's compromise,' said Fox as they stopped next to the van where four more armed officers waited. 'I'll give you one name – the name of someone who was one hundred per cent involved today. Just to show willing. And then you show me a little respect by letting me travel with my hands cuffed in the front. Look at all these people escorting me. It's not as if I can do anything anyway.'

Tina thought about it. There were twelve armed officers in the convoy, plus herself. It was more than enough to keep Fox on a tight leash. And if she was honest with herself, she saw an opportunity to look good by squeezing out a second name before the real questioning had even begun.

'Go on then. Give me a name.'

'Cecil Boorman. Ex-soldier. Very reliable. He should have been involved at the Stanhope, but he had salmonella of all things. He'll be part of this too, although not at a senior level. Cecil's just a grunt.'

Tina remembered Bolt telling her earlier that Boorman was the man his informant had been trying to get close to. 'And you've got evidence to back this up?'

'Plenty.'

Tina sighed. Agreeing to Fox's request went against all her instincts, but he'd now given her two useful names – more than anyone else had done.

'OK,' she said. 'Let's do it.'

Sixty-seven

21.20

The key is to stay conscious. If you shut your eyes, even if it's just for one moment, then that's it. You're dead. That's why the medics keep talking to you while they wait for help. Because they know it's the only way they're going to keep you alive.

But when there's no one there to talk to you, it's hard. Jesus, it's hard.

I had no idea how long I'd been lying there for. An hour. Two hours. Maybe even more. I'd tried crawling out of my hiding place but had managed barely a few feet on my belly before what little energy I had left simply slipped away. Now I was half in, half out of the tangle of bushes, lying on my side on the gravel curled up in a foetal position, surrounded by the blood that was dripping steadily from my wounds and wondering how long I had left. I could see the lights on in the old lady's flat, no more than twenty yards away, yet it might as well have been twenty miles for all the good it would do me. I was stuck there, alone in the freezing cold, and it was taking all my resolve to keep myself fighting through the minutes, waiting for someone to turn up in the car park and see me.

I had a vague recollection of a car containing two men turning up some time earlier. Of them getting out and walking round to the front of the house, missing my neighbour's corpse completely, before coming back. At least I thought they must have come back, because the car was no longer there, and neither were they.

Lying there now, I was reminded of a time just after I'd arrived on my first tour of Afghanistan. Our platoon had been stationed in an old brick fort five miles away from the Forward Operating Base in Southern Helmand, and one day we'd gone out on patrol and walked straight into a 360-degree ambush. Surrounded on all sides by dozens of Taliban fighters, and hopelessly outnumbered, we'd taken refuge in an irrigation ditch. As we engaged the enemy at close quarters, the radio operator tried to call in air support, only to discover that the radio had been hit by enemy gunfire and was totally useless. So there we were, trapped in no-man's-land, with no hope of rescue, fighting for our lives, as the bullets and the RPGs whizzed around us, and I remember thinking at the time that if I had to die, I'd want it to be here, surrounded by my friends and fighting. The adrenalin was incredible. Like nothing you can imagine.

And then the platoon commander, a good guy with a calm head called Mike Travers, got hit by a Taliban bullet. He was only ten feet away when he went down into the knee-deep, sludgy water clutching his shoulder, his face screwed up in pain. As some of the guys went to help him, he'd shouted for them to get back to the fight, which was typical of him. He didn't want to be fussed over. But within a few minutes he'd gone very pale and, as the medic stripped off his body armour and examined the wound, things took a serious turn for the worse. The bullet had severed a major artery, and without a rapid blood transfusion there was no way he'd survive. The medic patched him up as best he could, but the commander kept bleeding, his blood turning the muddy water red as it dripped steadily out of him.

We had to make a decision. Stay put until either we got the radio working or FOB realized we were missing and sent reinforcements, or fight our way back to base, carrying the commander as we went. The sergeant, who was now in charge, chose the latter, and I'll always remember those brutal twenty-five minutes as we made our way along the irrigation ditches, before finally breaking cover a hundred yards from the base and running along completely open ground, firing as we went, faint and exhausted in the murderous forty-five-degree heat, knowing that at any moment any one of us could be the next casualty. Two of our number had volunteered to carry the commander over that open ground, knowing that as the slowest group they'd make the biggest and easiest targets. One of those men was Cecil. The other was me. He had the front. I had the back. And we'd done it. As Cecil had pointed out afterwards, if the Taliban had been as good shots as we were we'd have been peppered with more holes than a cheese grater, but the fact was they weren't, and because we'd had the guts and the determination, we'd made it against all the odds.

The commander didn't make it, though. He died in the helicopter en route to Camp Bastion, having completely bled out.

I was going to bleed out too now unless help came, and it was a supreme irony that one of the men who'd put me in this position was Cecil, my fellow soldier and friend.

The war had fucked him up.

But then, I thought ruefully, it had fucked me up too.

Ten or so feet away the body of my neighbour, Rupert, lay motionless next to his car, a long dirty blood smear running down its paintwork where he'd slid down it after Cain had shot him. An innocent man, nothing to do with any of this, caught up in somebody else's war. He was lying on his side facing me, eyes closed, a peaceful, almost bored expression on his face.

You never think it's going to happen to you. Death. If you did, you'd make a crap soldier. And I would never have got involved in half the things I'd done – especially those I'd been involved in today – if I'd thought I was going to end up like this, dying alone in the cold.

I didn't want to die. The thought came almost as a shock. I wanted to live. To watch my daughter grow up. To find a woman who'd love me for what I was: a flawed guy, but a decent one, I was sure. To settle down and have a steady job and a steady income. I no longer even wanted revenge against the people who'd murdered my cousin in the Stanhope Hotel.

I just wanted to be like everyone else.

My eyelids felt like lead weights. If I just closed them for a moment, maybe I'd be able to reserve my energy. Just a moment.

They began to flicker, then close ever so slowly, curtains shutting out the harshness of the outside world.

The sound of tyres on gravel followed almost immediately by the harsh glare of headlights startled me, and as I forced open my eyes, I saw a car come into the car park and pull up a few yards away.

I tried to call out but no words came. I tried to lift my arm but that didn't work either, and I wondered grimly if it was already too late.

Sixty-eight

21.22

The back of the police van was cramped, hot and airless, but when you'd spent over a year in a closed prison you were used to that kind of atmosphere, and Fox was visibly more relaxed than the four other men in there with him.

He was sitting between two of them – big guys in helmets with plenty of body armour – while two more sat opposite him, resting the MP5s on their laps, the barrels pointed at his gut. As well as the four cops in the back, there were two in the front, and a car at each end of the convoy, each one containing three officers. In all, twelve armed men surrounded him. It was an impressive number and emphasized his importance to the authorities, as well as the danger he still represented.

He caught the eye of the cop sitting directly opposite him, a young mixed-race guy with a ridiculously square jaw and the build and looks of a rugby player. His dark eyes were simmering as he stared at Fox.

Fox held his gaze, noticing with interest that the cop's finger was instinctively tightening on the trigger.

'Try anything,' said the cop in a cockney growl. 'Anything at all. Because all I need's the slightest fucking excuse and I'll put a bullet right through your skull. I'd love that.'

Fox shrugged. 'You and a couple of million other people, I'm sure. The point is, most of them wouldn't have the spine to pull the trigger. They might think they have, but when it comes down to it . . . I don't think so.'

The cop's lips formed an exaggerated sneer. 'I could.'

'Really?' Fox couldn't resist a small smile. 'Ever killed anyone? Or do you get your kicks from firing that thing down on the range? Shooting paper targets that can't shoot back.'

'I get my accuracy from firing it down the range, so when it comes to it, I won't miss.'

'All right, shut it, you two,' grunted one of the older cops, who was clearly in charge, which suited Fox just fine. He had no desire, or need, to get involved in slanging matches with slow-witted coppers over whether or not he deserved to take a bullet for what he'd done. Of course he did. He was a bad man. He'd committed terrible crimes. He deserved to die. At least he had the self-awareness to confront it, unlike a lot of people.

But of course he had no intention of dying any time soon, or even spending much more time in custody.

Tonight was the night he was going to demonstrate how easy it was to outwit the people holding him. They'd searched him thoroughly as he'd left the prison, put him through a metal detector, made sure there was no way he could be carrying anything that would help him escape.

And he wasn't carrying anything. But only because he'd already swallowed it. A postage-stamp-sized GPS unit, made entirely of plastic. If it worked – and Fox was very confident that it would – it would give the people following its signal his location down to the nearest yard.

He settled back in the seat and stretched his shoulders.

Checkmate.

Sixty-nine

21.23

'Right,' said Cecil, 'they've just left the B158 heading east in the direction of a village called Epping Green.'

He was sitting with a Macbook Air on his lap watching the progress of Fox's GPS unit, while Cain drove at a steady fifty miles an hour along the B157, three miles to the south of them.

Cain nodded, pleased with the way things were going. 'Good. Then they're definitely taking him to a safehouse, and it can't be too far away.'

Cecil gave him a sideways glance. 'How the hell are we going to do this, sir? Now that there are only two of us?'

'The same way we'd have done it if there'd been three. By stealth. We get the location, we scope it out, and we move in. We'll have the element of surprise on our side. They won't be expecting a thing. If they were they'd never have taken him to a safehouse. And it's not like we're dealing with the SAS here. None of these coppers will have ever fired a gun in anger, I can guarantee you that.'

'It's still dangerous.'

Cain turned and glared at him. 'This whole damn thing's dangerous, Cecil. But that's the way it has to be. We're soldiers. It's how we operate.'

Cecil sighed. 'What if we haven't killed him? Jones, I mean. He can testify against us.'

He can testify against you, you mean, thought Cain. 'We shot him at least twice, and it's freezing cold out there tonight. He won't survive.'

'We never saw his body, and he's a tough bastard.'

'Then we'll take him out later if we have to. Accidents can be arranged, you know that.'

As he spoke, while still watching the road ahead, Cain could see that Cecil was looking at him suspiciously. Cecil had been in a difficult mood ever since he'd found out that Jones had to die, and Cain knew he had to keep his morale up while he still needed him.

'Look, even if Jones survives, the good thing is that he's in no position to talk to the police. He shot Dav in cold blood, remember? There's no way he can spin himself out of that one. His best bet's to keep his mouth shut, and he knows it.'

'But that's the thing,' said Cecil, and Cain could hear the pain in his voice. 'He shot the Albanian. He did the robbery this morning. He did everything asked of him. So I don't understand why he'd betray us.'

'Because he weakened, Cecil. Most men do. They take the easy option. We haven't.'

'Aye, and what good's it done us?'

Cain glared at him. 'Don't give me that. You know why we're doing this. And think of the money you're going to make when we break out Fox.'

Cecil quietened a moment at the thought of the reward on offer. Like most of the people Cain had ever met, he was greedy.

'And you reckon Fox has definitely got the money to pay us?' he asked eventually.

Course he hasn't, thought Cain. And if he did have it, he wouldn't pay us anyway. But he didn't say that. 'I know for a fact that Fox has got two million dollars stashed away in various foreign bank accounts. We're going to hold him until he pays us half of it. Us, Cecil. Me and you.'

In truth, Cain had already been paid by the man he reported directly to, Garth Crossman, to silence Fox once and for all. Cecil wasn't going to make it out either. Like Fox, he knew too much. Tonight, Cain and Crossman were going to make a clean break from their previous strategy of launching violent terrorist attacks. The attacks had served their purpose. They'd wreaked havoc, harmed community relations, and made the government look weak. Now it was time for Crossman to go political.

Cecil stared at the screen. 'OK. Targets have now turned right on to an unmarked road. The road leads down to a farm about half a mile north of us. It's the only building on that road.'

Cain felt his adrenalin kicking in. 'It's the safehouse.'

'OK, take the next right turn,' said Cecil. 'If we move fast enough we might be able to cut them off before they get there.'

Seventy

21.25

Bolt stumbled when he eventually got out of the car, and had to grab hold of the door for support. His headache had been getting worse, and every few minutes he was being hit by dizzy spells where his vision would blur and darken, each time for slightly longer. He took a couple of deep breaths, still waiting for this latest one to pass. He was going to have to get himself to a hospital soon, but he owed it to Jones to at least try and see if he was OK.

He blinked a couple of times as his vision returned to normal, immediately spotting Jones's old black Renault Mégane parked in the corner. It was too cold a night to be out walking, which meant he was probably here. Bolt felt a smidgen of satisfaction that his hunch had paid off, and turned towards the house, stopping suddenly as he spotted the ground-floor window hanging open, only partially visible behind one of the cars.

Jones had a ground-floor flat. It was unlikely to be a coincidence.

Bolt walked towards the window, his pace slow and unsteady, but as he passed a parked BMW he saw a body lying on the ground.

Even in the darkness, he could see it was a white male in his thirties dressed in a suit, and he felt a guilty relief that it wasn't Jones. The man was on his side, one arm outstretched towards a briefcase a few feet away. His shirt was heavily bloodstained, as was the car itself, and he had a large hole in the centre of his forehead, where he'd been shot at close range. It was also clear he was dead.

The sight didn't make Bolt feel sick. He'd seen too many murder victims for that, but it did make him feel terribly sad. Here was someone who'd come home from a hard day at work and whose life had been ripped from him in what must have been a terrifying last few seconds. It reminded him far too much of his own mortality.

The moan was almost inaudible, but Bolt turned round immediately, causing his vision to blur again. As it cleared, he saw a second body poking a little way out of a thick leylandii bush that bordered the property, partially obscured by a parked car.

It was Jones.

Even as he reached him, Bolt could see he was in a

bad way. He was only visible from the chest up, his face buried in the gravel, and he wasn't moving. The blood was everywhere, drenching his clothes and spreading across the gravel beside him.

Crouching down, Bolt turned him over as gently as he could, and looked down at his pale bloodstained face.

Jones tried to focus but couldn't seem to manage it, and his eyes flickered as he began to lose consciousness.

'You're going to be all right, Jones,' Bolt told him, aware that his own voice sounded weak. 'I promise. I'm going to get help right now.' He fumbled in his pocket for his phone. 'Stay with me, Jones. Come on, stay with me.'

Jones's eyes closed as Bolt dialled 999, and Bolt slapped his face to make him stay awake, the effort making him nauseous.

'I need an air ambulance right away,' he said when his call was answered, and gave the address.

The operator said he couldn't guarantee an air ambulance, that resources were severely stretched.

'My name is Detective Inspector Mike Bolt of Counter Terrorism Command. This man's a victim of today's attack. And he's the only person who can identify the terrorists. If he dies, you're responsible.'

'Are you all right, sir? You don't sound well.'

Bolt took a deep breath, feeling like he was going to faint. 'I'm fine. Just get here.'

He slapped Jones's face again. 'Come on, wake up.' He couldn't let Jones die. He just couldn't.

Jones's eyes flickered open and he looked up at Bolt, his lips curling in what could have been a smile or a grimace. But at least he was conscious.

'Who did this?' Bolt asked. 'Who shot you?'

Jones opened his mouth and let out a single word: 'Fox.'

Bolt frowned. What was he talking about? 'Did you say Fox?'

'Cain shot me,' whispered Jones, his words barely audible. 'After Fox.'

'What do you mean "after Fox"?'

Jones's face, white and bloodless, twisted in an expression of pain. It was clear that speaking was a huge effort. His eyes began to close again.

Bolt slapped him again, and asked him to repeat what he was trying to say. Because it didn't make any sense.

And then it hit him. Fox was en route to the safehouse. If Cain was 'after Fox', it meant he knew he was being moved, and was almost certainly going to try and break him out.

Bolt staggered to his feet, the sudden movement almost making him black out once again.

He had to warn Tina.

Seventy-one

21.29

They moved swiftly through the woods in total silence.

Cain could hear the sound of the convoy drawing closer, and was just able to see the first glow of the lead vehicle's headlights as it came round the bend a few hundred yards further up. He nodded to Cecil, and the two men split up, taking up positions twenty yards apart on the light incline that ran down to the road, using the trees as cover. Cain put down the AK-47 assault rifle he was carrying and removed a Russian-made RK3 anti-tank grenade from beneath his jacket, slipping his forefinger through the firing pin as the convoy made its steady approach along the narrow winding road – sitting ducks heading straight into an ambush.

He felt the joy of violence building within him. This was it. His final battle. All the months of planning, all the killing that had taken place today, was about to culminate in this last bloody act – an act that would so humiliate the government, it was difficult to see how they could survive it. Cain felt nothing but contempt for the police officers guarding Fox. They were establishment lackeys doing the dirty work of the politicians, and they deserved everything that was coming to them. There would be no mercy. And there would be no regrets.

A thin smile spread across his face as he crouched low behind the tree, away from the glare of the approaching headlights, his finger tightening on the firing pin.

It was time.

Seventy-two

21.30

'How come you always seem to get all the action?' asked the cop sitting next to Tina in the back of the final car in the convoy. There was a mixture of irritation and admiration in his voice, and enough of a smile on his lips to suggest he was only riling her. 'I reckon I've attended five hundred firearms incidents and you know how many times I've fired my gun?'

'Let me guess,' said Tina. 'None.'

'Exactly. See? It's not fair. You just have to turn up somewhere and the shooting starts. It's like you're a magnet for it.'

'I'm not usually the one doing the shooting, and things are a lot less fun if you're unarmed.' Which Tina had to admit wasn't entirely true. Unarmed or not, she got a huge buzz from the action she'd been involved in, although it also took it out of her.

As the three-vehicle convoy made its way down the

narrow country road leading to the safehouse where she was going to question Fox, she felt exhaustion beginning to overcome her. She'd almost been killed twice that day, had produced a month's worth of adrenalin in a matter of hours, and only through sheer force of will had she fought off the shock that had enveloped her afterwards in both instances. But now all she could think of was her bed, and she hoped that Fox would give them the rest of the names they needed without further delay. The fact that he'd told her about Cecil Boorman was encouraging, but she doubted if they'd get the more important people so easily. Fox was the kind of amoral egotist who liked to draw things out.

The cop was still talking and Tina was doing her best to listen, but she wasn't finding it easy. He was a nice enough guy – good-looking and friendly, which was usually a combination that worked for her – but she didn't like talking about her exploits at the best of times, and especially not near the end of a long day. She looked out of the window at the gently sloping woodland on either side of the road – the trees bare and forbidding, their branches like swirling skeletal arms – and was suddenly aware of the phone ringing in her pocket.

It was Mike Bolt.

'Where are you?'

She heard the stress and exhaustion in his voice and felt a stab of concern. 'On the road down to the safehouse. We're almost there.'

'Turn round now. Get back on the main road.'

The shots erupted out of nowhere – a ferocious hail of automatic weapon fire that tore through the side of the car, shattering two of the windows. A bullet seemed to explode in Tina's ear and blood splashed her face as the cop who'd been talking to her only a few seconds before tumbled sideways in his seat, already dead, blood pouring from an exit wound in the side of his head. At the same time the driver slumped forward, his hands dropping from the wheel, and the car veered to one side.

For a split second, Tina thought she'd been hit too, but she could feel no pain, nor the sudden, draining weakness that comes with a bullet wound. Mike had stopped talking and she realized with surprise that she was no longer holding the phone. It dawned on her that it had been shot out of her hand – probably by the bullet that had passed through the cop's head.

Jesus! She'd dodged a bullet for the second time that day.

There was another burst of gunfire, and more glass shattered as a round whizzed past somewhere in front of Tina's face before exiting through the passenger-side window. The shooting was coming from off to one side of them, and Tina thanked God she hadn't been where the cop was sitting, otherwise she'd be dead by now.

She reacted fast, ducking down in the seat, using

the cop's body as a shield. Reaching out, she pulled his pistol – a Glock 17 – free from its holster. She could have gone for his MP5 but, having never fired one before, she decided to stick with what she knew. As another burst of gunfire hit the car, shattering more glass, Tina leaned over and yanked down the door handle before rolling out of the car and landing on her belly, keeping low, because it was still possible there was a shooter on this side of the car as well.

The surviving officer in the front passenger seat rolled out the same way, taking up a firing position behind the bonnet and cracking off a number of single shots into the gloom.

A loud explosion shook the ground and Tina saw a ball of flame rise up from the front of the convoy. It looked like it had been hit by some sort of IED and, as Tina watched, a firearms officer staggered into the road, his clothes on fire, before falling to the ground and rolling over and over in a bid to put the flames out.

The van carrying Fox had stopped a few yards in front of them, but there was no obvious movement inside, and aside from the officer on fire and the one crouching next to her, she could see no one else. The whole thing was happening so fast and dramatically it felt like stepping right into the heart of a nightmare.

Tina looked round quickly. There were no muzzle flashes coming from the woods on her side of the car, which made her think there weren't that many attackers, although whoever they were, they clearly knew what they were doing.

The cop next to her was crouched down beneath the bonnet. He looked over as she crouched down next to him, leaning against the car and holding the Glock in both hands. He was older, in his forties, with the calm demeanour of a man who knew his job well. He asked if she was all right.

His voice was faint, thanks to the ringing in Tina's ears. She nodded. 'I think so.'

'Stay where you are and leave this to me.' He looked down at the Glock but made no comment. Now wasn't the time to be worrying about whether she was allowed to use it or not. Slowly, he peered over the edge of the bonnet, scanning the trees for movement.

He squinted, frowning, then opened his mouth to say something.

But the next second there was a single burst of fire, and he fell back into a sitting position, a hole in his forehead above the right eye leaking a long line of blood that pooled on his top lip before running over his mouth and on to his neck. Then he toppled sideways and lay on the ground.

Dead. Just like that.

And suddenly Tina was on her own.

Seventy-three

21.31

There's nothing like the element of surprise. It's particularly effective against people who've never been shot at before, and who have no experience of a bullet's ability to change things in an instant.

As soon as the initial burst of gunfire crackled across them, Fox hit the floor. He knew the first shots fired at the van would be aimed at the tyres to disable it, so there was no danger of him being hit. Even so, he was still the first one down, just in case his rescuers had a change of plan and decided to kill him. Fox was no fool. He knew he was a lot more use to the people he'd once worked for dead than alive, and it was going to take all his natural cunning to get out of here in one piece.

The second burst of fire hit a couple of seconds later, shattering the windows, but it didn't hit any of the cops, who were on the floor as well, several of them directly on top of Fox, crushing him into the van's cold floor.

The loud blast at the front of the convoy that Fox identified immediately as a grenade, followed by frightened shouts from the front of the van, seemed to galvanize the men in the back of the van into action. In a cacophony of yelling and shouting, they jumped up into firing positions and opened fire through the windows in all directions like cowboys trapped in a circled wagon – which was pretty much what they were.

'Out! Out! Out!' screamed one of the cops, reaching over and unlocking the rear doors. 'We're sitting ducks in here! That was a fucking grenade!'

No one needed asking twice, and they all started scrambling for the doors. This was all about survival now and, as the adrenalin pumped through the cops, they momentarily forgot about Fox. Which was a bad move.

Reaching up with his cuffed hands, which thanks to Tina Boyd were now in front of him, he grabbed the gun from the holster of the nearest cop – the big cockney one who'd dared Fox to give him an excuse to put a bullet in him – in a movement so quick that he had no time to react.

As the cop swung round, Fox leaned back against the van's metal partition and, with a cold smile, shot him twice in the face, swinging the gun round immediately and taking a second cop in the side of the head. Realizing what was going on, the other two made for the exit as Fox kept firing at them, not caring who he hit, or where, banking on the fact that as they spilled out of the van they'd run straight into the line of fire of his rescuers. He got one cop in the leg, sending him sprawling into the car behind, which had come to a halt at a forty-five-degree angle, its driver dead behind the wheel. But the other cop proved a more difficult proposition. He swung round fast, unleashing a volley of MP5 fire into the van at exactly the same moment that Fox hit him in the chest with a nine-mill round.

Luckily the shot knocked the cop off balance, but he didn't go down. He readied himself in the space of half a second and started firing again as Fox's last bullet, now aimed at the guy's head to avoid the body armour, missed him. Only then did a burst of automatic gunfire from somewhere out in the woods finally send the cop sprawling to the ground.

Scrambling to his feet, Fox grabbed the key to the handcuffs from the second dead cop and unlocked them with a remarkably steady hand.

He was free.

As the van's rear doors flew open, Tina saw two armed officers come stumbling out amid a series of gunshots from inside. One of the officers grabbed his leg as he was hit, and fell against the bonnet of the car Tina had been travelling in before falling to the tarmac so that he was facing her, his face etched with pain as he tried to wriggle round the front of the car to safety. The other officer turned round so he was facing the van and managed to get off a few shots before he was hit by a stream of automatic gunfire from somewhere in the trees. He dropped his weapon and fell to the ground too, momentarily disappearing from view.

Tina braced herself. The good guys were dropping like flies, and soon she was going to be the only one left.

Seventy-four

21.31

Mike Bolt had a cold feeling of dread in his gut that momentarily stopped his nausea. He'd definitely heard shots before Tina's phone went dead, and he had no idea whether she was alive or dead.

He called Commander Ingrams but his line was busy, forcing him to stagger back towards his car in the hunt for the police radio. He could hear the sound of a helicopter approaching, and as he looked up he saw an air ambulance coming in low over the horizon. His vision blurred again and he suddenly felt very faint. Grabbing the back of his car for support, he speed-dialled Ingrams's number a second time, knowing he had to hold on until he'd talked to someone at Scotland Yard.

'Mike, what the hell is it?' demanded Ingrams, picking up this time. 'I told you to go home.'

'The convoy carrying Fox has been ambushed. I just

heard shots down the phone.'

'Are you sure?' Bolt could hear the shock in Ingrams's voice.

'Hundred per cent. They're near the safehouse. Get reinforcements there now.'

The noise from the air ambulance's rotor blades drowned out the end of the call as it hovered directly above the car park.

Bolt pushed himself backwards, away from the car, dropping his phone in the process, waving up at the crew to try to attract their attention. A wave of pain, so intense that it made him cry out, surged through his head, culminating just behind his right eye. He lost his sight; he lost his balance; he lost every sense he had. All in that single, agonizing moment as he fell blindly into darkness.

Seventy-five

21.32

Poking her head just above the bonnet of the ARV, Tina saw the muzzle flash from the shooter's gun up in the trees, but she still couldn't see the shooter himself. It did, however, look like he was the only one firing. As she watched, a silhouette seemed to rise up from the ground twenty yards away and come jogging down the incline towards the convoy, keeping close to the undergrowth for cover, his assault rifle outstretched in front of him.

It was clear he hadn't seen her. She could have stayed where she was but she wasn't that kind of person. She didn't turn her back on trouble. This was a chance to even the odds, and she knew it. But she was scared. Damn scared. She could see at least two corpses of police officers only feet away, their blood leaking on to the tarmac, and knew full well that could be her in a few moments' time. Her whole body ached with exhaustion, and a heavy tension that made it hard to move.

A voice in her head told her to hide. It was a sensible voice – a voice of reason. To do anything else was madness.

But then she was jumping up and opening fire with the Glock, acting entirely on instinct.

Handguns are never the most accurate of weapons – a fact that's not helped when the person firing them hasn't fired one for a while, and is shooting at a moving target in near darkness – but Tina kept her hands steady and aimed low, cracking off five shots in rapid succession, before the gunman had even reacted to her presence.

But, crucially, she didn't hit him, and she was forced to dive for cover as he returned fire, his bullets spraying the spot where she'd just been standing. She landed painfully on her shoulder, knowing that she'd missed her chance, and would probably not get another one now.

At that moment, the cop who'd been shot in the leg, and who'd been lying on his side, rolled round so he was facing the gunman and let loose a burst of automatic fire from the MP5. Tina immediately got to her feet and peered back over the bonnet, seeing the gunman now running towards them, barely ten yards away, firing as he went as he tried to take out the firearms cop.

Smoke flew up from the cop's body armour as he

took rounds to the upper body, causing him to buck and jerk on the ground. Taking advantage of the distraction, Tina jumped up again and cracked off another three shots. She didn't know if it was her or the other cop who'd hit him, but the gunman suddenly went down on his side, dropping his weapon in the process.

She felt a surge of hope then that lasted the space of a second before suddenly Fox appeared in the van's doorway, a gun in his hand. He raised the gun, looking straight at her. She just had time to react by throwing herself backwards, firing as she went, as he pulled the trigger, narrowly missing her.

As she landed, she fired again, but Fox was already out of the van, moving fast. Keeping low, he jerked round and shot the injured cop in the face, then fired another shot at Tina. It bounced off the tarmac behind her as she kept firing back at him, but then he disappeared from view around the front of the car, and suddenly everything fell silent.

Seventy-six

21.33

Fox ran round the side of the van, then made for the cover of the trees. He hadn't run properly in a while, and his legs felt stiff. But adrenalin was keeping him going. Adrenalin and excitement. This was what it was all about for him. The hot joy of battle. God, he'd lived for those moments in the army, and in his time as a mercenary since.

And now here he was again, having planned his escape from prison down to the last detail.

The ambush had been perfect. All the cops were either dead or too badly hurt to offer any meaningful opposition. He didn't think he'd hit Tina Boyd, which was a pity. He'd like to have put a bullet in her. Not so much because of what she'd done to help scupper the Stanhope siege, more because it would be good sport to take out such an iconic figure, a woman who was a born survivor, and good at her job. But he'd defeated her. That was what mattered. He'd defeated all of them.

Ten yards away he could see the black-clad figure of one of the ambush team. He was lying on the ground clutching his leg, his face covered in black camouflage paint. Fox had been told that there'd be a minimum of three of them in the team, but this was the only one he could see right now.

'Help me, for Christ's sake,' hissed the shooter as Fox ran towards him, keeping to the undergrowth.

He recognized the Northern Irish accent immediately. It was Cecil Boorman, the man whose name he'd given to Tina earlier. He was no good to any of them, not now that he'd been shot.

Cecil sat up and put out a hand as Fox reached him.

Fox grabbed the hand to lift him up. 'Good shooting,' he said. 'Thanks for that.' Then he brought up the police-issue Glock and shot Cecil through the eye with his last bullet.

As Cecil fell back down, Fox grabbed his pistol – a Browning semi-automatic – from his waistband and turned and ran through the woods towards the front of the convoy. In many ways, this was the most dangerous part of the whole operation. If his rescuers were planning on killing him, then they were going to make their move now.

He heard movement to his left, and a silhouetted figure shot out of the darkness. His face might have been painted black, but Fox could see that the man coming at him out of the darkness was Cain. He'd recognize those pale, dead eyes anywhere. They'd known each other a long time through their association with The Brotherhood, but had always been rivals rather than friends, and Fox knew Cain wouldn't hesitate to put a bullet in him if it came to it.

But Cain's gun was down by his side, which had to mean that, for the moment at least, he didn't mean him any harm.

Even so, Fox kept his finger tight on the trigger of the Browning as the two men stopped in front of each other.

There was a moment's pause, and then Fox grinned. 'I knew you'd make it.'

'I don't make promises I can't keep,' said Cain, with a humourless self-righteousness that instantly reminded Fox of why he didn't like him. 'Have you seen Cecil?'

'He took a bullet in the leg. I had to finish him off.'

Cain nodded grimly. 'We've got to go. This place is going to be crawling with cops soon. Our car's over here.'

He turned and started running through the trees, with Fox following close behind.

'Haven't you got anyone else in the team?' Fox asked him.

'No. It's just you and me now,' answered Cain as they emerged on to a narrow single-lane track where a black BMW 5 Series was parked. He ran round to the driver's side and jumped in.

Fox could hear no sound of sirens or approaching helicopters and, as he got in the passenger side and Cain started the engine and pulled away, he briefly considered shooting the other man then and there, chucking his corpse out on to the road, and simply driving away himself. It would be a clean break and save any problems later if Cain chose to double-cross him. But he decided against it. It was best to put a few miles between him and the massacre here without complicating matters.

Cain roared on to the road and made a hard right away from the convoy. Behind them, the flames shooting up from the lead car dominated the view, illuminating the bodies of two cops lying nearby, one of whom was still on fire. As Cain hit the pedal and the BMW accelerated away, Fox felt a huge, all-consuming elation. For the first time in over a year he was getting a taste of freedom, and by God it tasted good.

And then the rear windscreen exploded in a hail of gunfire, and suddenly the BMW was veering out of control as Cain desperately turned the wheel. But the tyres had been blown out and he no longer had control as the car left the road and mounted the bank, giving Fox only a couple of seconds to brace himself before it smashed headfirst into a tree.

Seventy-seven

21.34

Tina saw the whole thing.

Having radioed Control to call for urgent assistance, she'd reloaded the Glock and was walking along the side of the road towards the front of the convoy, holding it in both hands as she tried to locate Fox and his rescuers, when a black BMW saloon lurched out of the woods twenty yards in front of her in a screech of tyres and accelerated away in the opposite direction.

She'd known straight away that Fox was in the car and that she was too late to stop him. Even so, she'd assumed a firing position, aiming at the rear windscreen, when from somewhere to the left of the burning armed response vehicle she heard an intense burst of automatic gunfire that sent her diving to the ground.

When she looked up, the BMW had left the road

and was heading straight for a tree. It struck it with a loud bang, and she could see the airbags deploying inside. The engine stalled, and an eerie silence descended on the woods.

Tina was on her feet in a second. Through the smoke and flames, she saw one of the armed officers emerge from behind the lead car and advance on the BMW, holding his MP5 in front of him. He looked shocked but unhurt.

Tina shouted over to him, and he turned round, recognizing her instantly.

'I've called for help, but for the moment we're on our own,' she told him as they walked slowly towards the BMW, weapons at the ready, keeping a few feet apart so they wouldn't make such an easy target.

'Jesus,' he said, and she noticed that he was very young, mid-twenties at most. 'Is everyone else down?'

'I think so. Look, I know this is going to be hard, but we've got to try to take Fox alive. He has information we need.'

'If he tries a damn thing, I'm going to take his head off,' said the cop, keeping his eyes fixed straight ahead. 'He's just killed some very good friends of mine.'

Fifteen yards ahead of them, the BMW's front doors slowly opened, and Tina's finger tensed on the trigger. She had no idea how many gunmen were in there, or what they were armed with, but she knew they weren't going to come quietly. The adrenalin was making her hands shake, and she had to fight to stay calm as they continued to advance on the car, step by slow step.

The first sirens cut across the night sky, still some distance away.

Nothing moved inside the car.

Tina and the cop exchanged glances, stopping five yards short of the vehicle.

'Stay calm,' she told him. 'We can stay like this until help gets here. It's not far away.'

Before the cop could answer, there was movement from inside and two men slowly rolled out of the car, one from either front door.

'Get your hands where I can see them!' yelled the cop, who was covering Fox.

Tina was covering the man who'd rolled out the driver's-side door. He was now lying on his side facing her, one of his arms squashed beneath him. He was dressed entirely in black, with black face paint covering his features, and even from some distance away she could see that his eyes were cold and alert. She didn't like the fact that she couldn't see the hand that was squashed beneath him, and she shouted at him to bring it out from under his body, working hard to keep the tension out of her voice.

He didn't move. Just stared at her with those cold eyes.

'Do it!' she snarled, aiming the Glock directly at his

chest.

The sirens were getting closer now.

The man smiled at her.

And then, in one whip-like movement, he brought the gloved hand up from beneath his body, already pulling the trigger.

Tina fired back twice, hitting him in the chest, leaping out of the way at the same time as his bullets whipped past her, conscious of the sounds of automatic weapon fire and shouting coming from the other side of the car.

As she hit the ground, landing on one shoulder, the man was already bringing his gun round to fire again, the two bullet holes in his chest smoking from where they'd struck his body armour. There was no fear on his face, simply a look of contempt, as if she was little more than a fly to be swatted away.

Tina cracked off a third shot, more in desperation than anything else, hardly having time to aim it at her target.

And struck lucky.

The bullet hit him in the neck, knocking his gun hand off balance so that when he pulled the trigger, his own bullet passed over her head.

A look of surprise crossed his face, as if he hadn't been expecting that, but he was up on his knees now, still holding on to his gun, and Tina wasn't taking any chances. She fired again.

This time the bullet struck him in the forehead. He

wobbled for a moment, and the look of surprise on his face seemed to melt away beneath the blood running down it, and then, without a sound, he tumbled sideways on to the tarmac, and stopped moving.

Tina was on her feet in an instant, which was when she saw the cop rolling on the ground and clutching his shoulder, his MP5 beside him. Ten yards beyond him, Fox was running into the trees, holding a pistol, but she could see by the stiff, awkward way he held his upper body that he too had been hit.

Shaking with tension, she raised the gun and aimed at Fox's running figure, knowing it was completely illegal to shoot a suspect who was running away, and knowing too that if she killed him, the secrets he claimed to know would stay hidden for ever. But he was already disappearing into the undergrowth, and she knew she'd never hit him from where she was.

And then she heard it. The sound of an approaching helicopter, coming in fast. Fox couldn't escape now. He was trapped.

Even so, the adrenalin was tearing through her at such a rate that she couldn't even think about not pursuing him.

Shouting to the injured cop that help was on the way, she took off after Fox.

Fox ran fast, ignoring the pain in his arm from the gunshot wound and the nausea that was trying to envelop him. He wasn't the type of man to give up, even though it was now clear his plan had failed. It had always been hugely risky, but he'd come so close that it hurt to fall at this, the final hurdle.

The sirens were coming from all directions, but it wasn't them that concerned him. It was the sound of the helicopter coming in fast somewhere ahead of him. Soon it would pick up his body heat and track him until he was finally cornered.

There was no way he was going back inside. How could he? There'd never be another opportunity like this one to escape their clutches. They'd throw away the key this time, and never move him outside the prison walls again. He couldn't have that.

He wouldn't.

But things weren't quite finished yet. Fox was nothing if not resourceful, and there was one last chance to snatch success from this situation. It was slim in the extreme, but what choice did he have?

He slowed down, hearing the sound of footfalls in the trees behind him.

It was time for one final throw of the dice.

Seventy-eight

21.36

Tina sprinted through the woods, Glock in hand, hunting round for Fox. She'd already caught several glimpses of him running ahead of her, one arm hanging loosely by his side, but now, as she came over a slight incline, looking down towards where the wood ended and open fields began, she could no longer see him. The trees were bare and spaced a few yards apart, and aside from the odd holly bush and bed of ferns, there weren't many obvious places to hide. She slowed down, working hard to keep her breathing quiet, keeping her finger tight on the Glock's trigger.

'Drop the gun,' a voice called out to her side, cutting through the noise of the approaching helicopter.

She turned as Fox emerged from behind a tree a few yards away, pointing his gun at her face. He took two steps forward, and even in the near darkness she could see that his face was contorted with pain.

'It's the end of the road,' she told him. 'There's no way you can get out of here now.'

'I can, with your help. Now, I'm only going to say it one more time. Drop the gun.'

But she didn't. Instead she turned and raised it so it was pointed at his chest. 'And I told you. It's over. You're surrounded. There's nowhere you can go. And don't even think about trying to take me hostage. It happened once a long time ago. I'm not going to let it happen again.'

'I could shoot you right here.'

'I could shoot *you* right here,' she answered, having to use all her willpower to keep her gun hand steady.

Out of the corner of her eye she could see the bright swirl of flashing blues lighting up the woods as reinforcements finally arrived. They'd be following her trail through the woods any minute now. All she had to do was hold her nerve.

They were suddenly bathed in the glare of the helicopter's searchlight. Fox squinted up towards it, then glanced towards the field at the end of the wood, about fifty yards distant, before turning back to Tina.

'I'm not going back inside,' he said, almost plaintively.

She could see a change in him now. The determination in his features was gone. Now he just looked thoughtful. It was clear he was contemplating his options and concluding that, like it or not, she was right: he didn't have any.

'It doesn't have to be thirty years' hard time,' she told him. 'We can still come to some arrangement.'

This time he managed a smile, though there was no humour in it. 'No, I think we've gone too far for that now, don't you?'

'If you cooperate, some good can still come out of this.'

'Not for me it can't.'

'Give me the names of the people we want, Fox. What do you owe them? Nothing. They're not the ones facing years and years in prison, are they? But they're happy to hang you out to dry. Come on. Don't protect the people behind this. Think of yourself.'

Fox shook his head dismissively. 'You don't understand, do you? I'm fighting for a cause. I always have been. And it'll live on long after I'm gone. I'm not going to betray the people still fighting for it.'

'Bullshit. It's over. Can't you see that? You've failed. Your friends have failed.'

He looked at her, his lip curled in a dismissive sneer, and Tina imagined it was the look he'd worn as he'd killed the hostages inside the Stanhope Hotel. 'You're wrong. We've only just begun. And the next time you hear from us, it'll be from a place you least expect. You won't even know we're there.'

To one side of her, Tina could just about make out a line of half a dozen black-clad armed officers approaching them, moving quickly but carefully, all of them with weapons outstretched.

'This is your last chance, Fox,' she told him, trying to keep her voice even. 'Talk to me now, and we might be able to salvage something.'

The cops slowed as they drew closer. They were only just outside the helicopter's glare now, all of them pointing their weapons at Fox.

'Armed police, drop your gun!' shouted one, working hard to make himself heard above the din.

But Fox's expression was utterly defiant. 'Unless you back off I will shoot her.' His finger tightened on the trigger, and he didn't take his eyes off Tina.

At that moment they were absolutely stone cold, and she realized he didn't give a toss that he also had guns, including hers, pointed at him. Was perhaps even willing her to use the Glock.

'You have five seconds,' Fox shouted. 'Pull back and lower your weapons, or I'll kill her.'

No one in the line of police moved.

Tina swallowed. The barrel of Fox's gun was barely two yards away from her. This was a ruthless and desperate man with nothing left to lose. A man who would rather go out in dramatic fashion than spend the rest of his life rotting in a prison, and in the end, who could blame him? In the same position, she too would prefer a quick death. An end to everything. But right now, Fox could just as easily shoot her, and get his quick death from the police bullets that would inevitably follow.

'Five!' he shouted, a terrifying decisiveness in his voice. 'Four!'

Tina knew the police wouldn't want to fire on him while he wasn't aiming his gun at any of them. It was too risky, leaving them potentially open to manslaughter charges. And there was no guarantee that his gun wouldn't discharge anyway, wounding or even killing her.

'Three!'

A picture formed in Tina's mind of the officers lying dead and dying on the road where she'd left them, their blood pouring all over the concrete. She didn't want to die. She didn't want to be like them. She wanted to travel. To meet someone. To have children. Suddenly, in a huge flurry she wanted all those things, and standing there, surrounded by colleagues, but utterly alone, she knew she risked losing it all. And in the next few seconds.

'Two!'

Fox was staring right at her now, a maniacal energy in his eyes.

She knew he was going to pull the trigger.

'One!'

And then the shot rang out, echoing through the cold night air.

Seventy-nine

21.39

For a few seconds, Tina didn't even breathe. Then, slowly, she exhaled and lowered the gun as the armed officers raced over to her. She made no move to resist as the Glock was carefully removed from her fingers. Instead she stared down at the man she'd just shot.

Fox lay on his back, convulsing and gasping for air, his hands down by his side, his eyes wide with shock. His gun had dropped from his hand and was now out of reach – not that he was in any position to use it. She'd shot him once, in the chest, and already his movements were beginning to slow as his heart stopped working.

A group of officers approached him carefully, pointing their MP5s down at his torso, but none made any move to help him. Only when his eyes closed and he stopped moving altogether did someone shout for medical help, but by that point Tina was already walking away from the scene, almost in a daze, her heart hammering in her chest, as she tried to come to terms with what had happened.

One of the officers walked with her. Putting an arm round her shoulders, he asked if she was OK. She wasn't. She was shell-shocked. She'd seen too much in one day – more than her mind could quite take in. But she shrugged off his arm and told him she was OK, and he didn't try to stop her, even though she was going to have to make a statement.

More people were coming up the incline now, a long, straggling line of police officers, the majority of them armed, and ambulance crew. They were hurrying, some glancing across as they passed, but no one saying anything. Whether they knew who she was or not, it seemed as though they all wanted to give her a wide berth. Blue lights flashed through the trees in a wide and ever-growing arc as the emergency services continued to arrive in large numbers – but too late, as so often, to prevent the bloodbath.

Tina sighed. She'd been played. They all had. She'd fallen for Fox's lies. She'd believed that he was genuinely going to cooperate. So, it seemed, had a lot of other people, including members of the government, who'd authorized his move to a safehouse. No one had believed that the individuals they were dealing with would have dared launch such an audacious rescue attempt. But perhaps they should have done. Audacious attacks seemed to be these people's forte. Jesus, they'd even attacked the Shard.

But ultimately they'd failed. London had been shaken, but it was still there, just as it had been when the attacks had started this morning; and the perpetrators hadn't been able to achieve their goal of making it look like the work of homegrown Islamic extremists, further diminishing the effect of their bombs.

Fox, too, had got the fate he deserved. Tina found it hard to believe that she'd been the one who'd killed him. She'd killed before, more than once. Two of those killings had been legal and were out in the public domain. One wasn't, and never would be. But the shock of ending a life always hit her like a hard, physical blow, especially when it was done at close quarters. She wasn't a soldier. She hadn't been trained to kill. She was just a copper, for Christ's sake, although after tonight, she wasn't sure for how much longer.

Still, she was too tired to worry about that now. Reaching into her jacket with shaking hands, she pulled out a cigarette and lit it, savouring the hit as the smoke flew down her throat and into her lungs.

Before she called it a day, though, she needed to do one more thing.

Eighty

21.50

After he'd broken the boy's neck, Voorhess allowed himself a well-deserved sigh of relief.

Given the numbers of police who'd been trying to catch him, he'd been extremely lucky to have made it this far, but Voorhess was a firm believer in the maxim that ultimately you made your own luck. He'd remained calm when others would have panicked, had adapted his plan to suit the rapidly changing circumstances, and even though he'd been betrayed, he'd outrun his pursuers and beaten their roadblocks.

On the seat next to him, the boy sat facing Voorhess, his neck tilted at an awkward angle. Voorhess pulled the boy's baseball cap down over his face so that he didn't have to look at him. The boy had told him that he was eighteen, and Voorhess felt a pique of sadness that he'd had to kill him. At least it had been quick. As the boy had pulled into the parking space, Voorhess had reached over, slipped an arm round his neck, like they were old rugby buddies, and done it in one swift movement, so that the boy hadn't had to suffer. Eighteen was a very young age to die, just when you were on the cusp of adulthood, with a whole bright world of adventure about to open up. But it didn't look as if this boy – with his bad skin, his poor looks and his terrible taste in music – appreciated life in the way he should have done, and as a result, in Voorhess's mind, his death was less tragic than it might otherwise have been.

He got out of the car, closing the door gently behind him, and stretched. It had been an uncomfortable as well as nerve-racking journey here, and his back was aching. Rolling his shoulders, and keeping his head down, he looked around. He was on the fourth floor of the short-stay car park at Heathrow's Terminal 4, parked in a dark corner, and at this time of night it was mostly empty. Surprisingly, he could still hear the sounds of the occasional plane taking off and coming in to land, which meant that despite his missile attack, flights were still going in and out of Heathrow.

A lift bleeped, and Voorhess stepped into the shadows as a couple walked out pushing a luggage trolley. He waited until they'd got in their car and pulled away before transferring the boy from the driver's seat to the car's boot, so that he was hidden from view, only just managing to squeeze him in

Then, grabbing the bag that contained his few

possessions, he flung it over his shoulder and walked away from the car, feeling a sense of satisfaction at a job well done, and already dreaming of sunshine and money.

Eighty-one

23.00

Mike Bolt was lying in the hospital bed with his eyes closed, a bandage round his head, when Tina walked in. She'd had to beg the officers from CTC to let her come here before they took her away to Paddington Green Station for questioning about her part in what had happened that night. So far, she wasn't under arrest, even though she'd shot dead two men using a police-issue gun she wasn't authorized to use. But she guessed this was only because so far no one had figured out exactly what to arrest her for, given the unprecedented nature of the night's events. As soon as they did, she'd be facing charges of some sort.

The doctor had told her that the results of the CT scan they'd given Mike when he'd arrived at the hospital had shown no major head trauma and that it looked like the concussion he was suffering from was mild. Now he just needed to rest.

Tina approached the bed. Looking at him lying there, she felt a sudden urge to cry that she only just managed to suppress. She'd promised the doctor she wouldn't wake him, but as she stopped by the bed, taking a deep breath to push down her emotions, his eyes opened, taking a couple of seconds to focus on her.

'You're OK?' he whispered.

She put a hand on his. 'I'm fine. Everything's all right now.'

'I heard shots over the phone. What happened?' His voice was weak and he sounded exhausted.

'They tried to break out Fox. They failed. Cecil Boorman's dead. So's Fox. And another gunman they think might be Cain.'

'Did Fox talk before he died?'

'Not enough to give us anything useful.'

He sighed. 'Then we've failed.'

Tina shook her head and squeezed his hand. 'No,' she said, 'we didn't. The men behind today's attacks are dead, the Shard's still standing, and Jetmir Brozi's in custody facing charges that are going to keep him in prison for the next twenty years. I'd call all that a success.'

Bolt managed a weak smile. 'That's what I like about you, Tina. You don't let things drag you down.'

'And nor should you.' She bent down and pecked him on the cheek – a gesture that surprised both of them. 'Go to sleep now,' she said. 'I'll come back to see you tomorrow.'

'You're not in any trouble, are you?' he asked as she said goodbye and turned towards the door.

She smiled. 'Course not. You know me.'

And with that, she went back out into the corridor where the CTC officers were waiting.

Eighty-two

23.45

Alone in his spacious living room, Garth Crossman smiled.

It had been a difficult few hours watching the stories unfold on the TV screen. A huge part of him enjoyed the seemingly non-stop scenes of chaos: the Shard spouting flames; the Prime Minister pale and shaken as he addressed the nation; the burning prison surrounded by riot police; the aerial view of the police convoy that had been escorting Fox, with one of its cars on fire and the bodies of several black-clad police officers clearly visible on the ground. These scenes were the electric shock treatment that the nation needed to jolt it from its complacency, and they demonstrated Crossman's power, because he had made them happen. But they'd also shown his vulnerability. Such was the scale of the attacks that the hunt for the perpetrators would be intense and all-consuming, and for the last two hours Crossman had had to wait to discover whether either Cain or Fox – the only two men who knew his part in all this – had been captured alive after the botched attack on the convoy.

The reason for his smile was that the news anchor had now confirmed that not only was Fox dead but so were the two as yet unidentified gunmen who'd helped him escape. Since Crossman knew that Cain had only used one other man in the attack, that meant that he too had to be one of the fatalities.

It had been, Crossman would be the first to admit, a close-run thing, but ultimately the day had been a success. It had always been a major priority to get rid of Fox. The problem was that Fox was cunning, highly intelligent, and he played by his own rules, which meant he couldn't be trusted. Crossman had therefore decided to concoct a plan to break him out from prison before he opened his mouth to the wrong people. He'd considered having someone try to kill him inside, or indeed paying extra to the man they'd used to attack Fox to actually kill him. But in the end, he'd concluded it was best to play it straight until they had him somewhere where he could be disposed of properly and efficiently.

But now there was no longer any need for such subterfuge. The war was temporarily over, and without anyone left who could point the finger at him, Garth Crossman was, as far as the world was concerned, a victim in all this. It still made him shudder to think how close his wife had come to ruining everything. He would have to be careful that others didn't discover the secrets he'd worked so hard to hide.

He stood up, poured himself a glass of brandy from the drinks tray, and took a long sip.

It was time to contemplate the next stage of his career.

ONE MONTH LATER

Eighty-three

I used my stick for support as I walked across the park. I'd been out of hospital just over a week, but this was my first time outside on my own. If my doctor knew what I was doing, he'd blow a gasket. According to him, I had to take everything very, very slowly. It was, he claimed, a miracle I'd made it through at all. I'd lost three-quarters of my blood by the time they got me to the hospital and, apparently, had died twice on the operating table, although I don't remember any out-of-body experiences or seeing a bright light at the end of the tunnel, or any of that kind of thing. In fact, I slept through the whole lot.

The medical people hadn't wanted me to leave hospital. Apparently, I was only 50 per cent into my recovery and they'd wanted me to remain under observation for another week at least so they could monitor my progress. But, to be honest, I've never been one for hospitals, and the one I was in reminded me too much of prison, so I'd exercised my citizen's rights and walked. Or hobbled at least.

Also, there was something I needed to do. A wrong that needed righting.

The weather was sunny and unseasonably warm, and the world had returned to normal after February's seismic events. In fact if Cecil and Cain had still been alive, they'd have been mortified to see how little long-term effect all their actions had had. The Shard was being repaired and would soon be back to its former glory; the government might have tottered a little on the day, but it hadn't fallen; and there'd been no race riots on the streets. In fact, people had pulled together in the face of the barbarity that had been inflicted on them. The whole bloody day had been a colossal waste of lives, including very nearly my own. If Mike Bolt hadn't found me when he did there's no way I would have made it, and for that I'd be forever grateful to him.

Around me, the park was bustling with activity. A group of schoolkids were playing a loud, anarchic game of football; people were walking dogs; others just sat soaking up the sun's rays; young mothers chatted and laughed as they pushed prams; an old couple walked hand in hand. This was what it was all about. Ordinary life.

And yet, in truth, I'd never been able to settle back into it since leaving behind the army, and the two foreign wars I'd fought, all those years ago. The real world – this place of reality TV shows, anti-social behaviour, obesity and obsession with Z-list celebrities and the weather – seemed so utterly meaningless when compared with the things I'd done and seen, and the friends I'd lost or who'd been maimed for life by the RPGs and the roadside bombs. These people enjoying the park in the sunshine knew nothing of what was going on in hellholes like Afghanistan, in their name, or of the sacrifices that were being made every day on their behalf. They didn't even really know what was going on all around them, of the tide of crime being committed by a vast and ever-growing army of thugs whose activities were only just being kept in check by an overstretched and embattled police force. These people lived in a cocoon.

But, you know, maybe that's the best way to be. I no longer felt bitter about the way things were. People had been good to me since the events of a month earlier. I'd been treated as a hero in the media – the man who'd infiltrated the terrorist cell and narrowly escaped death when the terrorists had turned on him. Somehow, too, there'd been no mention of the gun battle at the scrapyard with the Albanians, which was being looked at as a separate murder inquiry. The investigating officers from CTC seemed to accept my story that I'd only seen the Stinger after it had been obtained and had no idea where it had come from. A businessman hearing about my plight had offered me the use of his company apartment rent-free for as long as I needed it. Gina and Maddie had visited or spoken to me every day, Gina telling me how proud she was of the part I'd played in trying to stop the missile attack. Incredibly, it turned out she'd been in the Shard when it had been attacked, and had only narrowly escaped death herself. I'd been shocked to the core when I heard that. If anything had happened to her, it would have killed me, given my own involvement in procuring the Stinger.

It wasn't the only shock I'd received regarding Gina either. It also turned out that she'd been inside the Shard with the man she'd been seeing for the past few months. I can't tell you how much it hurt when she told me that. It was like a physical blow. At the time, I didn't say a word. I simply turned round, walked out of my old house, and didn't stop walking for about two hours afterwards, trying to come to terms with the fact that my marriage was now irreversibly over.

But you know what they say about time and healing, and since then I've at least got more used to the idea. The important thing is I've still got Maddie, and as long as she continues to stay in my life, nothing else really matters.

There was a bank of three payphones on the pavement just beyond the park. Two of them were Phonecard only but one still took coins, and that was the one I went to. I dialled a number that I knew by heart and waited.

It rang a long time – at least a minute, maybe even two – before it was finally picked up at the other end.

'Who's this?' growled a male voice.

'I've got a message for Nicholas Tyndall.'

'I don't know anyone of that name.'

'Yes you do. You tell him that the man who set up LeShawn Lambden for that robbery a month ago was one of his crack dealers, Alfonse Webber.'

The voice at the other end was silent for a moment. 'How do you know this?'

'Because I was one of the robbers, and the man who gave me the information was Alfonse Webber. He was paid five grand to help me set up the robbery. He told me all about Tyndall's eleven crackhouses; the vehicles LeShawn used when he was out collecting money; who he travelled with when he was doing a collection. All of it. Check him out.'

'If you're lying—'

'I'm not.'

I put down the phone and limped away, knowing I'd probably sentenced Webber to death. Nicholas Tyndall wasn't the kind of man to tolerate people trying to ruin his business, especially when they were trusted employees. It was why he'd lasted as long as he had as one of north London's premier crack dealers. The irony was that Webber, one of the biggest lowlifes I'd ever met, was actually totally innocent of this particular crime. I'd used knowledge about Tyndall gained during my time as a cop to carry out the robbery of LeShawn, and I knew Webber worked in one of his crackhouses, which meant he was easy to set up.

I didn't feel bad about it. Why should I have done? Webber was a violent, cowardly criminal who'd used the very system he cared so little about to put me behind bars.

I looked over at the people in the park going about their daily lives, and felt the sun on my back. My revenge was complete now. The past was the past, and it was time to start thinking about the future.

For the first time in a while it felt good to be alive.

Eighty-four

'So, tell me. Is the job offer still open?'

'I don't remember making one.'

Mike Bolt grinned at Tina across the table. They were sitting in his local pub in Clerkenwell, just down the road from his flat, and he looked to be back to his old self after his recent spell in hospital. The stitches in his head wound were gone now and already his hair was growing back to cover the scar.

'Do you really want to be part of the team?' he asked her.

She shrugged. 'I don't know. I'm not even sure what my position is at Westminster CID any more.'

In the end, Tina had never actually been arrested for anything, but she'd been on indefinite leave ever since the day of the bombs. Not suspended exactly, because that would have sent the wrong message. As far as the media were concerned, Tina had done everything she could to stop the attacks, and had killed Fox, the individual the *Mirror* had dubbed 'The Most Evil Man in the Country'. But she was pretty sure her bosses in the Met would love to be rid of her once again. In the end, she was far too much trouble, and now that she was facing a protracted IPCC investigation over the killings of Fox and one of his would-be rescuers, the longer she stayed on leave the better.

Bolt finished the pint of lager he was drinking. 'I'm not even sure how long Special Operations are going to be continuing for now,' he said. 'There's talk of winding everything down.'

'Well, they shouldn't. There are still people out there who were involved in the attacks. I'm convinced of it.'

'There may well be, but the leads have completely dried up, and there's no one left who can help point us in the right direction. We even tried leaning on the girlfriend of Eric Hughes, as you suggested, but she didn't say a word, and we haven't got a thing on her, so that's another dead end.'

He put down his empty glass. Tina finished her own drink, a pint of orange juice and soda water. Outside, the early spring sunshine was fading rapidly as night made its approach. It was at times like this – relaxing with a friend over an early evening drink – that she could really do with a nice glass of Rioja, and she felt a pang of sadness at the thought that she'd never be able to have one again.

She asked Bolt if he fancied another pint.

He shook his head. 'No. Let's go back and eat.'

'What are you cooking me?'

'Lamb rogan josh. It should be ready' – he looked at his watch – 'right about now.'

They got to their feet and headed for the exit, keeping a respectful couple of feet apart. It had been Tina's idea to meet up. Having spent a reclusive couple of weeks wandering the countryside near her home and hardly seeing anyone, she'd had a real urge to catch up with Mike away from a work setting. The fact was, she was lonely and she missed him. So she'd called him up, and asked if he'd like to go out for a drink one night, steeling herself against the distinct possibility of rejection.

But the conversation had gone really well, and instead of a drink he'd invited her to dinner. She had no idea if he was just being friendly, or whether he wanted something more. And she still didn't. But she didn't care either. She just wanted a nice evening in good company, and if something happened, well, she probably wouldn't say no.

As they passed the bar, Tina looked up at the TV on the wall. It was showing footage of a good-looking older man in an expensive suit talking at a news conference. Tina recognized him instantly. It was Garth Crossman, wealthy businessman and husband of one of the coffee-shop bomb's victims. He was telling the assembled reporters of his much-publicized plan to form a new independent political party that would campaign on a pro-business, anti-crime platform. 'Our People First' was his slogan.

She slowed down to watch it. Crossman sounded passionate as he talked about his dead wife and his desire for her not to have died in vain.

The barman was watching him too, as was a customer sitting on one of the stools. There was something in the way he spoke that grabbed people's attention.

'I reckon he's going to be a real breath of fresh air,' said the barman, looking at Tina. 'Better than the rest of that bloody shower in Westminster.'

'Who knows,' she said, and turned away to follow Mike out of the door.

But something Fox had said to her just before she'd shot him suddenly crossed her mind, and she stopped.

The next time you hear from us, it'll be from a place you least expect. You won't even know we're there.

Mike turned round. 'What's wrong, Tina? Having second thoughts about my curry?'

She remembered something else Fox had said, when they'd first met in the prison interview room. He'd told her that the ultimate aim of The Brotherhood was to get into politics.

Could Garth Crossman be something to do with them?

She dismissed the idea immediately. She was getting paranoid.

'Course not,' she answered, smiling at Mike. 'I'm starving. Come on, let's go.'

She slipped her arm through his, and they walked out of the door together into the last of the day's dying light.

Hi there,

I'm guessing that if you're reading this then you finished *Ultimatum*, and I really hope you enjoyed it. I'd love to hear what you thought of the book, so feel free to drop me a line via my website or Facebook page if you have any questions or comments (about this or any of my books).

In case you're wondering what I'm doing next, well I promise you I'm keeping busy! I've got a new digital novella – a thriller set amongst the jungles of Panama – which is out in ebook in November. Then, in January it'll be the release of book number 13, which is going to feature Scope, a favourite character of mine from *Siege*, who finds himself fighting for his life against some particularly nasty characters, when he agrees to help an old friend. I'm really pleased with both offerings, and I'm hoping you will be too.

Cheers

In the Dock with Simon Kernick

Shakespeare or Dickens?
Dickens. *Great Expectations* was my favourite book of 1989. Shakespeare, for all his talents, still reminds me of school.

Sherlock Holmes or Hannibal Lecter?
Hannibal Lecter. I like charismatic baddies.

Homeland or The Killing?
Homeland. It has more pace.

The Sopranos or The Wire?
The Sopranos just shades it, because when I'm watching TV I do sometimes prefer escapism to gritty reality.

Beatles or Stones?
Beatles, but only because George Harrison used to drink in my local pub and gave my mate a signed guitar. Oh, and because Lucy in the Sky with Diamonds is such a great song.

French Fries or potato wedges?
French fries. I can shovel them in ten at a time.

Wine or beer?
That's unfair. I love both. Forced to choose, red wine. It's a sign that I'm getting older.

Hardback, paperback or ebook?
Until last year it was the physical edition. Now, I'm converted to ebook.

Diet or gym?
Gym

City or countryside?
Countryside. I'm a smalltown boy at heart.

Bath or shower?
Shower. No time for baths!

Mike Bolt or Tina Boyd?
Tina. She's sexy.

Eiffel Tower or ... The Shard?
Ho ho. The Shard. It's v pretty, and would look good even with a hole in it.